Blood

&

Steam

By

Jamie Sedgwick

Look for these and other exciting titles by Jamie Sedgwick:

The Tinkerer's Daughter Series

Aboard the Great Iron Horse (New Steampunk Series Coming December 2013)

Hank Mossberg, Private Ogre Detective Series

The Darkling Wind

The Shadow Born Trilogy

Karma Crossed

Acknowledgements:

Special thanks to Janice, who gave me an amulet of light in a dark place. Also, a very special thank-you to Jeramiah, without whose imagination and insight this book would not have been possible. Last but not least, my eternal gratitude to Tanja, my first and last editor and my greatest fan.

Blood & Steam, Part One:

Prologue

I never knew my mother. I was little more than a babe when she headed out into that vast frozen wilderness known as the Wastelands in her old spring-powered plane, searching for the fabled lost city in the ice. According to legends, the city is a strange mystical place filled with wild magic and incredible advanced technology. My mother believed she might find something there to help us, some superior weapon or science that might give us an edge in the war against the Vangars. She never returned.

My mother left me in the care of an eccentric old inventor who raised me as his own. I loved him like a father. I called him Tinker, but I never knew his real name until after he died.

I was born on the side of a mountain in the spring. It was the year the Vangars invaded, the year they killed our king, decimated our cities, and forced our people into slavery. The banks of the Stillwater River were swollen with the runoff from the melting snow in the Blackrock Mountains. Stories say the river ran red that year, that it overflowed its banks and flooded the plains, and all of the land from Anora south to the Badlands became like a river of blood.

Before she left, my mother named me River. It was no mistake she chose that name, in that year. I've done my best to live up to it ever since.

Chapter 1

I emerged from the alley like a wraith, wings of smoke and shadow curling up behind me, the filtered moonlight splashing like blood against the rusted and decaying buildings that surrounded me. Down the hill and to the west I could see the flickering lights of Dockside's shanties in the fog, and I heard the distant rumble of a steam locomotive rattling along the tracks towards Avenston with a load of freshly hewn timber and raw Blackrock steel.

I watched its dark shadow pass through the southern end of the city, moving deeper into Dockside. The train's whistle sliced through the night, echoing back and forth through the maze of darkened streets. Somewhere in the distance, a child began to cry.

A chill ran up and down my spine as I saw the red crescent moon peeking through the thick layer of smoke that blanketed the city, and the words of Tinker's eerie warning echoed through the back of my mind. I shuddered, remembering the wild look in his eyes:

"Don't go out tonight, River, it's a blood-moon. Dark forces are working against us!"

It was terrifying and tragic all at once, seeing one of the greatest minds of our time given over to dementia and superstition like a common peasant. I had been watching Tinker's mental health decline for several years. I could tell that the end wasn't far. His health had been failing ever since the Vangars took him captive, before I was born. All these years later, he still wouldn't talk about what they had done to him.

In the last few months, Tinker had begun to lose his grip on reality. He saw things: ghosts and monsters, demons from his past. His occasional moments of lucidity were stretching further and further apart, and it was all I could do sometimes just to keep him sedate. I had soothed him with calm words and a warm cup of tea before leaving our Dockside shanty that night- the tea laced with a pinch of powdered duskwood, a mild sedative that would help him sleep through the night. I hated doing that to him; hated drugging the man who had raised me as his own child. I felt I owed him more than that, and yet I had nothing more to offer.

What I did, distasteful as it may have been, was for his own protection. I knew what the Vangars would do to Tinker if he wandered out into the city during one of his fits. Even if they didn't recognize him (which they probably wouldn't) a crazy old man like Tinker would have been like a plaything to them. They would have toyed with him like cats torturing a field mouse, bringing death in the slowest and most painful ways that their twisted minds could conceive.

No, it was better just to let the old man fade away. As long as I could keep him comfortable and well-fed, Tinker would be all right. Heartbreaking as it was, I could give Tinker nothing else. He had peace and comfort, and that was more than most.

I drew my attention back to the street and my fingers twitched nervously for the familiar grip of my revolver, though I knew it was still resting on the bookshelf by the stairs at home. I'd had a feeling in my gut all day, and not just because of Tinker's superstitious ranting. Something just seemed *wrong*. I should have taken a weapon with me, but I didn't dare break the law by arming myself in public, even late at night and under the cover of darkness. There were too many suspicious eyes on the streets, too many turncoats ready to sell out to the Vangars for a better job or a few extra coins.

The people of Astatia were weak, dependent on their overlords. They had lost their honor, had their senses numbed by fear and starvation, their pride destroyed by decades of slavery. Most of us had nothing left to live for except the instinct for survival itself. Few still had the courage to fight. Those of us who did knew that nothing would come of it but our own inevitable deaths. If nothing else, we had the desire to spill the Vangars' blood. For some, that was enough to keep us going.

I hurried into an adjacent alley, my heart pounding as I exposed myself to the weak light of the gas lamps. The sense of impending doom intensified. *The blood moon,* I thought, gazing up into the thick, black, polluted sky. *It's just superstition, that's all.*

If only it were so easy to believe.

A gust of ocean breeze swirled up the smoke and fog, and for a moment, I almost thought I could see the stars. Then the clouds and vapor closed back in, smothering the life out of the sky. I relaxed as the shadows enveloped me. The dark streets of Avenston were my environment, my home. The place had molded me. It was where I had learned to fight, to survive, and to kill. That last one was the most important of all. To survive in the streets of Avenston, one must always be prepared to kill.

I slipped down the alley and cautiously made my way to the back door of a dilapidated old engine factory. Like most of the city, the tin-sided building was in a bad state of disrepair. Most of the windows had long since broken out and the siding was peeling away from the underlying structure in numerous places. It was the type of place that even the Vangars tried to avoid after dark, and that was what made it a perfect place for the sleepwalkers to meet.

The hinges creaked noisily as I pulled the door open. I yanked on it and stepped inside, blinking at the darkness. "It's me," I said in a whisper.

I heard a shuffling noise and someone pulled the cover away from a lantern. The dim light barely illuminated the faces that peered at me from the darkness. "Are you alone?" Kale said.

I nodded, stepping closer. Kale and the others had gathered around a table covered in a pile of gears and machinery parts. The skeletal frames of engine hoists and factory equipment rose up from the shadows behind them like obelisks. I glanced at their faces as I stepped up to the table, taking a mental roll call. All of the regular sleepwalkers were there.

"Sleepwalkers" was what we called our little group of rebels, because we only dared meet late at night, under the cover of darkness. It gave us a way to refer to the group in code, so that if the Vangars or other outsiders overheard us talking, they wouldn't know what we meant. We were the only resistance, a small handful of revolutionaries plotting and scheming against our overlords in the hope that some day we would throw off the yoke of oppression and drive the Vangars back to their homeland across the Frigid Sea.

Hatch and Shel Woodcarver were there, as always. They were the oldest of the group. The couple had been married longer than most of us had been alive. In fact, they'd raised a child who would have been old enough to be my father if he hadn't been killed when the Vangars invaded.

Hatch was a wily old sailor with a scar on his cheek and a twinkle that came to his eyes every time he talked about killing Vangars. Shel was his perfect match, an age-wizened woman with long wavy gray hair who knew how to take care of herself. The others: Breck, the butcher with broad shoulders and a missing left arm, cut off at the elbow by Vangars in his youth. Tasha, the tailor from the upper crust Hillcrest District whose entire family had been slaughtered by the Vangars. She had since married and had three children, but still met with us in secret once a week to keep her dream of vengeance alive.

There were a few others, but not many. Less than a dozen. Our number had been three times that once. Some of us had been killed over the years; others had simply given up hope. The sleepwalkers were dwindling fast.

"Tinker couldn't come tonight?" Hatch said.

"No, he hasn't been feeling well."

"Tell him we miss him," Shel said. "And we hope he gets better soon."

I nodded quietly. I didn't have the heart to tell them Tinker wasn't going to get better.

"Did you miss me, gorgeous?" Kale said, brushing up against me. He gave me a mischievous smile and I pushed him away.

"Stop it. You know you're like a brother to me."

"Like a big, muscular, sexy brother that all your friends are in love with?" he said. Laughter broke out around us.

"No. More like a very special brother who needs a cork on his fork so he won't put his own eyes out."

The others hooted at that one and Kale turned slightly red. I was impressed with myself. Being the ruffian he was, Kale wasn't quick to blush. He had a way with the ladies. He always had, ever since he hit puberty at the ripe old age of eleven. I couldn't help but think that his only interest in me was due to the fact that I always rebuffed his advances. Or perhaps he just did it to get a reaction out of me. Kale was like that. He had a bit of a mean streak.

Like many of us, Kale had his scars to bear. His entire family had been slain during the Vangar invasion, except for his father who died after a year of hard labor in the Vangar slave mines. Kale had a bright red scar on the side of his face the size of a man's hand. From a distance, it almost looked like he had been slapped, but up close it was obvious that he had been badly burned. That happened when a Vangar warrior threw a spear at him, but missed and instead impaled the boiler on the back of the steamwagon next to him. Kale bore the scar proudly now, claiming it as proof that the Vangars couldn't kill him.

"Every scar makes me stronger," he told me once. "One day I'll be nothing but scars, and then you'll know all the Vangars are dead." Of course that was but one of many boasts, and I took everything Kale said with a grain of salt.

"We've got some good stuff this time," Hatch said, gesturing at the table. I glanced over the pile of parts.

"Well, what do you think?" Kale urged. "Can you use this stuff?"

I shuffled through the mess, looking for anything useful. "Gears, springs, a few bits of Blackrock steel," I murmured. "No welded pipe?"

"Not this time," Kale said. "The Vangars got there too fast."

I arched an eyebrow, wondering just what Kale had done to get those materials. I decided it was better if I didn't know. "I can't make weapons without good steel pipe," I said. "Guns need a barrel."

One of the gifts I inherited from my mother is the ability to build things. Or perhaps I just picked it up from Tinker. There's no magic to it, I just have a knack at putting the pieces together. I'm something of a mechanic, but my abilities are nowhere near Tinker's, nor my mother's, who could reach into a machine and *feel* the parts with her mind.

"Maybe not a gun then," Kale said hopefully. "Can't you come up with something else?"

I glanced at him and then at the rest of them. If gray hair and wrinkled skin could have made an army, we'd have been in great shape. Kale and I were the only sleepwalkers left under the age of thirty.

"I'm not an engineer," I sighed. "I can fix things or build weapons if I have the right parts, but what can I do with a pile of gears and springs?"

"Maybe Tinker could look at it, see what he thinks?"

I glanced around the room and saw the disappointed looks on their faces. So much of their hope depended on Tinker. If they knew how bad he was, they might give up altogether. I sighed. "I suppose

I could show him, if he's up to it," I said. "Put this stuff in a bag and I'll take it with me."

"Excellent!" Kale said. "I know he'll figure some-thing out."

I smiled weakly, already working on the problem in the back of my mind. I knew it would fall to me, because Tinker simply didn't have the capacity to build things anymore. It had been two years since he'd been in the workshop below our home. That was when he'd finished his last big project, a machine we both referred to as the *boneshaker*. I wasn't sure if he even remembered about it anymore.

The others began moving away from the table, talking in low voices as they scattered around the factory. Our meeting was over. In a few minutes, they would all begin quietly making their way back home. I looked at Kale and then back at the pile of materials, wondering what I would possibly make from it all. It was up to me to make something useful out of that pile of junk and I didn't have the slightest idea where to start. I had almost nothing to work with.

A feeling of hopelessness washed over me as I realized how pathetic we were. A handful of revolution-aries with no weapons and no army. Kale and I were the only real fighters in the group. As much as we liked to celebrate our minor victories, I knew we couldn't ever accomplish anything meaningful. Not like this. Not hiding out in abandoned factories, trying to plan an insurgency with a pile of rusty nuts and bolts. The best we could ever hope to accomplish was to kill a Vangar now and then, or help a few slaves escape from the mines. That wasn't enough. Our resistance was dying.

"I know what you're thinking," Kale said, stepping closer.

I arched an eyebrow. "Is that so?"

"Yes. I can see it on your face. You should remember that any one of them would die for our cause."

"They probably will, eventually," I muttered. "If old age doesn't get them first."

Kale laughed. He started to say something but at that moment a massive explosion went off near the front end of the building. I saw a flash of light and heard the sound of tearing metal. A cloud of dust and smoke poured into the factory, filling the front of the building. Screams filled my ears.

Someone shouted, "Sentinel!"

I exchanged a glance with Kale. We had crossed paths with sentinels before. If this truly was a sentinel, we were in a lot of trouble. Sentinels are Vangars, but they aren't entirely human. Soon after invading our country, the Vangars learned that half-breeds like my mother possess certain gifts. They have the ability to work magic on both machines and living people. The Vangars used this to their advantage, forcing magic-users to create strange abominations of man and machine.

They experimented first on victims of the war, creating new arms and legs for them, giving fallen soldiers the ability to continue living and working. These artificial limbs were powered by springs at first, but they quickly evolved. It wasn't long before the Vangars were looking for ways to *improve* their sub-jects. With springs and steam power, they created pow-erful robotic arms and legs, and integrated weapons into the soldiers' bodies.

These experiments went on for years, until the Vangars finally created the ultimate warrior. They called it the *sentinel*.

Sentinels stand nine feet tall and have the strength of twenty men. Their armor and helmets protect them from conventional weapons, making them nearly indestructible. The sentinels remain slightly human, but not enough to have any empathy or conscience. If they ever had any, that is. They are Vangars, after all.

Sentinels are the perfect killing machines. They have very few weaknesses, and even those are deceptive. For instance, the grated metal visor at the front of their helmets appears to be an opening, but the plate is made of specially treated Blackrock steel. It's nearly impossible to damage, even with a firearm. Most of their armor is similar, and it covers their entire bodies. Against warriors like this, we were helpless.

Instantly, we were moving. Kale disappeared into the shadows off to my right and I raced back to the metal stairway at the center of the building. I leapt over the banister and flew up the stairs. I landed on the catwalk above and paused, scanning the front of the building for a clearer view. At first, I could only see smoke. Then a massive section of the wall gave way with a shrieking sound and the old lumber collapsed inward, crashing across the floor.

The smoke drifted out through the opening and a sentinel stepped through, his massive steel boots thudding against the floor as he moved. I heard the unmistakable whirring sound of the gears and springs that powered his suit. My gaze went to the scattergun he wore in a long holster at his side and then to the massive sword strapped to his back. I sized him up, calculating my chances of winning a battle with this creature. I scanned the area for a weapon, wondering what damage I might do with a length of iron pipe or a scrap of board.

Not much, I thought cynically.

As the smoke cleared, the sentinel crossed the front of the factory and I saw another dark form appear in the opening behind him. My heart fell as a second sentinel appeared, and then a third. *Three sentinels!* We were doomed.

In unison, they raised their scatterguns and began firing indiscriminately into the building. A chorus of screams went up in the smoky darkness below me. I heard the sounds of the other sleepwalkers scattering throughout the factory, running for their lives. I broke into a run, flying down the catwalk towards the front of the building. I didn't have a plan at that point. I only knew that I had to distract the sentinels before they killed everyone. I reached the end of the catwalk and without slowing down, I leapt onto the guardrail and plunged forward, hurling myself over the edge.

The sentinels had spread out at the front of the building. I landed directly behind them, touching down as gracefully as a panther. I rose to my feet, glancing at the backs of their suits, wondering at the technological genius that made all of those gears and springs work together, meshing flesh and bone. I'm good with machines, but not that good. The half-breed engineers who created the sentinels were pure genius. Mad genius.

I heard the faint clicking and whirring of the machinery under their armor and noted the steady rattle of the steam condenser and boiler that drove it all. The boiler housings on the back of their suits looked like rectangular boxes made of copper-plated steel. Being an obvious vulnerability, the Vangars had gone to great lengths to protect their power source. I doubted even a high-powered rifle could puncture that boiler.

One of the sentinels noticed me. He turned, swinging his scattergun in my direction. I latched onto his arm and heaved myself upward. I moved gracefully, without hesitation. Before he even realized what I was doing, I had climbed his suit just like a tree. I stood over the Vangar's helmet, straddling it with one foot on each shoulder. He waved his gun in the air trying to knock me off, but I easily dodged out of reach.

"Meva!" he called out to his companions. "Help!" At the sound of his voice, the others ceased their firing and turned to see what was the matter. They raised their scatterguns to shoot me, but the sentinel cried out, "Naya, Naya!"

If they shot at me, they'd probably kill him, too. His armor could protect the Vangar from a weapon like that, but the steel mesh on his helmet was an obvious weakness when it came to scatter-guns. He didn't want to risk it.

I smiled grimly. I noticed a latch on the side of his helmet and on a hunch, I pulled the linchpin. I bent my knees and yanked back as hard as I could, thinking that I might have found a way to remove the helmet. It moved slightly, but it was fighting me. I had missed another latch somewhere.

I stood up and kicked it. Instead of pulling free, the helmet twisted sideways, binding against the rest of the suit, leaving the Vangar inside half-blinded. He dropped his scattergun and reached up to straighten the helmet, but his large clumsy hands broke a piece of copper tubing in the process.

Hot oil spurted out of the tube, splattering painfully across my arm. I sprang backwards, deftly landing on the ground behind him. As my feet touched down, I heard the warrior inside the suit screaming. The hot oil was working its way through the cracks, burning his skin. I glanced down at my arm and saw a dozen small blisters beginning to form. I almost felt sorry for the Vangar. Almost.

The other sentinels had their scatterguns trained on me, but they didn't dare shoot for fear of injuring their companion. Instead, they lowered their weapons and rushed me. I took a cautious step back, making some quick mental calculations, and then dashed for the hole in the wall.

I leapt through the opening as the heavy *kathud* of a scattergun went off behind me. I dove for the ground, hoping the stonework foundation might offer some protection. Projectiles riddled the wall above me, tearing holes through the tin siding and hammering into the brick building across the street. The pellets whistled as they ricocheted off the brick wall, sending puffs of dust up in the air.

The first shot was high. Luckily, I had gone low. I rolled aside as I landed and came to my feet at the corner of the building. Another shot went off, closer this time but still wildly inaccurate. I cursed myself once again for not bringing a weapon. I should have known better.

Standing at the corner of the building, I took a step back, positioning myself at an angle to the adjacent building across the alleyway. With a burst of speed, I ran straight at it. I had learned the trick from a Tal'mar thief when I was a child. He was the only full-blood Tal'mar I'd ever met, and he made his living picking the pockets of Vangars and other corrupt businessmen of Avenston. Unbeknownst to Tinker, I had followed the Tal'mar around for a while, learning his trade. I helped him occasionally, and for this he gave me trinkets and coins that I used to buy food. More importantly, he taught me certain skills that came in handy later in my life, especially at moments like this.

When I reached the corner of the adjacent building I leapt up, climbing the wall several steps, and then pushed away, twisting as I flew over the narrow alley. As I hit the outside corner of the factory, I curled my legs up like springs. The tin siding rattled noisily as I rebounded, pushing back toward the first building. Just like that, in two jumps I was within reach of the roof. Or so I thought.

Out of the corner of my eye, I saw something dark and massive hurtling towards me. I twisted awkwardly in midair trying to avoid the object. As I turned, a massive axe *whooshed* by my head, missing me by an inch. I contorted my body, struggling to regain my balance, straining to reach the roof of the building. As I reached the arc of my flight, I barely caught the ledge with my fingertips. I instantly knew it wasn't enough of a handhold to support my weight.

Using my momentum, I swung myself forward, gliding along the side of the building, trying to bring my feet up to the level of the roof. I swung my legs up over my head, curving my knees back towards the ledge. I vaulted upside down and gently came to rest hanging by my knees with my back against the wall. My hair dangled down beneath me, my arms at my side, fingers searching desperately for a handhold. The hard cobblestone street stretched out below, taunting me.

I took a deep breath, analyzing my precarious situation. I had spent my momentum. There was nowhere else to go. I bent my torso, trying to reach up to the ledge of the roof. My foothold immediately started to give. I felt myself sliding away from the ledge and I quickly straightened out, pressing my back up to the wall. I turned my head to stare awkwardly at the sentinels as they stepped around the corner. They raised their weapons, training their sights on me. I closed my eyes, measuring, calculating.

I couldn't drop. Not that far and not at that angle. I'd never make it to my feet. I'd break my neck in the fall, and that was if I was lucky. If I wasn't, I'd survive long enough for the sentinels to make me wish I *had* broken my neck.

I heard deep taunting laughter from below, and the unmistakable click of a scattergun round being loaded into the chamber.

Chapter 2

I was as good as dead and I knew it. I was tempted to let go, knowing that at least I'd rob the Vangars of a kill. *No,* I thought. *Better to let them shoot me. It'll end faster.*

"Why don't you cowards fight a real man?" a voice shouted below. I cringed. I glanced sideways and saw Kale rushing the sentinels with a length of soft iron pipe. One of the sentinels turned to face him just in time to take the full brunt of that pipe across his face. His helmet rang like a bell. The pipe bent, bowing slightly at the middle.

Unfazed, the sentinel lashed out with his scatter-gun. Kale leapt deftly aside, responding with a hammering blow to the sentinel's midsection. Inside his armor, the Vangar warrior laughed.

The second sentinel watched this interplay for a moment. He decided his assistance wasn't needed, and then turned his attention back to me. He raised his scattergun to shoot me but then paused. For some reason, he thought better of it. He replaced the weapon in its sheath and looked up at me. Through the cage of his helmet, I saw a glint of teeth as he smiled wickedly. Suddenly, I understood. I clenched my jaw, my fingernails clawing at the brick wall.

The sentinel's suit chugged and whirred as he stepped up to the corner of the building below. He tilted his head back and gazed at me for a moment, and then took a swing at the wall. Bricks exploded outward as his large metallic fist hammered into the structure. A wave of energy rushed up and down the side of the building. A small scream escaped my lips. The surface of the wall behind my back rolled like an ocean wave. The sound of shattering bricks and plaster was almost like breaking glass.

I lost traction and slid a few more inches. The leather of my boots caught the ledge and I blinked slowly, taking a deep, shuddering breath. The Vangar nodded approvingly at his handiwork. He smiled again, and then took another swing.

This time, the wooden stud inside the wall snapped and the entire corner of the building dropped several inches. I dropped with it, momentarily freefalling. As the building settled, my legs caught the ledge again. I slid a few inches to the side and came to a bouncing halt, my heart racing in my chest, blood rushing dizzily through my head.

The wood framing behind the wall creaked and groaned like the hull of a ship in a hurricane. Bricks trickled down. The sentinel let out a deep, rumbling laugh as they bounced off his armor. I twisted my head frantically from side to side looking for something - anything- to latch onto. I realized that during the partial collapse, the edge of the building had opened up a handhold. I saw exposed timbers, but they were just out of reach. If I could just swing a little closer, I might reach the opening at the edge of the building...

Kaboom!

The sentinel's fist smashed into the wall again and the entire corner gave way. The building made a moaning, creaking sound as the top of the wall separated from the structure. It tilted awkwardly outward from the rest of the building, dangling me out over the street. I caught my breath as I realized the entire building was about to collapse on top of me.

I twisted my body in a desperate attempt to swing toward the crumbling ledge. As I reached out, I felt the entire section of wall give way beneath me. I reached for the corner that was no longer there, and felt my hand close on one of the wall studs. I grabbed it with both hands, pulling myself forward as the bricks collapsed around me.

Chunks of brick and plaster rained down, pulverizing my arms, my legs, and the back of my head. I cried out, unable to let go, not daring to look up for fear of having one of those bricks smash me in the face. The board swung out and away from the building as it collapsed. I held on as long as I could, until the stud slid from my grip and the inertia threw me into a freefall.

I saw the street coming at me. I did my best to twist into a position where I could roll when I hit the ground, hopefully absorbing some of the impact. I'm not sure if I actually succeeded because the next thing I knew, everything was silent.

I was lying flat on my back. My eyes fluttered open and I sucked in a deep breath. A cloud of dust filled the air, so thick that I couldn't see more than a few feet in any direction. I instantly started to cough.

I felt hands on my shoulders and twisted my head to see Kale trying to lift me. I turned, pushing awkwardly to my feet, and let out a cry as my hands scraped across the cobblestones. I held them out, examining my bloody palms. The board that had saved my life had also rubbed the flesh from my palms and left splinters and gashes all over my hands. I grimaced, pulling one of the larger splinters from my exposed flesh.

Kale gave me a dark look. He handed me his gloves and nodded that I should follow him. I accepted them gratefully, wincing as I slid them over my exposed flesh. My mind flashed back to seeing him wielding that iron pipe. "What were you thinking?" I said quietly, wincing as I flexed my hands in the gloves.

"What?"

"What were you thinking, attacking that sentinel with a pipe? Are you nuts?"

He smiled cavalierly. "I had to do something to save you."

I rolled my eyes. "Idiot," I mumbled.

He shot me a mischievous grin and then broke into a run up the street. I took off after him, ignoring the painful bruises up and down my body. I took half a dozen steps before I realized that I was running with a limp. I glanced down and realized that my leg too, had been injured. A shard of wood several inches long was sticking out of my thigh.

"Wait!" I called out quietly. I stopped and bent over to pull the shard free. Kale looked horrified as I yanked the splinter out and a stream of blood trickled from the open wound.

"You need a doctor," he whispered.

I was going to say I was fine, but I didn't get a chance. We both heard the unmistakable sound of heavy steel boots coming up the street behind us, and we broke into a run.

I threw a glance over my shoulder as we ran, and I caught a glimpse of the sentinels racing towards us through the smoke and the dust. Their armor looked red under the light of the moon and Tinker's warning again came to mind. *Perhaps,* I thought grimly, *I should have listened to the crazy old man.*

I saw a flash of color on the cobblestones and realized it was my blood. I was leaving a trail that would lead the sentinels directly to us. I threw my gaze up and down the street, trying to formulate a plan. A narrow, winding street opened up to my left. I recognized it as one of the old routes that led down into a seedy southern Dockside neighborhood.

"There," I said, pointing. Kale nodded, and ran that direction. I let him get a few strides ahead of me and then I turned and ran the other way. By the time he'd realized what I'd done, it was already too late. The sentinels were between us.

I had forced them to either split up or choose one of us to chase. As expected, they chose me. I swerved to the right, climbing north up a narrow street into Hillcrest. Two and three story buildings loomed over me. These were the homes of the working class, the merchants and laborers who were either clever or weak enough to avoid becoming slaves in the mines. Of all the people in Avenston, these were the ones who led relatively normal lives. Hillcrest was about as good as it got.

I reached the summit and saw the rest of the Dockside District stretching out below. A smile turned up the corners of my mouth. Those were the streets I knew best. If I couldn't shake the sentinels in Dockside, I deserved to die.

I heard thundering footsteps coming up the hill behind me and I took off at a run. My plan had seemed clever enough at first: lead the sentinels into Dockside and then lose them in the maze of warehouses, shanties, and dark alleys. I'd done it before. It shouldn't have been hard. The one thing I didn't count on was the second patrol of sentinels waiting for me at the bottom of the hill.

Halfway down the street, two more sentinels stepped around the corner and leveled their scatter-guns at me. I was running downhill so fast that I couldn't possibly turn aside without injuring myself. Instead, I used my momentum to leap to the top of a five-foot wall that ran along the street. I flew along the top of the wall and then leapt up onto a second-floor balcony, slamming into the rail as I landed.

I grunted, forcing air back into my lungs, and climbed over the rail. The sentinels opened fire, and scattergun pellets ricocheted behind me. Chunks of plaster rained down.

I broke into a full-out run, launching myself from the balcony rail, and caught the edge of the next building. I pulled myself up onto the roof, turning to the northwest, running deeper into Dockside. I made it to the edge of the roof in just a few steps. I leapt into the air, vaulting towards the next rooftop. My leg screamed in pain as I landed, but I forced myself to keep moving.

Behind me, I heard the familiar *kachunk, kachunk* of a sentinel's brisk walk. One of them had climbed the wall of the building behind me, ripping out bricks and siding all the way up. The entire building shook as he charged across the roof. I caught glimpses of three more sentinels in the street below and I began to worry.

Fighting a sentinel is a lot like fighting a bear. All weaknesses are simply illusion. They may seem clumsy until you're standing in front of one, just trying to stay out of reach. They might seem slow, until one of them is chasing you. That's when all of your preconceived notions vanish and you realize that you'll be lucky just to get away alive.

Those were my feelings as I bounded from rooftop to rooftop at full speed, heart pounding in my ears, eyes searching for another way to shake them. I was fast. I had never met a human who could outrun me. Only the Kanters, the tattooed giants from the slaves mines might match my speed. Or, of course, a sentinel. And these sentinels were unusually determined.

I don't know how long the race lasted. I only know that my body was screaming with pain and I couldn't go on much longer. My lungs ached. I was beginning to feel dizzy from the loss of blood. We had crossed the rooftops of more than a dozen buildings.

I went back down to street level and ran into the narrowest, darkest alleyway I could find. Working my way back and forth through the dregs of Dockside, I was sure that I would lose the sentinels eventually. It had worked in the past. Sooner or later, they would give up the chase.

But this time was different. There were more of them, for one thing. And they had never pursued me with such vigor in the past. It was almost as if they feared to return without me... perhaps that was the reason. Perhaps they had been told to bring me back once and for all, or they would suffer.

Regardless, it soon became clear to me that I couldn't go on. I had to find shelter. I had to rest and lick my wounds. I couldn't shake the sentinels long enough to even catch my breath. Every time I came out of an alley, it seemed there was another sentinel waiting for me on the other side. Every time I vanished into the shadows, it seemed more of them came out of the woodwork. There was simply no escape.

And suddenly, strangely, I found myself at home.

I wasn't entirely sure how I'd gotten there. My mind was a blur of streets, dark alleyways, and roof-tops. They were all familiar to me, but in my state of mind, they were all more or less transient. It wasn't until I found myself climbing the front stairs of our two-story shanty that I realized what I had done.

Halfway up the stairs I paused, realizing my horrible mistake. I turned back and saw three sentinels chugging down the street towards me. It was too late to turn back. I had nowhere else to go. I stood there for a moment struggling with my mistake, slowly coming to the realization that I only had one choice. I must give myself up. If I didn't, they would find Tinker.

Even as I thought his name, I looked up and saw Tinker standing at the front door. The open door behind him hung awkwardly to the side, dangling by a broken hinge that had needed fixing for more than a year. In his arms, Tinker held an old blunderbuss. I recognized it as a weapon he had modified years ago. It didn't shoot bullets or small projectiles. It shot half-rounds of cannon charges. It was powerful enough to knock the shooter off his feet if he wasn't careful.

My eyes widened as I saw him. "Tinker, get inside!" I said in a desperate panic. "Hide!"

He stepped forward, brandishing the weapon. "Get behind me!"

He raised the gun over my head and fired. I had just enough time to duck and cover my ears. Tinker twisted sideways from the recoil as he fired, and I felt the concussion of the blast go all the way through my body. Tinker steadied himself and began to reload. I glanced up the street and saw one of the sentinels standing still, his body tilted at an awkward angle. Then I saw the liquid running down his armor and realized it was a mixture of oil and blood. Tinker had killed him.

Behind the dead sentinel, many more were coming. I leapt up the stairs and grabbed Tinker by the arm. "Hurry!" I shouted. "We've got to get out of here."

He shrugged me off, locking another charge into the chamber of his weapon. "Get behind me, Breeze! Go out the back."

I narrowed my eyebrows, staring at him. "Tinker?" I said, my voice cracking slightly.

"Hurry up now," he said. "Get down to the water. They won't follow in the water. Go, Breeze!"

Tears stained my eyes as I stared at him. "Tinker, I'm not Breeze. I'm River."

He stared at me for a moment and then a sly smile broke out across his face. He nodded at me and said, "Go on, child. GO!"

The whole world crashed down around me. Tears streamed down my cheeks. I no longer felt the pain of my bruised bones or the laceration in my thigh. I didn't feel the grated skin of my palms or the blisters on my arm. I only felt my heart breaking inside of me.

I stared at him confused, wondering. Did he know what he was doing? What was going on in the old man's mind? He must have known he couldn't survive a fight with the sentinels. What he was doing was insane. It didn't make any sense.

Tinker impatiently shoved me backwards through the doorway. As I stumbled inside, he let loose another round. "Come on, then!" I heard him shouting. "Come get your medicine, you filthy Vangars!"

Suddenly, it all became profoundly clear. Tinker didn't want me to save him. All that he wanted was for me to escape. He wanted me to get away, so that I might come back some other day and exact our revenge. He was placing all of his hopes in me, the same way that he had in my mother before she died in the Wastelands.

I knew then that there was nothing I could do for Tinker. He had chosen to sacrifice everything to give me that chance to escape. I owed it to him to survive. I owed it to him to come back and hunt down those sentinels one by one.

I turned and ran through the upper room of our shanty, knocking over furniture, leaping into the narrow staircase that led down into Tinker's workshop. I paused on the stairs to grab the spring-powered revolver that I had inherited from my mother. It was resting on the small bookshelf like an old knick-knack. I snatched it up and shoved it into my belt.

I flew down to the lower level, racing toward the back door that led out onto the docks. Halfway through the shop, I stopped cold in my tracks.

Tinker's workshop was a long, narrow room, like a tunnel. I was standing next to the bench on the outside wall covered with tools and odds and ends -Tinker's usual assortment of junk- but that wasn't what caught my attention. It was something else: it was the thick dust-covered canvas resting directly adjacent to the workbench. Or rather, it was the thing *under* the canvas. It was the *Boneshaker.*

Hurriedly, I yanked the canvas off and knelt down, opening the fuel inlet from the tank. Tinker's boneshaker didn't run on steam or springs like most of his inventions. This version, the only one he had ever built, used an engine from one of the Vangars' larger gyroplanes.

The boneshaker was something Tinker had called a "mechanical horse" when he designed it. It wasn't so much that it looked like a horse, but rather the fact that it was long and thin, as opposed to the common wide-bodied steamwagons and similar vehicles. The boneshaker was something different. It was a simple steel frame resting on two wheels, with a handlebar to steer and a seat just big enough for one person. Tinker had designed it to be fast. It was supposed to be a quick and economical way to get from one place to another, a vehicle for the poor.

Of course, that was all before Tinker had lost his senses. Soon after finishing the boneshaker, Tinker lost interest in his work. Sadly, the thing had been sitting under the canvas in his shop ever since.

I hastily checked the pipe connections and blew the dust off the carburetor. Satisfied that everything was in place, I sat astride the boneshaker and kicked the engine over. It rolled the first time without promise. I kicked again, this time rewarded with a small *chugging* noise. The third time was a charm. I kicked, and the engine came to life. A cloud of sooty black smoke puffed out the tailpipe.

Smiling, I kicked the thing into gear and revved up the throttle. A moment too late, I realized I hadn't bothered to actually open the back door *before* going through it. The rotten old wood exploded as I hit it, shattering around me as I burst through the doorway. I went roaring down the dock, shaking off the shards of wood, ignoring the slivers in my knuckles and shoulders.

As I bounced down the uneven surface of the dock, I noticed a jarring pain moving up and down my entire body. I suddenly remembered why we had decided to call the vehicle a boneshaker. It didn't have any suspension. It vibrated like a hammer beneath me, rattling the teeth right out of my head.

Over the roar of the engine, I heard the explosions of Tinker's blunderbuss in front of our shanty, and the loud bursts of the sentinels return fire. I hit the brakes and spun in a half circle, craning my neck for a clear view. For a split second everything seemed to go quiet. Tinker had retreated into the shanty. The sentinels followed him inside.

Three seconds later, the shanty exploded. There was a massive wallop and a fireball rolled up into the air, riding a cloud of smoke that mushroomed out in a broad circle. All of Dockside shook, and the sound of the explosion echoed back and forth across the city. For a moment, the flames lit up the night sky and the entire city turned bright red. I stared with my jaw hanging open as bits and pieces of burning wood started raining down.

Bystanders began to gather along the docks to stare at the hole where our shanty used to be, stamping out the fires before they spread to the buildings nearby. It took a moment for me to realize that the sentinels were gone. Tinker had tricked them into following him inside before setting off the massive explosion. He'd done it on purpose.

Tears flooded my vision. I couldn't help but think of my father. He had done the same thing to save my mother. He had sacrificed himself, dive-bombing a Vangar dragon ship with his gyro to help her escape. And now, Tinker...

Two fathers had been taken from me by the Vangars. My blood-father so many years before, and now my adopted father. Both sacrificed themselves to save me. I wiped the tears from my cheeks, my lips curling with rage. Under my breath, I swore that I wouldn't rest until every Vangar was dead. I didn't care how long it took or what I had to do, I would pay them back for what they had done.

I gunned the throttle and disappeared into the night, my blood boiling for revenge.

Chapter 3

With Tinker gone, my thoughts immediately turned to Kale. He was the closest thing I had to family, the only person who might know what I should do. I left Dockside and roared up the city streets, making my way back to the area where I'd last seen him.

I don't know what I was thinking. I wasn't in my right frame of mind or I would have known how unsafe this was -that the sentinels were still on the lookout for me. I was in shock and I wasn't thinking clearly. After several minutes of searching the area where we'd split up, I rounded a corner and saw half a dozen Sentinels marching up the street. I hit the brakes, skidding sideways. My chest tightened as I recognized Kale's limp body hanging over one of the sentinel's shoulders.

Hearing the boneshaker's engine, the sentinels all turned at once. Four of them immediately came at me. I gunned the throttle, fishtailing back and forth as I took off in the opposite direction.

I flew through the streets of Avenston, not entirely sure of where I was going. It was clear to me now that I shouldn't try to contact anyone I knew. Going to the other members of the resistance would place them in too much danger. I had to do something else. I had to think of somewhere else to go. And I had to find a way to help Kale.

The boneshaker bounced along the cobblestones, jarring my body painfully. I gripped the handlebar with all my strength, weaving through the streets. I knew all the dark alleyways and the narrow winding tunnels. I had used them all at some time or other. It only took a glance over my shoulder to tell me that the usual tricks weren't going to work this time. If anything, I seemed to have picked up a few *more* sentinels along the way.

Their speed surprised me. I had never seen sentinels move so fast. I supposed that was because I had always been on foot when they chased me, and they couldn't run at top speed through the narrow streets and alleys where I led them. On the boneshaker, things were different. Now they had to run to catch up. I had never seen them run before.

As I drifted around a sharp corner and began climbing back into the Hillcrest District, I realized the sentinels were driving me into a corner. Hillcrest pushes up against the north wall of the city. Being next to the palace, it's the most protected place in the city. The wall presses into a sharp corner at the western edge of the palace. Beyond it is a straight drop several hundred feet to the rocky shoreline. If I kept going in that direction, I'd be trapped.

I hit the brakes and spun around, barreling back down the hill. I hit the brakes again as I reached the corner, sliding sideways into the turn. I hit a loose cobblestone as I rounded the corner and the boneshaker nearly went out from under me. As I struggled to regain control, a sentinel flew around the corner at top speed, nearly plowing into me.

The sentinel didn't seem to recognize me at first. He was running so fast that he took me as an obstacle. He leapt into the air, trying to avoid a crash. As I skidded sideways, inches from the ground, the sentinel flew over me. For one surreal moment, I looked up and saw the Vangar's face looking back at me from inside his helmet. His eyes widened with recognition and he twisted, trying to reach out for me.

I ducked, gunning the throttle, and came upright just as the sentinel hit the ground. Twisted as he was, the sentinel didn't have a chance. He landed on his side and bounced backwards across the street, slamming into the building on the corner. I heard the crash and turned my head back to see a cloud of dust billowing up around his still form. I laughed. The fool had knocked himself unconscious.

It didn't take long for the other sentinels to figure out I had backtracked on them. I caught glimpses of them running along parallel streets and racing around corners behind me. My little maneuver had bought me some time, but not much. I still couldn't shake them.

Suddenly, I knew what I needed to do. I had to leave the city. There were too many sentinels chasing me, and they were determined to catch me at any cost. They wouldn't give up this time. Not unless I gave them a good reason. Getting out of the city was the only thing I could think of.

I took a sharp right and headed for Main Street. The long, straight boulevard leads right through downtown and out the city gates.

I turned onto Main and opened the throttle with the sentinels just a second behind me. The boneshaker took off like a rocket. It was all I could do just to hang on. The carburetor made a loud whooshing noise as it sucked in air and fuel, and I felt the front end of the boneshaker lift off the ground. I leaned forward, hoping my weight would keep the front wheel down. The machine threatened to pull out from underneath me as it accelerated. I could only hang on for dear life.

Buildings flew by in a blur, gas lamps flashing against the shadows of alleys and side streets. Tears streamed down my cheeks and I blinked rapidly, trying to keep my vision clear. I could barely breathe from the force of the wind against my face.

As the boneshaker approached top speed, the front end settled down. To my relief, I felt myself regaining control. Then I noticed something unexpected: the boneshaker wasn't shaking anymore. I was flying across the cobblestones so fast that they had become like a flat surface. The ride had completely smoothed out.

A triumphant shout escaped my lips. Then a bug smacked me in the middle of the forehead and exploded like a firecracker. I wiped if off with a grimace, ignoring the sharp pain, and twisted around to get a look at the sentinels. I saw something I had never seen before. They had dropped down on all fours and were running like wild dogs, coming straight down Main in great leaps and bounds. Every time they landed, cobblestones shattered and exploded out around them. I had hardly gained an inch on them.

I concentrated on driving as I flew through the city gates and across the drawbridge. The boneshaker bounced unsteadily as I traversed the uneven terrain, then it smoothed out again as I reached the open road. I revved up the throttle confidently. Now I knew what the boneshaker could do.

I had never been outside the city before, but I knew that the stone road built by my ancestors stretched all the way to the ruins of Anora. I was willing to go that far if I had to. I just hoped my fuel would outlast the sentinels'.

I felt an odd sensation in my gut as I left my familiar surroundings. I was fearful at first, heading into that vast unknown territory. The tall buildings and crooked streets of Avenston had always been my home. I didn't know how I would survive without them. I saw the landscape open up around me and the sky stretching from horizon to horizon in a way that I'd never seen before. The Blackrock Mountains were sharp angular shadows stretching skyward across the horizon, and the stars... *The Stars!*

Gradually, mile by mile, the thick black smoke of the city thinned out and gave way to the jeweled heavens. For the first time in my life, I saw the flashing stars and the silvery moon, clear and bright in all their splendor. The sight was like something out of a poem or a painting. It was breathtaking.

I noticed that the air outside the city was clean and sharp, heavy with the scent of sage and earth and some other sweetness that I didn't recognize. The plains stretched out tirelessly in every direction, offering themselves up to me with the promise that I could ride forever. I threw my gaze back and forth along the endless miles of wild grain, tempted to steer off the road just to see what it was like.

Unfortunately, that was a risk I couldn't take. The sentinels were still there, determined and tireless, unrelenting in their pursuit. I couldn't do anything that might give them an advantage. I couldn't even release the throttle long enough to shake out the cramps in my hand. For the moment, it seemed we were evenly matched. It was a race now to see whose fuel would last the longest.

An hour passed in this manner, and then another. The brass gauge on the side of the fuel tank warned me that I was perilously low on fuel, but I had been unable shake the sentinels in all that time. A quick glance over my shoulder told me that they were still there, great black shadows bounding along the plains behind me like giant wolves, a steady cloud of dust rising in their wake.

Up ahead in the distance I could see the ruins of Anora, dark sections of stone walls thrusting up out of the earth, unnatural and alone, jagged edges cutting against the horizon. I saw the tortured remains of buildings, their burned timbers stretching skyward, roofs and walls collapsing in upon themselves.

I had heard many stories about Anora. The frontier city had once been second only in splendor to the capital city of Avenston. Those were the days of kings and nobles, a time of order and a renaissance of human understanding and growth. Remembering Tinker's stories made it even stranger to see what had happened to this once-great city.

As Anora goes, so goes the kingdom, I thought. Under the rule of the Vangars, Astatia had fallen into ruin. With the exception of Avenston, they had destroyed all of the great cities. Smaller towns and villages had been abandoned, most of them burned to the ground as the Vangars terrorized the countryside. Anora had been the defenders' last hope. I had heard the story of its demise a thousand times. It was different seeing it in person, though. It was haunting. It was as if the remains of those old buildings were tombstones, and they cast long shadows over the graves of not only the people who had once lived there, but the entire civilization.

Somewhat cynically, I realized that it might make a great place to hide. The sentinels were powerful, but they didn't have superhuman senses. They couldn't chase me down in the dark and sniff me out like a dog, and they didn't have backup here like they had in Avenston. Anora looked like it might be exactly what I needed.

I sped toward the city, my eyes scanning the area past the tall wooden beams that once housed the city gates, searching for a good place to vanish. I saw the remains of a few tall buildings scattered here and there, and I wondered if they had any strength left in their old timbers. However tempting the shelter might look, I didn't want the sentinels pulling a building down on top of my head.

Suddenly, the ground vanished beneath me. I tumbled forward, stars and darkness flashing through my vision. The boneshaker streaked away from me in the darkness, the engine roaring like a caged animal. I vaguely remember a sense of weightlessness, and the world spiraling away as I fell, and then something solid struck me in the head. I lost consciousness and the cold, painful darkness swallowed me up.

I didn't dream. I woke feeling like my entire body had been crushed by some giant machine. When my eyes fluttered open, I found myself staring up at a large timber beam. The scent of earth and moss mingled in my nostrils and I groaned as a wave of pain washed over me. I reached for my head. It felt like it was being crushed in a vice.

"Drink this," a woman's voice said. She appeared next to me, her face hidden in shadow as she bent forward, pressing a cup to my lips. The liquid spilled over my face as I sipped it. I swallowed quickly and the liquid was already down my throat before the bitter flavor overwhelmed me. I started to gag.

"Hold it down," she said gently. "It will ease your pain." She reached out, touching my forehead with a warm, calloused hand. I noted wrinkles and age marks on her skin as she pulled away. My eyelids grew heavy and consciousness danced just out of reach, like a bird on the wing. Once again, I succumbed.

As I drifted back to sleep, I saw something strange. I blinked as the old woman moved across the room and a man appeared next to her. He was tall, dark haired, dressed in the traditional clothes of a Tal'mar. I had just enough sense to realize that what I was seeing didn't make sense, and then my eyelids slid shut and the world twisted away.

Hours later, or maybe days, I woke. I gradually became conscious of the sound of the old woman quietly humming to herself. The scent of food filled my nostrils, and my stomach rumbled hungrily. I opened my eyes and once again found myself staring at that heavy wooden beam. Beyond, I saw earth and stone and realized that I was in some sort of cave.

I lowered my gaze to watch the old woman. She was seated in an old rocking chair next to a makeshift fireplace. It was little more than a fire pit in the cave wall, with a series of tin pipes for a chimney leading up through the ceiling.

"Smoke," I mumbled awkwardly. "Sentinels."

The old woman turned to look at me, a smile warming her wrinkled features. "Don't worry about them," she said. "The creatures that were chasing you are gone."

"Sentinels," I said weakly, my tongue thick in my mouth. I moved, trying to push myself upright. My body ached right down to the bones, but not as badly as before. Gradually, I made it to a sitting position. I glanced down and realized that I had been sleeping on a cot, covered in heavy furs. A glass of water rested on a small table next to me. I reached for it and gulped it down.

"Slowly," she said. "You haven't eaten in three days. You'll get sick if you don't take it slow."

My stomach rumbled queasily in agreement. I glanced around the room, taking it in. The woman had decorated her cave with sparse furnishings that looked like stolen antiques. I saw a small oak table with matching chairs, a bookshelf, and several other odd, out of place furnishings. I noted that all of them were either small enough for one person to move, or could be disassembled and moved one piece at a time. The old woman had been living there by herself for some time, possibly years.

"Where is the man?" I said weakly. "The Tal'mar?"

She glanced at me and then turned her face back to the fire. "You've been dreaming," she said. "There's no one here but the two of us."

I frowned, trying to force the images in my head to clear. Perhaps she was right. Maybe it had been a dream. I couldn't tell. "How long have you been here?" I said.

The old woman paused in her knitting, considering my question. "To be honest, I don't exactly know," she said. She shook her head and laughed quietly. "The days sort of bleed together. I suppose I lost track at some point, and never bothered to catch up. Sometimes I fall asleep when I'm reading. When I wake, I'm not sure if it's the same day or the next." She bent her head down and went right back to her knitting.

"This is your bed," I said with a hint of guilt in my voice. "Where have you been sleeping?"

"Here in my chair, of course. Don't feel bad. I do it all the time. I like it here, close to the fire. It warms my old bones."

I watched her for a few minutes, trying to make sense of the strange old woman. Judging from her skin and face, she was about seventy. I couldn't understand what she was doing in this place all alone. How had she survived?

"Where are we?" I said eventually. "Is this one of the Vangar mines?"

"No, this tunnel is older than that by a few hundred years, at least."

"Who built it?"

"The men who first came here, I suppose. The men who first started mining copper and iron to make things."

She spoke in a distant voice, almost as if she could remember the time. Judging by her looks, I wouldn't have been surprised. "Is that stew?" I said, nodding toward the kettle on the fire.

"Nearly done," she said. "Give it a few more minutes. It will be worth the wait."

I was so starved I was about to gnaw off my own hand, but I kept my manners. I stood up from the cot, hoping to take my mind off the hunger pains in my stomach. Jolts of pain instantly shot up and down my body. I glanced down at the wound on my leg and saw that the old woman had cleaned it and sewed the skin back together. It looked hideous. I groaned.

"Gently," the old woman said. "Don't move too fast yet."

I stepped out into the middle of the room. I saw a cave-in blocking off the path to my right, and the long open stretch leading out into darkness the other way. "Is that the way out?" I said.

"It can be," she said cryptically. "If you know the way."

I frowned, wondering if she was planning on keeping me down there. It wouldn't have surprised me. The old woman was probably desperate for company. I wasn't too worried. I knew I could get out of there if I really wanted to.

"I'm River," I said, hoping to learn more about her. "What's your name?"

She pulled her gaze away from her knitting long enough to look me up and down, and then she went right back to work. "Ana," she said distantly. "My name is Ana." She leaned forward and lifted the lid off the stew. "Bring bowls," she said. "From the cabinet there. And some bread..."

We didn't speak much as we ate. The old woman stared at me most of the time, which I tolerated because she had been kind to me and because I was too starved to do anything but shovel food into my mouth anyway. It was only after dinner that I started feeling normal enough to consider my situation.

"Did I really sleep for three days?" I said.

"Mostly. You talked in your sleep a lot, about wild dogs and boneshakers, whatever all that means. The fever will do that to a person, make you rant and rave senselessly."

I nodded, drawing my gaze to the fire. I didn't bother explaining that I knew exactly what the rantings meant. "Did you move down here when the Vangars came?" I said.

"No. I came here after they left."

"Why here? You could have gone to Avenston, where you'd be safe."

"Safe?" she said, laughing quietly. "Do you really believe that? No one is safe with the Vangars around. Sooner or later, they kill everyone."

I considered that and found it hard to argue. I thought of Tinker and of Kale. *Kale!* It had been three days since the sentinels captured him. I rose from the table abruptly. "I have to go," I said.

"Nonsense. There is nowhere to go." She reached out to take my hand, but I pulled it away.

"You don't understand," I said. "The sentinels captured my friend. He's in danger. He might already be-" I couldn't bring myself to finish the sentence.

"You can't do anything for your friend now," she said patiently. "You need to rest, regain your strength."

I turned away from her, walking toward the dark end of the tunnel. "I'll find my own way out," I said. I snatched a lantern off the table and started walking. As I vanished down the tunnel, the old woman took a deep breath and sighed.

Chapter 4

I quickly realized the meaning of Ana's cryptic comment. Just a few yards away, the tunnel branched out in two different directions. From there I could see more tunnels spreading out in various directions. It became obvious that if I started randomly picking tunnels, I'd get hopelessly lost. I heard a shuffling sound and turned to see her coming my way, leaning heavily on a walking stick.

"Always right," she said. "Don't ever go left. The second one on the left leads to a bottomless hole. There might be more."

"Bottomless?" I said. "That's not possible."

She pulled the lantern from my hand and held it up between us, staring into my face. "If you don't believe me, then go throw yourself in and find out!" She turned and went ambling down the tunnel to the right. I followed, biting my tongue, reminding myself that the crazy old woman probably hadn't talked to a real human in years.

A minute later, we reached the end of the tunnel and climbed a narrow stone staircase up to a trapdoor. I shoved it open and found myself in the shell of a burned-out building. Ana followed me up. I helped her step across the crumbling remains of the foundation.

It was late afternoon and the heavens were painted in a hue of deep blue. Puffy scattered clouds broke up the sky, their texture so vivid and color so bright that I thought I might reach up and touch them. I glanced at Ana and saw her blinking against the light.

"Don't get up here much these days," she said. "It's been a while."

I considered that. "How do you find food?" I said. "I'm surprised you haven't starved."

"Oh, lots of root cellars down in the tunnels," she said. "Lots of rats and ground squirrels, too."

My stomach churned uneasily. "Ana, what kind of stew did you feed me?"

She smiled wickedly. "Probably best you don't know." She looked the other way and mumbled something under her breath. I distinctly heard the words, *City girl.*

Ana raised her walking stick and pointed down the street, toward the south end of the city. "What you're looking for is down there," she said. "That steam contraption of yours."

"The boneshaker?" I said. "It's not steam powered."

She frowned, twisting up her face. "Burns oil then, like the Vangars?"

"Yes."

She shook her head and spat on the ground. "Steam's better. If Tinker taught you anything, he should've taught you that."

My jaw fell open. "Tinker? You knew him?"

She waved me away and started back toward the tunnel. "Go get your contraption. See if you can fix it. I need a nap."

I watched her curiously for a moment, my head suddenly full of questions. I could tell from Ana's attitude that she wasn't in the mood to answer them. She disappeared back into the tunnel. I shook my head.

"Crazy old woman," I mumbled.

Following her instructions, I headed south down the street. I noticed that some of the buildings appeared almost whole, but I could tell by looking at them that they'd probably collapse on top of the first person who opened the door. They looked oddly out of place though, as if the owners had just left. I almost expected a light to go on in the upper windows of one house, even though the building next to it was nothing but a foundation and a few rotten timbers.

Further down the street I found the façade of a saloon, the boardwalk out front almost as good as new. The sign that dangled from the roof beckoned to the empty street as if the ghosts of the city's past might come walking in at any moment. I cautiously stepped over the weeds and creaking boards in the boardwalk to peer through the broken windows. I saw grass growing up through the floor, and mold and mushrooms covering the walls. A few tables and chairs sat undisturbed, but most of them had been overturned and broken, probably during the Vangar invasion.

I saw bits and pieces of life here and there: the shredded remains of an apron on the bar, the tilted paintings and rusted curios on the walls. I suspected that there was far more of interest inside, and I was tempted to crawl through the window and go snooping around even though I knew the risks. I could scarcely imagine what sort of fascinating things might be waiting for an adventurer foolhardy enough to discover them. And not just in the saloon, either. The entire city was full of relics and treasures waiting to be discovered.

Not for me, though. Not now. Grudgingly, I pulled myself away and continued my journey toward the edge of town. There would be time to explore the ruins of Anora later. For now, I had other things to worry about. I had to find Kale, to free him, and wreak my vengeance on the Vangars.

As I passed through the remains of the city gates, I noticed the shattered and burned-out hulls of several dragon ships. Tinker had told me about the battle of Anora many times when I was younger, but I hadn't paid much attention. I was mostly interested in hearing the parts about my mother and father. I vaguely remembered Tinker explaining that the city's defenders had shot down several dragon ships using the Vangars' own cannons. I scanned the area along the edge of the city and saw several of them, aging and discolored, barely visible in the deep grass.

That was the moment it became real to me. I realized that my mother and father might have stood or even fought on that very spot. It took my breath away. Pride welled up inside of me and I stood there soaking up the feeling. I turned slowly, taking in everything, noting the broken pieces of machinery peeking out from under the weeds and the wild grain. In my mind's eye, the scene came to life and I heard all of the old stories echoing through my mind:

Vangar airships washed over the city in the middle of the night, pummeling the resistance with heavy cannon fire and flamethrowers. The citizens fought back using the Vangars' own cannons against them, forcing them to land and bring the fight to the ground. With muskets and swords, the citizens could not overcome the Vangars, but the Vangars would pay a heavy toll.

They lost a thousand fighters before the uprising finally collapsed. In the process, the Vangars took the lives of several thousand insurgents. It was the last stand of the resistance and the bloodiest battle of the entire invasion. The fall of Anora soon became the stuff of legends...

At last I began to walk. I hardly noticed the weeds growing up through the cobblestones in the road. I kicked something and heard the clatter of metal against stone. I looked down and realized I'd just found my revolver. I scooped it up, examining it for damage. A few scratches, nothing more. I turned slowly, looking for the boneshaker, and saw it laying in the grass just a few yards off to my right.

I cautiously stepped off the road, remembering that somewhere in the area I had fallen into a collapsed tunnel. I had no desire to repeat that mistake. I tested the ground, slowly making my way over to the machine. Even before reaching it, I noticed that the front forks were twisted and a piece of metal had pierced the top of the engine. My heart fell. If I'd had the right parts and tools I might have been able to rebuild the boneshaker's engine, but not there. Not among those ancient ruins, a hundred miles or more to the nearest civilization.

I slumped my shoulders. How was I going to free Kale if I couldn't even get back to Avenston? That hike could take days. Out of anger and frustration, I kicked the front wheel and it made a *click-clicking* sound as it slowly spun around. Irritated, I bent over and grabbed the handlebar.

It took all my strength to get the boneshaker upright. I rested it on the kickstand and took a step back, surveying the damage. The forks needed rebuilding, as did the top-end of the engine. The carburetor had been knocked loose and I wasn't sure what it would take to repair that. The fuel pipe had also been broken, allowing the fuel to run out all over the ground, not that there had been much left.

"Perfect," I said, scowling. Even if I did get the engine repaired, where would I find the fuel to make it run?

I glanced at the old tool bag strapped to the handlebar and remembered that there had been a pair of saddlebags on the boneshaker, too. Was it possible that Tinker had stored some spare parts? I glanced around and saw them lying in the grass a few feet away.

As I bent to retrieve them, a cold chill crawled down my spine. I turned, my eyes searching the ruins around me. I was sure that someone had just been watching me. I saw nothing out of place. No color, no movement, just the ever-lengthening shadows creeping across the ruins of a long-dead ghost town.

I nervously threw the saddlebags over the seat and started pushing the boneshaker back into the city, my eyes scanning the buildings, my hands never far from the revolver tucked into my belt. Even though I couldn't see anything, I knew well enough to trust my senses. Somewhere out there, something was watching me.

Ana shared her stew with me again that night, and I cautiously avoided the subject of the ingredients. I noticed during the meal that her eyes kept straying to the chair where I had left Tinker's saddlebags, with my revolver placed neatly on top. Eventually, I offered to let her see it. She accepted the weapon in her shaking old hands and turned it over. A slight smile turned up the corners of her mouth.

"Fine piece of craftsmanship," she said.

"It was my mother's," I said proudly. "My father gave it to her as a gift when the Vangars invaded. This gun has spilled much Vangar blood."

"You seem eager to spill more," she observed, handing it back to me.

I nodded, taking a bite of bread. "Someday, the Vangars will beg for death," I said around the mouthful of food.

She stared at me, the look on her face indecipherable. At last, she spoke: "I suppose you'd better get that machine running then."

I reached for the saddlebags, and plopped them down on the table. "Hopefully, Tinker left some spare parts in here," I said.

Ana frowned as I dropped the bags on the table. "You have the manners of a barn cow," she muttered.

"I'm surprised you remember what barn cows are," I said sarcastically. I pulled open the flap on one of the bags and found a book of some sort. I pulled it out and saw that the cover was blank. I flipped it open and saw pages of clean, precise handwriting.

"What have you there?"

"I'm not sure." I scanned the first few pages, expecting to find some of Tinker's recipes for powder charges or chemical ingredients. As I began to read, my mouth fell open. The first words on the first page read:

"My only clear memory of my father is from the day he left me. That frosty autumn morning remains vivid in my memory as if I were there now watching

the scene play out, though I can't seem to recall any other day before it..."

My breath caught in my chest. "It's my mother's journal. I never knew Tinker had this. Why didn't he tell me?"

"Perhaps he was waiting until you were ready," she said.

I considered that. "I think he may have forgotten. His memory wasn't very good towards the end."

"A tragic end for such a great mind," she said.

"You knew him, didn't you?"

She tilted her head sideways, remembering. "I knew of him. Everyone knew of Clay Tinkerman."

"Clay?" I said. "That's an odd name. Are you sure we're talking about the same person?" This was the first time I had ever heard Tinker's given name. I had only ever known him as *Tinker*.

She smiled. "Indeed. He hated that name. Everyone called him Tinkerman until he adopted Breeze. She's the one that came up with *Tinker,* and it stuck."

I frowned. It bothered me that the old woman knew more about Tinker than I did. I suddenly wondered what else she knew. "Did you ever meet him?"

"Oh, in passing," she said with slight smile.

I considered that. "What was he like then?" I said. "Before the Vangars came, I mean."

She stared at me with glistening eyes. She began to speak, but not about Tinker. Not at first. She went further back, to the beginning of it all. Her words were not the tale of a lonely old woman living in a cave, but that of a historian who has made a long and careful study of the world.

She described the thousand-year war between the Tal'mar and the humans. She told me about the feuding nature of the two races and how a handful of good people had tried many times over the centuries to end the warfare, but their efforts were always in vain. Over time, the hatred ran so deep that the two kingdoms continued to fight without even knowing why.

Ana described a soldier named Bran Vale who spent his entire life trying to forge a treaty between the two cultures. Bran had been my grandfather, of course. He abandoned my mother with Tinker in order to bring a peace accord to the Tal'mar. His mission failed when he was murdered, but his actions set many other things in motion that ended up changing our world.

I didn't know much else about him. I was about to say so, but she *shushed* me and continued on. Ana began to talk about the old inventor named Tinkerman and the young half-breed named Breeze who became his daughter. As she spoke, I began to realize that Ana knew far more about my own past than I did. I pried for more information and at times, it almost seemed she spoke straight from her memory, as if she had forgotten I was even there. That night, Ana finally confided the truth to me. I had been listening to her stories for hours, and then the realization hit me:

"You knew them, didn't you," I said. It wasn't a question, but a statement. "You knew my mother and father, and Tinker... who are you?"

She sighed. "My name is Analyn Trader," she said in a sad voice. Your mother and father were dear friends of mine, as was Tinker."

I stared at her for a moment, trying to put it all together. Tinker's old stories swam through my mind. I remembered the name Analyn and connected it with the teacher who had befriended my mother. She was the woman who had led the rebellion against the Vangars. "You're the queen!" I said.

"No. Not now, not ever."

"But you're king Ryshan's daughter."

"And King Ryshan is dead, and so is our kingdom," Analyn said.

I slammed my fist on the table. "No! You're the rightful heir to the throne."

"I know when I'm beaten," she said in a flat tone. "Perhaps you should learn that as well."

I rose from the chair and began pacing back and forth. "All those years," I said. "All of those things that happened... how could you just abandon your people?"

Analyn pursed her lips and turned her gaze on the fire. "I did what I must to keep us all alive," she said. "As did Tinker."

I considered that, and slowly realized what it meant. "You were there with us on the mountain, when I was an infant. When my mother died."

"Yes."

"But what happened? How did we end up in Avenston? How did you end up here?"

"Tinker and I had to do something," she said. "The two of us couldn't raise you and Kale up on that mountain alone. It wouldn't have been right. Avenston seemed the safest place. There you could be around others. We hoped there were enough refugees in the city that the Vangars wouldn't notice you. I see now that it worked."

"What about you?" I said. "Why didn't you come?"

"For what?" she said. "So the Vangars could capture me once and for all? So they could parade my corpse around the city and guarantee that no one would ever rise up against them again? No, I did what I must. I did what was best for all of us."

I leaned closer, staring into her eyes. "I'll tell them!" I said. "I'll go back to Avenston and let everyone know that their queen is still alive. That'll put a fire in their bellies."

"You'll do no such thing!" she said angrily. "The people, *my people* are not ready for this."

"How do you know? You haven't even seen them in years. You've let them all think you died up in the mountains. How can you say they're not ready for the truth?"

"Because I told her," said a low voice, somewhere down the tunnel.

I spun around and saw a tall, broad-shouldered Tal'mar man step into the light. He wore a dark green cloak with the hood slid back over his shoulders. I saw the glint of steel daggers hanging from his belt.

I sized him up, frowning, trying to decide if he was truly a Tal'mar or not. He wore the clothes of the Tal'mar and his face looked Tal'mar. So did his ears. But he was so tall, so broad in the chest and shoulders. I had known a Tal'mar when I was young, and seen a few more, but never one so tall. And those dark brown eyes... those were not Tal'mar eyes.

My gaze danced back and forth between the two of them, putting it all together. "You're the one from my dream," I said. "You lied to me, Analyn. You said we were alone."

"One of many lies, I'm afraid. I couldn't tell you the truth until I was sure of how you would react. I had to know-"

"Know what?" I said angrily. "That I'm not a turncoat? That I would keep your secret?"

"Yes," she said patiently. "Yes, that and so much more."

"We had to know what had become of the refugees," the stranger said. "We couldn't risk that you were a spy."

I eyed him up and down. "Who are you? What do you have to do with all of this? You don't look like a Tal'mar to me."

"That's because I'm not," he said. "Not fully, anyway. I'm a half-breed, like our mother."

"You're not-" I broke off midsentence.

Our mother? What did he mean by that? Was this some sort of trick? I wasn't sure, but I did know that his story wasn't adding up. My mother had died just after my birth. I spun around, snatching up my revolver as I rose out of the chair. I released the safety and lined the barrel up at his chest.

"I don't know who you are, but if you don't give me some straight answers I'll put a hole through you the size of a cannonball," I said.

"Calmly, River," Analyn said behind me. "I don't think you want to kill your own brother."

My chest rose and fell quickly, my heart drumming in my ears. "He's lying," I said. "He tricked you." I fixed my gaze on the stranger. "What do you want? What's your game, Tal'mar?"

"You're wrong," he said calmly. "I know you believe our mother died, but you're wrong. She found it, River. She found the city in the wastes."

I shook my head, gripping the revolver as if it was the last solid thing in the world. Analyn stepped close behind me. She put her hand on my arm, forcing it down. In my ear, she whispered: "This is your brother, River. *Your own blood.* His name is Crowasten'-Talbresha. It means *vengeful sword of the north wind.*"

"Call me Crow," he said with a half-smile. "My name is such a mouthful. I don't know what our mother was thinking, giving me that name."

My mind raced. How could I know if this was the truth? Was it possible that Crow was truly my *blood*? *My own brother*? It was too much to grasp. I'd lived my entire life believing that I had no blood relatives left alive. Tinker and Kale were all I'd had in the world; the closest I had ever come to family.

I stared at him, doubtful, wondering. Did he look like her? I couldn't be sure. I had only seen one faded old painting of my mother, and that was from when she was very young. I couldn't see a family resemblance. There was something in the face, though. Something in the cheekbones. And those shoulders and dark eyes... he must have stood head and shoulders taller than the rest of the Tal'mar. Had Crow inherited those features from our human grandfather?

I slumped into a chair to keep my knees from buckling underneath me. Analyn took the revolver out of my hand and set it back on the table. "I'll make some tea," she said softly. "Crow, have a seat. Give your sister a few minutes."

He settled down across from me, staring at me, grinning like a fool. I stared back, boring into those dark eyes, still not daring to believe. After a minute, I couldn't tolerate it anymore.

"Why are you staring at me like that?" I said angrily.

"Because all of my life I have dreamed of the day I would meet my big sister, and this is that day."

I lowered my gaze to the table and covered my face in my hands so he wouldn't see the tears moistening my eyes. I hate it when people see my cry. It makes me angry. Only this time, I couldn't be angry. I could only think that somehow, miraculously, it was all true. This Tal'mar was my brother. *My own blood.*

"My mother is alive?" I said quietly to the table.

"Yes. She wants very much to see you. I'd like to take you to her, but we don't have much time."

I wiped the tears away and raised my head to stare at him. I barely noticed Analyn setting the teapot on the table next to us, quietly filling three cups. "If it's true, why didn't she come to me?" I said, my voice tainted with anger. "If you're really my brother, why are you here now? You've waited this long, why bother come at all?"

"It's not as simple as that," Analyn said, settling down beside me. "Your mother found the city, but she wasn't able to return. Be patient. Crow will explain everything."

"This was our first opportunity," he said. "You must believe me, things in Sanctuary are complicated. Our mother would have returned, but it wasn't safe until now, not even to send me. You must understand that."

"But I don't understand," I said. "Why can't she leave? Why isn't it safe? What is this city that she found?"

"How can I describe Sanctuary?" he said, throwing his gaze up to the ceiling. "It is a place of magic and wonder. It is *the source*. You won't truly understand until you see it."

"Why is it called Sanctuary? What does that name mean?"

"It is a word from our ancient history. Tens of thousands of years ago, our ancestors believed their gods lived on an island called Sanctuary. It was the home of immortals, and the source of magic. It was an important part of their culture."

"So they named the city in the wastes after this island?"

"No, not them. They were dead for many thousands of years when the city was built. The name Sanctuary had become part of mythology by then, only remembered by a few scholars and historians."

"I'm afraid I don't understand any of this," I said.

Analyn handed him a cup of tea, and the steam curled up around his face as he considered my questions. "Let me explain it simply," he said. "We don't know the entire history yet, but we're studying the libraries. Soon all will be known. We have discovered that many civilizations have come and gone throughout the history of our world. Mankind has gone through golden ages of high technology and incredible power, as well as dark ages of superstition and ignorance. It seems to be an eternal cycle."

"I wonder where we are in that cycle now," I mused.

He laughed. "Perhaps we will see that more clearly in the future, though it is a complicated study. Outside forces often influence the cycles. Weather patterns and seasons change, among other things. Something spectacular happened to our ancestors, for example."

"What do you mean?"

"Three thousand years ago, a massive cataclysm destroyed everything. It was something monumental, something that changed the face of the entire world. It killed millions of people overnight, and millions more in the weeks and months that followed."

"Millions?" I said skeptically. "Are you saying that there were millions of people here, once?" That seemed highly unlikely. Avenston was the largest city in the entire kingdom, and it was only home to eight thousand people. At its peak, just after the Vangars drove everyone into the city, Avenston still only had a population of sixteen thousand. As far as I knew, it was the largest city that had ever existed.

"We don't know much about them yet," Crow said. "But here's the important part: after the cataclysm, a few scattered survivors were drawn together by a bright light in the sky. It led them north, deep into the wilderness. When they found the source of the light, they also discovered the cause of the cataclysm. A giant stone the size of a mountain had fallen from the heavens. When it struck the earth, the dust cloud blocked out the sun for years. It lowered temperatures across the entire world, destroying harvests and covering entire kingdoms in ice. According to records, the seas even froze over."

"But there were survivors?"

"Yes, because of the stone," he said with a sly smile.

I rolled my eyes. "A stone saved people? You just said it killed millions."

"The light of the stone brought the survivors together, to a place where they might help each other, and it also made it possible for them to build a city."

"The stone helped them build a city?" I said skeptically.

An amused look crept over his face. "The survivors discovered that the stone was made of some strange new element, something that had never been seen in our world before. Most importantly, the stone possessed a strange, powerful energy."

"Energy?" I said. "Like fuel?"

"Yes, in a way. The stone could be used to power machines."

"So that's how they built the city," I said.

"Exactly."

"And the city is still there," I said. "That's what my... *our* mother found?"

"Yes."

"What are the people in Sanctuary like?"

"There are none. When our mother found the city, she found it deserted."

"What happened to the survivors then, to their descendents? Did the Vangars destroy them?" He laughed. I shot him a glare. I don't like being laughed at.

"Don't take offense," he said. "I understand why you might think that, but no, it was not the Vangars. It was the stone. The very stone that saved them all, almost killed them,"

Analyn had settled into the chair next to me and had been listening to our conversation quietly. I glanced at her. "You believe all of this?" I said.

She smiled wisely. "Listen," she said. "Wait until you've heard the entire story before you form your opinion."

I sighed. "Fine. So the stone that somehow saved all these people then turned around and killed them?"

"Something like that," Crow said. "The history books are vague. From what we can discern, the people of the city had been mining this element out of the stone to use it in their machines. They had been quarrying it and keeping it in large containers. Gradually, over time, the properties of the stone began to change. First it cooled, and eventually it turned into liquid. Several containers burst, releasing the liquid into the water supply."

"What it poisonous?" I said. "Is that what killed them?"

"No, but it sickened them. As the citizens worked to shore up their storage of the remaining material, they realized the stuff was making them ill. It was affecting their minds, giving them unnatural visions and hallucinations. In less than a year, almost everyone in the city had migrated away, moving south through the Blackrock Mountains and back out into the world of their ancestors. Only a few hundred people stayed behind to continue with the repairs."

"And staying in Sanctuary killed them," I said.

"Perhaps, some of them. They finished the repairs, however. When it was all done, those who had stayed behind had been *changed*. Some of the energy from the liquid had leached into their bodies, altering their very nature. They too, had to leave, for fear the liquid would eventually destroy them."

"And then the city was empty," I said as he trailed off. "But there's more to the story, isn't there?"

He grinned, glancing at Analyn. "Don't you see, River? Don't you understand what happened to the survivors?"

I shook my head. "I don't know. Did they die in the snow?"

"No," Analyn said in a patient voice. "What Crow is trying to say is that the last survivors to leave Sanctuary were the ancestors of the Tal'mar. Of all the races, they were the most changed because they remained in the city longest."

Suddenly I understood. "The humans were the first to leave," I said.

"Exactly, therefore they remain more or less unchanged."

"And the powers of the Tal'mar, the ability to see at night and to reach inside people with their minds..."

"All from the stone," Analyn said. "Or rather the liquid it became. It changed them into an entirely new species."

"That means we all started the same," I said. "We all came from the same race of people. But if that's true, what about the Kanters? The giants aren't like us at all."

"The same goes for them, and most likely the Vangars as well," Crow said.

"And the trolls in the Blackrock mountains, if there are any left," Analyn added. "And probably other races too, that we haven't found yet. You see, the stone changed us all, and it did so in different ways depending on certain characteristics we had within us. The Kanters were probably remarkably tall already, and the stone simply encouraged that natural tendency. And obviously, the Kanters experienced more exposure than humans, probably because they traveled along the northern edge of the Blackrock Mountains as they migrated towards the desert."

"Their water sources were likely contaminated for decades," Crow added. "It's reasonable to assume that the water carried the liquid to many unexpected places."

I shook my head, marveling. "I don't know what to think about all of this," I said. "Is it really possible that the Kanters and the Tal'mar came from the same ancestors?"

"It's a fact. They were once as alike as you and Analyn," Crow said. "The stone changed us all, in our own ways."

"And ironically we've been fighting each other over those differences ever since," said Analyn. "That's where the hatred between humans and Tal'mar began. It's what turned the Kanters into giants, the Tal'mar into magic users, and the Vangars into perfect warriors."

"It's so much to digest," I said. "It's hard to believe all of this actually happened."

"There is one more thing," Crow added.

"There is?" I said, suddenly unsure if I wanted to know what he meant.

"Yes. There's Blackrock Steel."

Chapter 5

I stared at him, puzzling out that statement. It was a well-known fact that ore mined in the Blackrock Mountains produced steel of special quality, but I had always assumed that it was just different. It had never occurred to me that there might be a scientific reason for this difference.

"Are you saying the ore in the Blackrock Mountains was changed by the liquid?"

Crow smiled knowingly. "Iron ore soaks up the element like a sponge soaks up water. In doing so, it changes. Just the way our ancestors did. The city's builders took advantage of this when building Sanctuary. They could use the steel to make many new things-"

"Wait!" I said. "Tinker once told me that pureblood Tal'mar can't touch iron. Does it have something to do with that?"

"Yes, you understand perfectly," said Crow. "Plain iron or steel that has not come in contact with Starfall will drain the energy right out of a Tal'mar. This is because of the changes that element has made to their bodies. The Tal'mar still possess some of that energy, and the touch of ordinary iron sucks it right out of them. Obviously, Blackrock steel came into contact with the element as well, and still possesses some of that same energy."

I was astounded. The powers of the Tal'mar and their aversion to iron were the stuff of legends. Their powers and weaknesses were as mysterious as the workings of the universe itself. My own mother's ability to touch steel because of her human ancestry had seemed miraculous to the Tal'mar of her generation. Now that I knew the truth, it all seemed so simple.

"Amazing," I muttered. "But how did the liquid get into the Blackrock Mountains? The stone must have landed miles from there."

"When it first struck the earth, the stone dug a massive trench all through the northern line of the Blackrock Mountains, deep into the area that became known as the Wastelands. The land wasn't covered by snow yet, so the trench filled with water and became a massive inland sea. Then, when the containers broke and the water was contaminated, it leeched into the sea and eventually found its way to the ore in the Blackrock Mountains.

"Gradually, the ice crept further south until it covered everything, all the way into the mountains. All along, the liquid was seeping into the mountains, drawn to the ore like a magnet. There the secret lay hidden until Tinker began his work with steam engines and springs. It was by mere chance that Tinker happened to be using mountain ore rather than the stuff in the plains. If he hadn't been such a hermit, Blackrock steel may not have been discovered for generations."

I leaned back in my chair, staring up at the ceiling. "Then it's all because of that stone. Our entire history is based on that stone."

"If it hadn't fallen onto our world, none of this would have happened," Analyn agreed. "And most likely, none of us would exist. We would never have been born."

I was dumbfounded. In just a few minutes, Crow had laid bare the entire history of our world, explaining every great mystery with such simplicity that I could only accept it as fact.

Lies are complicated, but the truth is always simple, Tinker used to say. Everything Crow had just told me was easy to believe because there wasn't any room in it for a lie. In my heart, I knew that this was what had happened. This was how we had become what we were.

I had never cared much about history. I knew about the Great War between the Tal'mar and humans, and Tinker had told me countless stories about the Kanters and the Vangars, but to me they were like fairy tales. It was hard to imagine the old world he described. Dockside was my world. The city was what I knew, and Tinker's old stories hadn't ever seemed relevant.

As I got older, I saw what the Vangars were capable of. I had seen them take my friends off to the slave mines. I had seen them hurt and kill innocent people. I had learned to be strong; so strong that eventually all I cared about was killing Vangars and making them pay for all they had done to us. My life became defined by that dream of violent and bloody revenge.

Crow's story was a revelation to me, but ultimately I decided this knowledge didn't change anything. Not really. Regardless of how we'd gotten where we were, we were still in the same mess. And for the moment, my priority was still the same.

"I have to go back for Kale," I said. "I don't know what to think about the rest of this, but what I do know is that he's still alive and he needs my help. I'm sure of it."

"That wasn't part of the plan," Crow said. He gave Analyn a look and she pursed her lips.

I arched an eyebrow. "You have a plan? What scheme have the two of you concocted?"

"It's not us," Analyn said, waving her hands in the air. "It's your mother."

I felt a strange stirring in my chest. I still hadn't fully digested the fact that my mother was still alive. *Our mother.*

"What is it, then?" I said. "Tell me Breeze's plan."

Crow took a deep breath. "The defenses of Sanctuary are formidable," he said. "When our mother found the city, she stumbled upon a technologically advanced society. There are weapons, things you couldn't even imagine. Things far more sophisticated than what the humans and Tal'mar created."

"Then we could defeat the Vangars," I said. "Is that her plan? To use all of this technology to win the war? That's what she went there for in the first place..."

"We would," Crow said, sighing, "but we *can't.*"

"I don't understand."

Analyn spoke up. "Your mother hasn't been alone in Sanctuary. There are other Tal'mar with her. Hundreds of them, along with the queen, your great-grandmother. They have become isolationists, cutting themselves off from the outside world. They refuse to have dealings with humans or anyone else. In fact, your brother just barely managed to escape."

I stared at him, stunned by the idea that he'd had to *escape* from his own people. "Why would they do that?"

"The Tal'mar blame humans in a way," Crow said. "They also fear the Vangars. Mostly, they want to rebuild their society and their culture without outside influence. And they have found the perfect place to do it. Nothing can harm them in Sanctuary."

I felt my fists clenching up as he spoke. "We have been suffering, living with the Vangars' boots at our throats for all these years and the Tal'mar could have stopped it at any time! They've hidden themselves away, ignoring the fact that their own people are dying in Vangar slave mines?"

"You're right," Analyn said. "It's unforgiveable, and regrettably, there's nothing we can do about it."

"Then what was your plan?" I said, the irritation clear in my voice.

"I was supposed to bring you home. Mother sent me to find you, as well as Analyn and Tinker and anyone else willing to join us. I'm supposed to bring you to Sanctuary where you'll be safe."

I shook my head, staring at the table. "I can't do that," I said. "I won't just leave like that."

"I didn't expect you to," Crow said. "The truth is that I had something more... *impressive* in mind."

I frowned. "What are you talking about?"

"Let me put it this way," Crow said. "If three of us return, we will be safe from the Vangars. If three hundred of us return, then we can make the *whole world* safe."

My eyes widened. "That's your plan? To bring so many?"

73

"If we can, yes. But that is dependent on us. The plan won't work unless we return in significant numbers. The Tal'mar will have to *know* they can't keep their secret anymore. We have to expose them in such a way that they are forced to recognize the outside world."

I considered that. Gradually, a smile came to my lips. I could see my mother's wisdom behind this plan. If the Tal'mar were exposed, they'd have no choice but to defend themselves from the Vangars. And their only defense would be a good offense. They'd have to attack the Vangars while they had the element of surprise on their side. And if their technology was as impressive as Crow had described it, the Vangars would be in for a surprise.

"I'll do it. I'd give anything to see the Vangars crushed like the vermin they are. But first we have to get Kale. I won't leave without him."

"You'll have to find others," Analyn said. "And you'll have to find a way to get them out of the city without the Vangars knowing. It won't be easy."

"First things first," I said. "When I know Kale is safe, then I'll worry about the rest."

"As you wish," Crow said quietly, sharing a glance with Analyn.

I started working on the boneshaker the next morning, with my vision bleary from lack of sleep and my senses dulled by exhaustion and emotional overload. I'd spent most of the night talking with Crow and Analyn, and I had far too much to think about. My thoughts were muddled, dull, and congested. I couldn't think clearly enough to use the right wrench to pull a broken pipe off the carburetor, much less absorb everything I had learned and make sense of it all. My entire world had changed. It was going to take some time to get used to.

Crow showed up and offered to help. I noticed that he had no problem fetching pieces of pipe or tools made of brass and copper, but he flinched at the touch of steel. "The element has affected you, too," I noted.

"I'm a lot more like a Tal'mar than our mother," he explained. "Physically, they say I look human, but the rest of me is Tal'mar."

"You have the *sight* then? You can see into things?"

"I can, but not so readily into a machine. As you have observed, touching steel is uncomfortable for me."

"But your daggers," I said, nodding toward his belt. "They're steel, aren't they?"

He drew one of them and held it up, smiling. I watched as he twisted his hand and sent the blade spinning into the air. It flipped half a dozen times and then landed, perfectly balanced on the palm of his hand, the blade still rotating. He flicked his hand again and the dagger danced across his wrist, rotating end over end until it slid down out of sight, somewhere up his sleeve. It reappeared as he raised his hand and closed his grip on the blade. He handed it to me, handle first.

"Not bad," I said, admiring his skill. "You should see what I can do with my revolver." I examined the dagger, noting the fine balance and perfect craftsmanship. I'd never seen a weapon so flawless. I also noticed a slight tingling feeling in my fingers as I held it, like tiny jolts of electricity. I quickly handed it back to him.

"As you can see it is steel, but it is more. Like Blackrock steel, this dagger has absorbed energy from the element. It has simply absorbed a great deal *more*."

"I don't like it," I said. "It feels strange to me."

"And now you understand my aversion to untreated steel," he said. "We are opposites, you and I, and yet of a type."

A slight grin turned up the corners of my mouth. "You talk like our mother."

His eyebrows shot up. "Oh? And how do you know that?"

"Because I've been reading her journals." I turned my attention back to the boneshaker. "This isn't going to work," I said, frustrated. "The engine and carburetor are destroyed. I'll have to find another way back to Avenston."

"Steam!" Analyn called out behind us. We both turned to see her making her way slowly down the street. "I told you already, oil is for Vangars. Steam is better."

I rolled my eyes. "What's better doesn't matter. I can't convert the boneshaker to steam without a steam engine and a boiler."

Analyn waved her walking stick in a broad arc. "Oh look!" she said in a sarcastic voice. "It's a whole city. I wonder if there's any steam equipment there."

I looked at Crow and we both started laughing.

Despite her sarcasm, Analyn was actually quite helpful in locating parts for the boneshaker's conversion. She had spent a lot of time wandering around the city over the years, more time than she'd initially led me to believe. She led us to an old steamsmith's shop, still full of useable tools and parts.

She also knew where to find a good anvil. What she couldn't do was help. She had no knowledge of such things. Unfortunately, Crow couldn't help much either. Even though his head was full of strange esoteric knowledge, he didn't have the slightest idea what I was doing. Crow had never touched a steam engine in his life. At one point, I asked him to hand me a pressure release valve and he just stared at me. I shook my head.

"Sanctuary must be quite a place, if nothing ever needs to be fixed there," I said.

"Oh the machines take care of all of that," he said.

I paused and twisted around to stare at him. "The machines?"

"Yes. When things break, the machines repair them. That is their... it's their fulfillment, their purpose. It's what they were designed to do."

"But if the machines break, then what?"

"Other machines repair them, of course."

I could only shake my head. It was just one more crazy story about Sanctuary; one of dozens he had already told me. I didn't bother asking him to explain because I knew he'd just confuse me trying to put it into words.

I stepped into the steamsmith's shop to find the valve I was looking for. I located it in one of the toolboxes and brought it quickly back outside. I had been working in the street for fear of the building collapsing on top of my head. Crow quietly watched as I went back to work installing the valve.

I worked late into the night, until Analyn insisted we douse our lantern and get back into the tunnels. "Vangars do still come around here from time to time," she warned us. "Considering you just barely escaped them, I would think you'd be more cautious. And there are other things out in the darkness to worry about as well."

She was right, and I was too tired to argue about it anyway. Crow helped me cover the boneshaker with an old canvas sheet. We returned to Analyn's tunnel for a quick meal. While we were eating, I noticed that at some point during the day Crow had located another cot for me to sleep on. I noted that he hadn't found one for himself. I asked him why.

"I don't sleep often," he explained. "Once or twice a week. While you rest, I'll go hunting. We've almost used up the venison."

"Venison?" I said. I shot Analyn a glare. "I thought you said we were eating rats."

She smiled wickedly. "Only a city girl wouldn't know the taste of real venison stew."

I glared at her as I took my bowl to the washbasin. She and Crow shared a laugh at my expense, which I didn't find amusing at all.

After dinner, Analyn went to her chair by the fireplace to do her knitting and I curled up on the cot Crow had found. I turned the lantern down low and opened my mother's journals. I began reading at the page where I'd left off.

The stories kept me up later than I should have, but I was riveted. I'd never known my mother. The insight into her life and personality was more than I ever could have asked. Somehow, as I scanned those faded yellow pages, I almost began to feel that I actually knew her.

The following morning, I went right back to work on the boneshaker. The process of restoring the old steam engine I'd located only took until midmorning, and then it was just a matter of installing a boiler. The old steamsmith's shop had a good supply of copper boilers, somewhat tarnished but all in good shape. I had my choice of sizes, so I picked the biggest one I could fit inside the boneshaker's frame. At last, I stood back surveying my work, a satisfied grin on my face.

"What now?" Crow said.

"Now we start the fire and test it out. We'll need to find some coal."

Crow reached into the folds of his cloak and pulled out a small glass vial full of phosphorescent blue liquid. "Try this," he said, offering it to me.

I took a nervous step back. "Is that the... is it the *element?*"

"Yes, we call the liquid form starfall."

"You used that word last night. I wondered if that was what you were talking about."

"None other. Don't worry, a very small amount like this won't affect you. It takes prolonged direct exposure to cause any harm."

I cautiously took it from him and looked it over. "What do I do with it?"

"Use it for fuel."

Frowning, I knelt down and placed the vial into the firebox. "What now?"

"Light it," he said, grinning.

Reluctantly, I pulled a match out of the tool bag and lit it. I took a step back and tossed the match into the firebox. There was a flicker as the vial caught fire, and dark blue flames danced up. I winced, expecting some sort of explosion or a powerful release of energy. Nothing like that happened. Not so much as a crackle. Just smooth dancing flames.

"Are you sure it's safe?" I said, eyeing the flames suspiciously.

"The vial won't break, but don't bother trying to put the flame out. It will burn for years like that."

I raised my eyebrows. "Years?"

"Truly. You wouldn't believe what we can accomplish with this fuel."

"I'm starting to get an idea," I said, closing the firebox.

Minutes later, the boiler was hot and the rapidly climbing needle on the pressure gauge told me it was time for a test drive. I mounted the boneshaker and dropped it into gear. With a twist of the throttle, I was off.

The boneshaker's new steam engine did not disappoint. It accelerated just as quickly as the old gyro engine, but with much less noise. Instead of the shrill, whining buzz of a combustion engine, the steam engine gave off a low *chug-chugging* sound that reminded me of a heartbeat. As I built up speed and wound the engine tighter, it *whirred* like a sewing machine, the sound accentuated by the deep pulsing drive of a locomotive. I found the sound quite pleasing.

I kept an eye on the pressure gauge as I drove, and I noted that even at full throttle, I never lost pressure. The boneshaker was at least as fast as before, and seemed to have a good deal more torque when I accelerated. It accelerated more smoothly, it was quieter, and to refuel, all I needed was water. I returned to the steamsmith's shop with a broad smile plastered across my face. I hit the brakes and skidded sideways, sliding right up to Crow.

"Want a ride?" I said, beaming.

He gave me a sly smile. "I'll race you!"

I laughed thinking it was a joke, but then he took off running down the street, toward the city gates. I rolled my eyes and gunned the throttle, expecting to easily overtake him. To my surprise, once Crow had built up speed, he leapt into the air and spread his cloak out with his arms, fanning it out like a giant wing. As it caught the air, I noticed rib-like shapes under the fabric. I also noticed that in key places, the cloak was attached to his body by thin metallic straps. They connected at his arms and shoulders as well as his waist and thighs.

I was completely confounded as the cloak caught the wind and Crow began rising into the air. Then I noticed trails of misty vapor shooting out from the ribs behind him, and realized that he was using some sort of advanced flight technology. The cloak didn't just look like a wing, *it was a wing*. And it was designed in such a way that he could control his flight by moving his arms and twisting his torso left and right. In this manner, Crow flew up into the heavens, made a spiral far overhead, and then plummeted back down to race alongside me.

I'd been idling along, staring at him, hardly aware of the fact that I was moving. When he appeared next to me with that grin on his face, the race was on. I twisted the throttle and leaned forward, cutting the wind like a knife. The boneshaker surged forward, the front end rising a few inches off the ground as I accelerated.

Off to my right, Crow threw his arms back, forming a tight "V" shape with his body, and took off like a bolt of lightning. He hurtled past me so fast I only felt a gust of wind and saw a dark green mass disappearing in the distance. I reached down to adjust the pressure valve, giving the engine even more thrust. The road beneath my wheels became a smooth red blur. The wind hammered at my face. And Crow vanished into the horizon like I was standing still.

Three miles outside the city, I found him sitting on the ground beside the road. He smiled and rose to his feet as I pulled up next to him. "How does that thing work?" was all I could think to say.

He mumbled something about compressed gas and superheated steam but it was mostly nonsense to me. I just sat there staring. "Do you want to try it?" he said at last. "It's quite easy to learn."

"No," I said.

"Are you sure? I can teach you."

"No. I'll keep my feet on the ground."

"All right. Perhaps another time."

Reality settled over us then, and we both realized that our fun was over. "I should say goodbye to Analyn," I said. "If we leave now, we can reach Avenston by nightfall."

He nodded thoughtfully. "I wish we had more time, sister."

"When this is over," I promised. "Then we can talk, and you can tell me all about Sanctuary and our mother."

"I'll do better than that," he said with a smile. "I'll show you." He spread his arms, somehow activating the jets in his cloak. He began to rise slowly in the air. "I will watch for you tonight!"

I couldn't help smiling back at him. "Until then, little brother."

With that, Crow *whooshed* out of sight into the clouds. I stared after him with that one word ringing through my ears: *brother*. All those years I had believed my mother was dead. Now that I knew the truth, I had a renewed sense of purpose. Before, I had been eager to spill Vangar blood. That was when I had only one friend left in the world and a heart full of vengeance. Now, I had something more. Now I didn't just have something to die for, *I had something to live for.*

My farewell to Analyn was brief. I still wasn't sure what to think of the crazy old woman, but I had decided that I cared about her. She had meant something to my mother and to Tinker, and that meant she was important to me. I didn't need to know any more than that. I didn't care about the fact that she was our queen, or at least that she might have been if things had been different. I also didn't care about the fact that she had an annoying way of thinking she was smarter than me. She may even have been right. Probably not, but maybe.

I left my mother's journals with Analyn. I wanted to be sure they'd never fall into Vangar hands, and I knew they'd be safe with her. I knew Analyn would care for them dearly. I thanked her for everything and then sped out of Anora, a trail of dust and steam rising in the air behind me, the late afternoon sun beating down as I roared down the old road towards Avenston.

I tried to focus on the details of the plan, but I had so many things rolling around in my head that I found it hard to concentrate. My mother was alive. I had a brother! And throughout all of those years, my mother had never forgotten me. She had been waiting, planning, biding her time until she could make her move. Breeze had risked everything to make this moment happen, and I wasn't about to let her down.

Chapter 6

It was already dark when I saw the black clouds
stretching across the sky and the lights of Avenston
twinkling in the gloom. I soon tasted the familiar acrid
smoke on my lips and felt it burning my nostrils, and I
smiled because I was going home. The stars and the
moon vanished behind the thick black veil and I
gunned the throttle, making a beeline for the city gates.

I expected a sentinel to be waiting at the gate and I
was not disappointed. The Vangars aren't concerned
about people entering the city, but they patrol the gates
and the city walls to make sure no one escapes. That's
why the sentinel was facing the other way when I
roared past him and disappeared down Main Street. By
the time he had put on enough speed to catch me, I was
long gone.

I left the boneshaker in a special place, in the
shadows under a small footbridge not far from
Dockside. It was a quiet little corner of the city, a place
shrouded in thick ivy and the dense foliage of lilac
bushes. I had spent much time there as a child, hiding
in the shadows, waiting for an angry Vangar merchant
or a sentinel to give up the chase so that I could go
spend my handful of stolen coins. It was the safest
place I could think of to leave the boneshaker.

Before leaving, I pulled my revolver out and laid it
across the seat. Now that I was back in the city, I was

going to have to follow my instincts to survive. Carrying a weapon like my revolver would just attract unwanted attention.

I heard a *whooshing* sound up the street and I peered through the bushes to see Crow landing in the shadows at the corner. I glanced at my revolver and then reluctantly left. Once again, I got that uneasy feeling in my gut, but I pushed the thought out of my head and jogged over to meet him.

"This way," I whispered, leading him into the nearest alley.

He followed after me, silent as a shadow. We made our way through the north end of Dockside, up to the rocky coastline south of the city wall. There, at the edge of the old neighborhood, I spotted the shanty I was looking for. It was an unremarkable place made of discarded lumber and salvaged tin siding like most everything in Dockside. I saw a chimney poking out through the roof and smoke curling up into the sky. The boardwalk out front was quiet and I heard the waves crashing on the beach in the darkness somewhere below. I glanced up and down the street and then moved closer for a better look.

Crow and I slipped through the shadows between buildings until we were right next to the shanty. Cautiously, I peered in through the window. I saw a lantern burning and an elderly couple playing cards at a small table. I watched them for a few moments, smiling inwardly. The innocuous looking gray-haired old couple were two of the most dangerous revolutionaries in the kingdom. Like Tinker, they remembered the old world. They craved a return of our freedoms, and equally for the destruction of our Vangar overlords. Like Kale and I, they would stop at nothing to make that happen. They were willing to give their lives to the cause.

I waited a few minutes to make sure that the sentinels weren't staking out the area. I had no way of knowing how many rebels had escaped after our meeting, or how much information the sentinels might have gleaned from the ones they caught. It was quite possible that I was walking right into a trap.

When at last I was satisfied that we were alone, I led Crow to the door and quietly knocked. I heard shuffling inside. A moment later, Hatch Woodcarver answered the door. His wife Shel hovered just behind him. He blinked against the darkness and then smiled as his old eyes adjusted and he recognized me.

"River!" he said, throwing his arms around me. "You survived! We were sure the sentinels-" He broke off as he noticed Crow hovering in the shadows behind me. He pulled away, giving me a wary look. "Is he-?"

"Yes, he's with us," I said. I glanced up and down the street. "Can we come in?"

"Of course! We were so worried about you, the way you disappeared. The rest of us escaped, but you... you shouldn't have tried to take on those sentinels like that."

Hatch ushered us inside. As we gathered in the middle of the room, I glanced at my surroundings. I had never been in the Woodcarver's home before. I noticed that they had built a makeshift kitchen at the south end, facing the docks, and that they had a small library of books on the opposite wall near the fireplace. I was impressed. Few people in Dockside have the pride or ingenuity to turn their shanties into real homes. Hatch and Shel had done well. It couldn't compare to the two-story home Tinker had built out of scraps, but few things could. It wouldn't have been fair to expect so much from anyone but Tinker. I saw them staring at my brother and smiled.

"This is Crow," I said matter-of-factly. "He's my brother."

Their jaws both dropped open. "I'm... I don't understand," Hatch said.

I watched them for a moment, grinning as they tried to put it together. They knew that my father had died while my mother was still pregnant with me, and that she had died soon after my birth. It hardly seemed possible, unless...

"Robie?" Hatch said cautiously. "Did he have a..." his voice trailed off as he realized how delicate the situation might be.

"No, of course not," I said, laughing. "My father was perfectly faithful to my mother."

"Of course he was!" Shel said, smacking her husband on the shoulder. "I've never seen a more dedicated man. Robie would have crawled across broken glass for your mother."

"But..." Hatch said, his voice trailing off as he stared at Crow. "I just don't understand."

I took pity on him and explained everything. I started with the story of my journey into the plains on that first night with the sentinels chasing me, and the accident that narrowly saved my life. Then I told them about Analyn and Crow and of course, my mother. They were quite shocked to learn that Breeze was still alive.

The Woodcarvers had all the same questions I'd had when I first met Crow. I tried to explain the situation to them, with Crow helping here and there. He told them about Sanctuary with the same cryptic descriptions he'd given me, and did his best to explain our mother's situation.

"This is all wonderful," Shel said, staring at Crow, "but I don't understand why the two of you came back here. Especially you, River. You made your escape! Why would you return? Surely you know what they'll do if they catch you."

I gave Crow a sideways glance. I wasn't sure how much I should tell them. For their own safety, it might be best to keep them in the dark about our plan. "I need to find Kale," I said cautiously. "The night of the attack, I saw him with the Vangars."

"They took him to the slave mines," Hatch said angrily. He drove his fist into the palm of his hand. "Probably beat him within an inch of his life first."

I considered that. "At least we know he's alive," I said. "They wouldn't have taken him to the mines to kill him."

"Not right away," Shel said. "Everyone knows the mines are a death sentence. It's just a slow death."

"Hold on now," Hatch said. "You're going to stage a rescue, aren't you? You'll be walking into all kinds of trouble if you go to the mines."

I sighed. I was trying not to give them any details, but they were guessing half of it. "I've got to get Kale," I said. "I won't leave him there."

"I should have known. What can we do to help?"

I glanced at Crow. "I don't think that would be a good idea," I said. "Crow and I have a plan, but-"

"Well let us help you then!" Shel said. "What can we do? Do you need a distraction? I think I still have a bomb in the kitchen cabinet."

I smiled. "No, no bombs. Nothing like that. I really shouldn't tell you any more."

They stepped a little closer, their eyes sparkling dangerously. I noticed Shel's hand slide into Hatch's, and he squeezed it. "We can do this, River," he said. "Whatever it us, let us help you."

"Don't keep us in the dark," Shel said, pleading. I stared at them, biting my lower lip.

"Have pity on a couple of old-timers," Hatch said. "Give us a little hope. Tell us your plan."

I looked at Crow. He shrugged. "All right then," I said. "But you must keep this quiet. Don't change your routine. Keep on behaving as if tomorrow were just another day."

Their eyes lit up and a devious smile broke out on Shel's face. "This isn't our first revolution, child," she said wickedly.

"You can count on us," Hatch added.

"Crow and I will see to Kale. In the meanwhile, if you truly want to help, we need the two of you to spread the word -very quietly and very carefully- that some of us will be escaping the city."

"How do you plan to do that?" Hatch said.

"Leave the details to us. For now, we just need numbers. We need a large group that can travel quickly."

"Mostly youngsters then," said Hatch. "All right, we can do that. When will you be back?"

"A day or two at most," I said. "I have to get inside the mines and find Kale. Somehow, we'll have to break him out."

"How will you get inside?" said Shel.

"I can only think of one way in," I said. "The same way everyone gets in."

Their mouths fell open. "You can't be serious," Shel said. "You're not thinking of getting caught *on purpose!* Have you lost your mind?"

Hatch agreed with her emphatically. "Don't do this, River. The Vangars will kill you."

"I'm in agreement with your friends," Crow said. "It's too great a risk. There must be some other way. If the Vangars decide to make an example of you, we may not be able to save you."

"I don't think they will," I said. "I'm even more sure of it now, because I know they kept Kale alive. And if they really want to make an example of me, they won't want me dead right away. They'll want to make sure others see what happened to me."

"But what if you're wrong?" Shel said. "What if they kill you? What if that's their example?"

I smiled reassuringly. "I've slipped through the sentinels' hands many times before. Don't forget who I am."

They couldn't argue with that. I wasn't sure getting caught was a great plan, but I knew it was the only sure way to get into the mines, and by far the quickest way there. If Crow and I tried to find the mines and sneak in, we would almost certainly be caught by the Vangars. This way, I knew exactly where I was going. Once I was inside, I'd simply find Kale and help him escape. It seemed like a simple enough plan.

Before we left, the Woodcarvers assured us that they would be very discreet in sharing our plan. They promised to have a group ready to leave in two days. I thanked them for their help and then we said our farewells.

Crow and I parted ways after we left the shanty. He gave me a hug and warned me to be extra careful. "I haven't come all this way to see my big sister get killed," he said.

"Don't worry. Just stay out of sight. Follow me to the mines and look for my signal. Once I find Kale, we'll be out so fast the Vangars won't know what hit them."

"Be careful, sister."

I smiled. Crow *whooshed* into the heavens and vanished in the clouds over the city. I watched him disappear and then took a moment to steel my nerves. I wasn't as confident about our plan as I had led Crow and the Woodcarvers to believe. There were so many things that could go wrong. But in the end, it was worth it. It was better to risk everything and be dead than to risk nothing and be a slave.

I passed through the alleys and side streets of Avenston, quickly making my way to the patrol station at the south end of the city. It was a tall brick building on the corner with the word "justice" in the Vangar language scrawled across the masonry above the front doors, accompanied by the Vangars' seal, a war hammer crossing over an axe. This was the place the Vangars pretended to have court, where they brought innocent people to trial, accused them, and found them guilty. Always guilty. There was no jury, no impartial panel of judges. Any Vangar could accuse any slave of a crime, and the slave's death was all but guaranteed. It was just one more way in which the Vangars kept the populace under their control.

This was also the home of the sentinels. Being as much machine as human, they needed constant maintenance. The mechanics at the patrol station looked after the sentinels day and night, replacing worn out parts, lubricating their machinery, and installing upgrades. With a dozen sentinels patrolling the streets, they had no problem keeping the mechanics busy.

When I arrived, I stood on the street outside for a moment, watching them through the windows. I saw a few Vangar soldiers sitting at a table in the front of the building, talking and gambling over a card game. Behind them, I saw a mechanic working on one of the sentinels, probably repairing the damage I had caused when I escaped the city. That brought a small smile to my lips.

I knew that there were more of them in there. More Vangars, more sentinels. I was walking into a lion's den. The only advantage I had was that of surprise. Tinker used to have a saying about war: *"Where the enemy is strongest, he is also weakest."* I wasn't sure what it meant, but I hoped it was true. I was about to find out. In the next few minutes I'd either be dead or on my way to destroying the Vangars once and for all.

I took a deep breath and thought: *This is it. This is what you've always wanted to do...*

I charged up the steps and kicked open the front doors. The Vangars looked up from their card game, their eyes widening with surprise as I leapt into the room and kicked the nearest warrior in the face. He flipped over backwards in his chair, crashing loudly to the floor. His legs shot up as he fell, knocking over the table and spilling cards and coins everywhere.

The soldier to my right leapt up from his chair and took a step in my direction, his hand forming into a fist. I lowered my center of gravity. As he came at me, my leg shot out like a piston. I focused every ounce of strength I had, aiming a kick at the side of his knee.

The heel of my boot connected solidly and I felt the bone cracking as his knee bent at an awkward angle.

The Vangar went sprawling, arms flailing, a wild howl escaping his lips. As he tumbled, I spun around and smashed my elbow into his nose. If my aim had been a little better, I might have actually killed him. As it was, the cartilage shattered and blood fountained down my arm as he dropped to the floor next to me. A third Vangar flew out of his chair and came at me with a dagger. I avoided him by leaping over the table. I landed directly in front of the sentinel.

He was sitting in a massive chair that had been specially designed to hold his weight. He couldn't move because he was still attached to some sort of machine, but he took a swing at me the instant I got within reach. The mechanic was between us, and he took the brunt of the blow. The sentinel's swing caught him on the side of the chest and the mechanic flew backwards, pushing me out of the way as he tumbled across the room. Glass shattered as he crashed through the front windows and landed on the sidewalk out front.

I stumbled back, reaching out to catch my balance on the back of a chair. Unfortunately, I fell right into the open arms of a very angry Vangar. I instantly felt the cold steel of his dagger at my throat and his hot breath on the back of my neck. It occurred to me that I may have made my entrance a bit too dramatic.

"Time to die, little girl," he said in his native language. After a lifetime of being surrounded by Vangars, I know their language well enough to understand most of what they say. I just never speak it.

The sentinel grinned and leaned back in his chair, watching us. The others circled around, licking their lips like wolves encircling a wounded deer. One of the others yelled, "We have her! We've got the girl!"

Off to my left, a door swung open and a man stepped into the room. I could see the dark blur of his shape in the corner of my eye, but I couldn't turn my head for fear of drawing that sharp blade across my neck. The man sucked in a deep raspy breath, and I heard the sound of machinery: *Click, whir, thump. Click, whir thump. Click, whir thump.* He exhaled slowly, and then sucked in another deep, rattling breath. *Click, whir thump, click whir thump.*

The sound followed him as he crossed the room, and I gasped as he appeared in front of me. He was an older man, around sixty, and most definitely not a Vangar. But he wasn't human anymore, either. He was as much machine as man. He wasn't like the sentinels, though. A brass mask of tiny gears and springs covered half his face and I saw them move every time he took a breath or made a facial movement. Several metal tubes coiled out of the mask and connected to a similar-looking metal plate mounted across the center of his chest.

Click, whir thump. Click, whir thump.

His left arm was gone, replaced by more machinery. From what I could tell, most of the mechanisms were powered by springs and hydraulic pressure, not unlike the sentinels. I'd never seen the man before, but I instantly knew him by reputation. He was *the overseer,* something like a governor. According to the stories I'd heard, all of that machinery didn't just make him stronger. It was keeping him alive.

"Can we have her, Overseer?" one of the Vangars said. That was the one whose nose I'd broken. He had a dagger in his hand and I could see that he planned to use it on me.

The overseer looked me over. "Bring her to my chamber," he said.

The Vangar behind me relaxed his grip, and the one with the broken nose tossed me over his shoulder. I put up a struggle as we headed for the stairs, but not too much. After all, I didn't actually want to escape. The whole point of me going there had been to get caught. I did take advantage of the opportunity to jam my elbow in his eye though, and I was rewarded to see instant swelling. His response was to twist suddenly sideways, ramming my head into the wall. It was painful enough that I gave up any pretense of fighting. I went limp as he hauled me to the next floor and down a dark hallway.

The Vangar paused in front of a set of tall wooden doors. He set me down long enough to open them, and then dragged me inside. A sense of unease washed over me as I glanced around the room. It was a large, luxurious space, but the furnishings were sparse and worn. I saw a tall brass bed off to my right, and directly in front of it, a set of heavy chains bolted to the floor. The dark stains on the wooden floor could only have been from blood. That was when I realized I may have gotten myself into more trouble than I could handle.

I tried to pull out of the Vangar's grip, but I may as well have been locked in a vice. "Keep it up," he said in a dark voice, taunting me. Then he twisted my arm within an inch of breaking it. A moan escaped my lips and he laughed. "I'll break you into pieces, girl."

"Not today, Wulvine." The overseer appeared in the doorway behind us. "You may leave now."

"But-"

"Leave," the overseer repeated. *Click, whir, thump.* "Notify me when my flight is ready."

Wulvine shot me a dark glare as he left the room. The overseer waited for the door to close before he turned to smile at me. I think it was a smile. It was hard to be sure under all that machinery. "Sit," he said, gesturing at the bed. I glanced at it and went tense.

"I usually prefer Tal'mar women," he said casually. "They're so delicate, so refined. *So breakable.* But you... there's something special about you, River."

"How do know my name?"

He smiled again, or something like it. His face whirred and clicked, and I saw teeth appear behind his thin lips. "Do you know who I am?"

"You're the overseer."

"Ah, yes, *overseer.* The judge, the mayor, the lord of this garbage heap." He leaned in close, staring into my eyes. "You don't really know though, do you? Tell me, have you ever wondered how a human came to rule over this city? How was it that I, a mere human, not only became accepted by the Vangars but even empowered? Why do you suppose they made me overseer?"

"You're a turncoat," I said, glaring at him. "You sold out your own kind."

"True. It's all true, but I don't think you know the whole story. Did the tinkerman ever tell you who I really am?"

He stood back, watching my face, smiling that twisted smile. "My name is Gile Rutherford. I used to be the mayor of Riverfork."

"What's a river-fork?" I said, raising an eyebrow.

He made a *tsk tsk* sound. "Old Tinkerman didn't tell you anything did he?"

"He told me how to kill Vangars!" I snarled.

"Oh, I believe that. I wonder why, though. I wonder why he never told you about me." He tapped his chin with a mechanical finger as he considered this question. Then he turned his gaze back on me. "Do you know that your mother saved my life once?"

I snorted.

"It's true!" he said. "There I was, with a knife to my throat and a thousand voices cheering for my death. Your mother touched me and somehow... somehow she knew that I had a bad heart. She took pity on me. She let me survive. Without her, I wouldn't have lived another day, much less all the years it took for me to gain this position. I owe all I have to your mother."

My fist knotted up and my arm flashed out. I took a swing at him without even thinking about it. I threw all my years of backstreet fighting into that one blow, and I expected to at least knock out a few teeth. I never even touched him. I saw a blur of motion and found my arm frozen in space, an inch from his face. The overseer's mechanical hand squeezed my wrist, forcing my arm back, twisting it around, his face contorted in a wicked smile...

The bone in my wrist snapped like a twig. A jarring pain shot up and down my entire body, and a primal scream escaped my lips. Bile churned up in my stomach as my hand flopped loosely in his grip. I tried to pull away but it was futile. Rutherford's smile vanished, and he gave me a shove. I toppled over backwards, flying over the couch. I landed in a heap across his desk. Parchment and inkwells scattered, spilling out across the desk, glass shattering as it hit the wooden floorboards.

Spots swam in my vision. I moved slowly, cautiously pulling my broken wrist out from under me as I struggled back to my feet. I turned, leaning back against Rutherford's desk, grabbing my broken wrist with my good hand. I twisted it, attempting to reset the bones. An involuntary scream rattled my throat as the bones ground together and I had to force myself not to vomit. Blood trickled from my nose.

I stood there a moment, swaying back and forth as I grappled with unconsciousness. Gradually, the floor beneath my feet became firm again. I blinked away the spots and cast a wary glance at the overseer. He hadn't moved.

I grimaced, my good hand searching the desk behind me for something -anything- that I might use as a weapon. My fingers closed on a dull steel blade and I recognized it as a letter opener. *Click, whir, thump.*

"As I was saying," Rutherford continued, "it was your mother who saved me. She set me free, knowing that I didn't have long to live. She was right about that. I made it out of the city, but I had to swim across the river. My heart gave out halfway across. Fortunately, an escaping Vangar warrior found me and brought me back to his masters.

"I survived, but my body was wrecked. I had lost the ability to speak, or even move half of my body. But the Vangars found a way to fix that." He held his mechanical fist in the air, smiling, admiring it. "They made me good as new... even *better.*"

The door flew open and Wulvine stepped into the room. He glanced at the mayor, confused for a moment, then saw me leaning up against the desk. A grin broke out across his face as he saw the blood running down my chin and my broken wrist dangling at my side.

"Overseer, your flight is ready. I can tell the pilot to wait-"

"No," Rutherford cut him off. "I'll finish this later."

Wulvine nodded and then turned his attention to me. "This way, girl," he said in an amused tone. I stepped away from the desk, deftly sliding the letter opener under my belt at the small of my back.

Wulvine guided us to an elevator down the hall and pulled the iron gate shut behind us. He kept a wary eye on me as he pulled a switch on the wall. Somewhere in the darkness below, I heard the hiss of steam and the groaning sound of gears turning. Slowly, we began to rise. The elevator ascended through the roof, settling in front of a landing pad.

Before us waited a Vangar dirigible, one of the smaller airships often used for short local trips and hauling light loads. Wulvine pulled back the gate, ushering us out onto the landing area. We stepped into the shadow of the ship's massive air balloon, and proceeded up the boarding ramp.

"Put her in chains," Rutherford said over his shoulder as he stomped toward the nearest stairwell. "When we dock, take her to my private quarters."

Wulvine gave me a shove toward the edge of the main deck. I saw shackles and anchors lining the floor, dangerously close to the cannons. I thrust my shoulder back against him defiantly and gave him a violent stare. He smirked and said:

"You want to fight me?"

I didn't. The pain in my arm had receded to a dull throbbing ache, so long as I didn't move my wrist. It was black and blue, and swelling quickly. I threw my gaze at the floor and trudged over to the chains without a fight. Wulvine followed with a smirk on his face.

He locked a slave collar around my throat and shackled my ankles to a chain. I'd seen the collars before. They were made of heavy leather and lined with steel that made them impossible to cut off. The process of clamping the collar together required tongs and a red-hot metal pin. I screamed as Wulvine pressed the hot metal to my throat. The smell of burning flesh filled my nostrils. He laughed at my pain as he put the tongs away. Then, for good measure, he threw another pair of shackles on my wrists. I begged him not to, but he did it anyway. A moan escaped my lips as the cold metal buckled over my swollen injury.

"Don't go anywhere," Wulvine said with a laugh as he turned away. He went to join the rest of the ships' crew and left me there. I mumbled something about killing him but my heart wasn't in it. I leaned up against the rail, biting my lower lip, hatred burning in my eyes as I watched him leave. I was going to kill him. I didn't know how or when, but I swore to myself that I'd do it. And the overseer, too. I was going to make Rutherford pay, not just for what he'd done to me, but for what he'd done to all of us.

The captain appeared on deck a few minutes later and began ordering his men to release the ties and trim the sails. As the ship finally took flight, the full truth of my situation settled on me. I had been too caught up in the moment to realize it until then, too concerned with my pain until I saw the ground fall away and I had the horrifying realization that I wasn't going to the slave mines at all. Overseer Rutherford was taking me somewhere else entirely.

Rutherford was taking me to Juntavar, the Vangar sky city that hovered over the plains east of Avenston, halfway to the Blackrock Mountains. I knew this for a fact because I'd seen the steam locomotives coming and going from the mines for my entire life. The railroad went straight to the mines and right through Avenston, right up to the docks. There was no need for us to board an airship to go to the mines when the train could easily get us there in a few hours. No, I was sure of it. We were going to Juntavar.

My entire plan had hinged on the fact that I'd be sent to the mines. My plan had already failed. Worse yet, there was no way that Crow could find me in the sky city. He wouldn't even get close without the Vangars seeing him. I was on my own.

Chapter 7

I settled onto the deck, trying to ignore the throbbing pain in my arm as I leaned back against the rail and stared at the great black mass of a balloon hovering in the sky overhead. *What now?* was all I could think. What could I possibly do now? I had made an incalculable mistake. I had handed myself over to the Vangars for nothing. I was a fool.

Given enough time and a bit of privacy, I thought I might be able to pick the lock on my shackles, but even if I did somehow manage to get out of my chains, I'd never make it back to the ground. The Vangars would be all over me in a heartbeat. The only way to escape them was to jump, and that wasn't an option. I closed my eyes, searching for an idea, and a wave of dizziness washed over me. I felt myself drifting into a comatose sleep. I shrugged it off. My body was in shock. It was important to stay awake, to keep my mind working.

I thought about Crow and my mother and reflected on all that I had learned. I was still getting used to the idea that I had real living relatives. I never would have expected it, but I found myself thinking of Crow less as a stranger and more like a part of me; a part I had never known but had always been there.

Then there was the city, Sanctuary, and the shocking history lesson Crow had given me. It was all so much to digest. On an emotional level, I was still recovering from it all. It was more than enough to keep my mind distracted, and almost before I realized it, the crewmen were preparing to dock.

I rose unsteadily to my feet and watched the lights of the city growing in the distance. Juntavar appeared first as a massive shadow, the lights twinkling like stars against the horizon. Then it began to take form. I had never seen the city in person, but I had heard stories of it all my life. The Vangars had designed their airships in such a way that they could be connected during flight. The reason for this became clear after their initial invasion, when they banded dozens of ships together to create a flying city. The idea was brilliant, and probably something they had conceived long before they ever came to Astatia. The Vangars had a long and violent history of conquering other kingdoms for their resources. A city like Juntavar was the perfect way to rule over conquered territories. Their subjects would never revolt and breach that city. Not without a hundred airships, and that would simply never happen.

Over the years, the Vangars had replaced the airships' wooden hulls with steel framing. From this foundation, the sky-city had grown into a structure that all but defied the principles of physics. The city was shaped like a diamond. Tall buildings thrust up from the middle of the deck, their towers pressing forebodingly into the clouds, thousands of massive black balloons stretching across the sky overhead. Likewise, the sprawling structure had grown downward, each successive level slightly smaller than the last so that the level above could support the extra weight.

Without Blackrock steel, none of it would have been possible. The Vangars had mastered the steel and found ways to utilize its unique strengths. The Vangars' experiments with Blackrock steel had paid off in many ways and this architectural masterpiece was a major one. They used similar processes to make thin-walled plate metal and tubes out of copper and brass. With these scientific advances, the Vangars had created a city that was beautiful and ominous all at once. I could only marvel at it as we floated up to the docking bay and tethered our airship.

To the left and right I saw runways for planes and gyros, and directly ahead a massive landing bay for the Vangar dragon ships and dirigibles. Gas lanterns flickered here and there in the darkness, marking the runways for incoming flights. The rest of the main deck was more or less the same, with runways and landing bays along the periphery, and at least a dozen tall buildings rising up from the center.

I found a strange beauty to the scene. The simplicity of the design was elegant in its own way, the shining metal walls almost surreal against the starry sky, and I found it hard to look away. When the gang-plank was ready, Wulvine unchained me and took me into the city. I almost forgot the pain in my arm as he guided me across the busy landing area and through a large set of doors into a hangar-like building filled with airships and gyros.

My head was spinning as I took it all in. I tried to absorb everything, the layout of the place, the exits and tunnels and stairwells, but ultimately I was just gawking. I couldn't wrap my head around this massive thing, this city floating in the sky. I was awestruck as we entered the darkened hangar. Even now, in the middle of the night, the place was a cacophony of grinding metal and machinery. Mechanics were hard at work building, repairing, and creating. They never rested it seemed, and no wonder. How else could they maintain that city day and night, without ever touching the ground!

It was here that I saw Vangar women for the first time. In all of my life, no female Vangar had ever set foot in Avenston. Some people joked that they had no women, that they didn't like them, but we knew better. The Vangars often sated their carnal appetites by stealing young human women off the street, never to be seen again. I had heard many horror stories about such things. The Vangars had taken an interest in me a few times, but I always turned out to be more of a challenge than they'd expected. Many young women were not so lucky.

The Vangar women were not as tall or fearsome as their mates, but they were nonetheless impressive. Of the dozen or more that I saw, they all stood head and shoulders over any human woman, myself included. Like the men, they had strong chiseled features and many had light blonde or red hair. I noticed that they seemed to have free rein of the ship, and that they were treated more or less as equals. This seemed strange to me, that the Vangars could so readily enslave an entire kingdom and yet treat their own kind so nobly. It was my first glimpse into the psyche of this strange, conflicted race.

Wulvine led the way down several tunnels and flights of stairs until we entered a dungeon somewhere in the bowels of that massive city. The place was dark and rank, reeking with the smell of mildew, urine, and death. I heard cries and moaning sounds in the darkened cells around me, and the sound of someone wailing out in some distant room. I tried not to wonder what unique tortures they had in store for me.

By the dim light of a lantern, Wulvine led me to the end of the tunnel and threw me into a cold dark cell. I had just enough to light to see that the nearby cells were empty, and then he turned away and darkness washed over me. I tried to find a clean, dry spot on the bare wooden floor. I settled down, leaning back against the wall, trying not to think about my broken arm as the groans and screams of the other captives filled my ears. At some point, I fell asleep.

I woke hours later to the sound of my cell door opening. I blinked against the weak light as a small, shadowy figure came into the room carrying a lantern. It was a Tal'mar woman, but she was dressed in Vangar clothes.

"Rest," she said, putting her hand on my forehead.

A sense of warmth and relaxation washed over my body, and a sigh escaped my lips. My eyes rolled back in my head and a warm, prickly sensation moved up and down my arm. I felt something happening there, something eerily unnatural that I couldn't quite place, but it didn't bother me. In retrospect it should have, because I remember having the distinct feeling that things were *moving* inside my arm. Whatever magic the woman worked to heal me had also sedated me like a cup of duskwood-laced tea. My entire body was warm, and I remember having a strange floating sensation.

"It is done," she said a few minutes later, pulling her hands away from my head.

"Good," said the overseer's voice from somewhere behind her. "Have her brought to me."

I blinked, trying to find him, but he was out of sight down the hall. The girl paused as she turned away. She gave me a dark look and then reached out, brushing my cheek with her finger. Her touch was faint, delicate like a ray of sunlight kissing the clouds, and it warmed my skin with a faint tingling sensation that quickly spread throughout my body. Then she turned away and vanished down the hall. Wulvine appeared in her place.

Wulvine caught me up in rough hands and tossed me out the door. I stumbled, tripping over my own feet, and ran headlong into the adjacent cell. I should have felt pain, but instead it was like the sound of someone tapping on a distant door. There was something wrong with me. Whatever the girl had done to me had left me dizzy and unfocused, as if I'd drunk too much wine. A dull numbness saturated my entire being. I couldn't even see straight, much less form a coherent thought.

"Enough!" Overseer Rutherford shouted at Wulvine. "This one is *mine!*"

Wulvine gathered me up and tossed me over his shoulder like a sack of flour. I turned my head this way and that, trying to get a look at things, but I couldn't seem to focus. Wulvine carried me through a maze of darkened tunnels that might have gone on for minutes or days, I couldn't tell which.

I vaguely recall our journey ending in a large room with plush carpets and furniture. Here, Wulvine tossed me onto a red sofa and stood back. He gave me an approving smirk, and then winked at me before he left. I stared after him, my muddled thoughts crashing into each other like broken gears as he disappeared through the heavy iron door.

I cast my gaze about the room, wondering but not really thinking. I made a small effort to push myself up, but found it too challenging. With a sigh, I settled back into the sofa, listening to the sound of my own breathing.

Rutherford appeared before me. He was dressed in a long fur coat, with gloves and a hat. Slowly, deliberately he stripped these items away as he stared at me. He placed them meticulously on a hanger near the fireplace and then stood by the fire, staring at me. I stared back, wondering, waiting. Somewhere deep down inside me, a voice was screaming:

"Run, get out of there! Hurry, before it's too late!"

But I couldn't consider the voice because I couldn't think. I couldn't postulate what was about to happen. I was helpless as a babe, lying there, waiting for the inevitable. I couldn't bring myself to care, much less stop it from happening.

Rutherford poured himself a drink of liquor from a bottle I didn't recognize. He sipped at it, watching me quietly, a grin playing at the corners of his mouth. *Click, whir, thump. Click, whir, thump.*

At last, he set down the glass and approached me. He clenched his mechanical fist and the smile vanished from his face like a wisp of smoke on the wind. He reached out for me and I dizzily pushed myself back into the couch. The soft cushion resisted, and I fell into his grip. The overseer caught me by the throat and lifted me into the air.

"This is a moment to celebrate," he said, looking up at me. "This is the first of many nights that I assure you, you will never forget."

I opened my mouth to say something, but my body wouldn't respond. Instead, a drip of spittle escaped my lips, falling straight onto his face. He must have taken this as a deliberate attempt to spit on him. A snarl twisted his misshapen features, the gears on his mask spinning wildly, and I gave him a crooked smile.

Rutherford roared like an animal as he threw me across the room. I smashed into the wall, shattering a display of fine porcelain in the process, and then fell face-first onto the floor. Strangely, I didn't feel a thing. My entire body was numb and tingling. I was unbreakable! I could have taken on a sentinel, if I only I could move.

I lay there on the floor, the soft fibrous rug cool against my face, the smell of the fire filling my nostrils. I heard distant movements, the sound of clicking, whining gears. I heard Rutherford's deep rattling breath as he came stomping across the room toward me. His shadow filled my vision, his rough hands grasping at the slave collar on my throat.

I won't speak of the things that Rutherford did to me over the following minutes, days, years, I didn't know which because I was barely conscious during those moments and my memories of that time are vague. I had no perception of time, no frame of reality against which to measure its passage. I was simply there, lost in the haze of the moment, unafraid and at times blissfully unaware. And then I was not. Then cold, familiar darkness. My cell.

The Tal'mar woman came back to me after the beating. I remember thinking that she wasn't a Tal'mar though, because Tal'mar didn't dress that way. But if she was a Vangar, I reasoned, then how did she heal me? How did she reach into me, cooling my flesh and mending my bones so effortlessly, so trivially? It was easier for her than drawing breath. With a touch she could master my body, commanding bones to heal, wounds to close, flesh to mend. I couldn't sort it out.

I tried to speak to her, the words falling out of my mouth in a jumble. She *shushed* me and went to work fixing the broken things so that Rutherford could break them again. This was the pattern that was to become my life. I don't know how many times Rutherford beat me, but without fail the woman returned to heal my body and dull my senses. Sleep always followed, and then the beatings began again.

In a rare moment of clarity, I wondered why she took the pain away. She didn't have to. She could have left the pain there, or even made it more intense if she wanted to. Did she do it to spare me the suffering? Was it a simple act of kindness, or part of Rutherford's diabolical plan to make sure I couldn't escape? I had precious few moments of consciousness in which to consider these questions, but there was one thing I knew for sure: she kept me alive. The girl kept me breathing so that Rutherford could beat me within an inch of my life.

Our lives were entwined in some sick, inexcusable way, but still I was grateful for her. Without her, Rutherford would have killed me on the first day. I didn't have any great desire to go on living at that point, but I did have my memories. They surfaced occasionally, reminding me that I had important things to do. That people I cared about were depending on me. I also had my dreams, but in my dreams I didn't save Kale or help my brother. I didn't even escape. In my dreams, the only thing I did was kill Rutherford over and over again.

On the third day, something changed. The overseer left. I wasn't aware of this until Wulvine came for me. The Tal'mar girl had just finished healing my wounds and I was like a cloud floating across the sky as Wulvine led me through the maze of hallways to Rutherford's room. It wasn't until he closed the door that I realized we were alone.

Wulvine spun me around, cursing at me in Vangar, and then backhanded me. I felt warmth spreading across my face as I splayed out on the floor. I looked up at him, curious and confused.

"Rutherford has returned to Avenston," he said, smirking. "Today, it's just the two of us. Today you will pay for what you did to me."

What happened next is mostly a blank spot in my memory. I know that he beat me of course, just like Rutherford. I also know that at some point, Wulvine hit me too hard and in the wrong place. Something broke inside of me. As numb as I was, I knew that something was wrong. My chest went tight and my breath came in shallow gasps. I doubled over on the floor, curling into a fetal position.

Before I lost consciousness, the last thing I saw was Wulvine calling for the healer. The look on his face was one of sheer terror. Wulvine thought he had killed me, the overseer's plaything, and he was terrified of what Rutherford might do to him. I think I may have smiled as darkness swallowed me up.

A short while later, I heard voices. One of them I recognized as my brother. My eyes fluttered open and I saw him kneeling on the floor next to me. The Tal'mar woman was next to him. Crow held my neck in his left hand, my upper arm in his right. The Tal'mar woman moved her hand slowly up and down my torso. Her body was twisted slightly, as if reaching for something. I lowered my gaze to see her second hand on Wulvine's bare chest. The Vangar was lying on the floor next to me, unconscious. I passed out after that.

When I came to, I was lying on Rutherford's bed. Crow and the Tal'mar woman were standing over me. "How do you feel?" he said in a low voice. "Can you move?"

I pushed myself upright, taking an inventory of my body. "I feel fantastic," I said. "Like I've slept for a week." That wasn't right, though. I couldn't have... I searched my memories, trying to understand all that had happened.

"I am glad to hear that," Crow said. "For a while, we feared you might not survive."

"Thank you," I said, still not sure exactly what had happened. I glanced at the Tal'mar woman and saw a flash of her in my memory. "You," I said. "You're the one who healed me."

She nodded. "I am Raehl Skyrider. A distant cousin of yours, I believe."

I turned my head, slowly taking in my surroundings. "You work for the overseer." My voice sounded more accusatory than I meant it to. The flood of disjointed memories that washed over me was making it hard to control my emotions.

"She had no choice," Crow said. "Raehl is a slave, like all the other Tal'mar here."

"I tried to ease your pain," she said hopefully. "There was little more that I could do for you."

"It helped," I said, looking around the room. "Where is Rutherford?"

"He's gone back to the city," Crow said.

"How did you find me?"

"It wasn't easy. I came here three nights ago, the night we parted. I immediately knew something was wrong when I saw the airship leaving Avenston and I saw you chained to the deck. I followed, hoping the Vangars were taking you to the mines as we had planned. It soon became obvious that something had gone wrong. When the airship landed and they took you inside, I could do nothing. I spent many hours trying to find a way into Juntavar. Thankfully, I met Raehl."

"He found me on the roof," she said. "I go up there for a few minutes of privacy, when I can."

"Raehl knew where you being held. She assured me that you were alive, but I couldn't come to you because Rutherford wasn't letting you out of his sight."

"Why did Rutherford finally leave?" I said.

"We provided some encouragement," Crow said grimly.

"What did you do?"

"I returned to Avenston. I went to the Woodcarvers and I asked them to help me plan a diversion, something that would demand the overseer's attention."

A sinking feeling washed over me. "What did you do, Crow?"

"We lit some fires," he said, smiling. "Your friends are quite devious in matters of warfare."

"Fires! What did you burn? Did anyone get hurt?"

Crow gave the Tal'mar woman a glance and then drew his gaze back to me. "We were careful. We wanted to be sure that no innocents would be harmed, so we bombed the patrol building."

My jaw fell open. "Are you insane? Don't you know the sentinels will take revenge on the people?"

"We should have known," he said. "In retrospect."

My heart fell. "Crow, what have you done? What happened?"

He took a deep breath and reached for my hand. "The sentinels lashed out, just as you said they would. They kidnapped random people off the street, torturing them for information. Some of the sentinels went down into Dockside, where they began attacking peoples' homes and interrogating everyone they found."

"We have to go back!" I said, pushing myself out of bed. "They need our help."

"More than you know," he said softly. "River, your friends had been spreading word of our plan, looking for people to escape with us. The people they spoke to were ready, even desperate for something to happen. When the sentinels began torturing them, they pushed the people too far, and the people began pushing back. A revolution has begun."

I grappled with that for a moment, amazed and horrified all at once. I felt a moment of hope. In all my life I had never believed the people of Avenston had it in them. Then I reconsidered my feelings. "They will all die," I said, shaking my head. "They can't fight the sentinels. Everyone who takes up arms will be slaughtered."

"Perhaps," Crow said cautiously. "However, from a certain perspective... we may be able to use this to our advantage."

I narrowed my eyebrows. "Our advantage? What are you talking about?"

"Our plan."

"We have no plan. Our plan failed the moment Rutherford brought me here instead of the mines."

"Not necessarily," Crow said. "Strategically, we still might benefit from the situation. We can still find your friend in the slave mines. In the process, we might draw the overseer's attention away from the city and spare a few lives. Failing that, we can also return to Avenston and help the rebels."

I felt my stomach churning. "Our plan is getting more complicated by the second," I said wearily. "Even if we manage this, how many will we sacrifice? It won't do any good to defeat the Vangars if everyone gets killed in the process. As it is, we won't last another decade. Human kind is going extinct."

"Then we must make sure that doesn't happen," Crow said.

"Either way, you must decide soon," Raehl said, nodding at Wulvine's corpse lying on the floor. "It won't be long until he's missed."

I glanced at the body and noticed that the skin looked withered like rotten fruit. "What happened to him?" I said.

Crow gave me a dark look. "You don't want to know."

I glanced back and forth between the two of them. "What did you do?"

Crow grimaced. "Your body was severely damaged," he said. "We needed... materials."

I felt vomit churning up in my gut. I took a deep breath, forcing it down. "I didn't hear that," I said. I steadied myself and fixed my gaze on Crow. "All right, how do we get out of here?"

Chapter 8

Raehl guided us through a maze of dark empty hallways and hidden passages, carefully avoiding the Vangars along the way until we reached a narrow hatch that led to the roof. We accessed the hatch by climbing a tall ladder that was mounted in the narrow space between two metal walls. The crawlspace was dark and uncomfortably hot, which Raehl explained was due to the fact that we were adjacent to one of the ship's massive furnaces. I realized just how close we were when we got close to the ceiling and the iron ladder grew so hot that I could barely hold onto it.

A few seconds later, we emerged from the crawlspace and found ourselves standing on the roof of the tallest building in the city. Large knots of thick fibrous rope were bound to each corner of the roof, reminding me of the balloons that held the city aloft. The ropes were tethered to the edges of the buildings, as well as hundreds of evenly spaced tie-downs along city's main deck.

Crow joined me near the ledge of the roof, smiling quietly at my awe as I gazed out over the city. "I must credit the Vangars, it's an impressive accomplishment," he said.

"Credit the slaves, not the Vangars."

He nodded. "Perhaps it will belong to them someday."

"I think I understand them now," I said absently.

"How so?"

"Tinker once told me about the locusts that invaded the Borderlands when he was young. He said they swarmed across the land consuming everything in their path, eating all of the wheat in the fields, stripping the trees bare, and then even eating the trees, too. He said they even ate shovel handles and the siding on houses and barns. When the cold weather came, there was nothing left. Tinker's family barely survived the winter."

I craned my neck around, staring into Crow's eyes. "That's what the Vangars are," I said. "They're locusts. They won't stop until there is nothing left."

"Their old kingdom was like the Wastelands," Crow said. "They didn't have any resources to begin with. No wonder they found ours so enticing."

"You don't have much time," Raehl said urgently behind us. "The guards will discover the body any moment, if they haven't already."

"What do we do?" I said.

Raehl turned her face skyward and pointed up at the mass of black balloons overhead.

"You want us to go up there?" I said.

"Yes. You cant see them from here, but each balloon has a platform to maintain the fuel tanks. You will be safe there."

I glanced at Crow, frowning. "Then what?" I said. "We can't just wait there, hiding from the Vangars until we starve to death."

"You won't be waiting," Raehl said patiently. "You will cut the tethers and fly away."

My mouth fell open. "You want us to float away on one of those balloons? That's insane! We'll float right out of this world."

"Raehl has already explained this to me," Crow said reassuringly. "We won't float out of the world. We can control the altitude."

Butterflies churned up in my stomach, and I shook my head slowly. "There must be another way…"

"It is safe," Raehl assured me. "Believe it or not, the Vangars have races with these balloons."

I frowned, staring at her and then up at the balloons. What she described didn't seem possible. "But how can you direct them?" I said. "There's no engine, no propeller."

"The winds," Raehl said. "The winds will guide you."

I winced, a sudden queasy feeling washing over me. "Crow-"

"We don't have time to discuss it now," he said impatiently. "I'll explain everything later."

He went to the corner of the building, grabbed one of the ropes, and hauled himself into the air. As he did, I noticed that the ropes separated, revealing webbing between them. This, I realized, was how the maintenance workers climbed up and down.

Crow easily moved up the ladder and I stood watching after him as his clothes melted into the darkness overhead. He all but vanished. "Go on," Raehl urged me. "The sooner you're gone, the better for all of us."

I sighed. I latched onto the webbing and began to climb. I moved quickly, my entire being focused on putting one hand in front of the other, moving up a step and then another, and another. The buildings shrank below me and a cold wind began battering at my face. I could see the platform in the darkness above, its shape silhouetted by the fire that fueled the balloon's hot air supply.

I glanced down and saw the entire city stretching out below, the lights twinkling like a winter solstice tree. A wave of dizziness washed over me and I closed my eyes, pulling tight against the ropes. The wind buffeted against me, chilling me right to the bone. The ropes swayed dizzyingly back and forth with the movement of the balloons.

"Keep moving!" Crow's voice whispered out of the darkness above. "Hurry!"

I took a deep breath and noticed that my hands were shaking. Suddenly, I wasn't sure I'd be able to hang on to the ropes if I let go. I pulled tighter, locking the webbing under my arms, hardly daring to move. I threw my gaze upward, deliberately trying not to look down. Crow disappeared over the edge of the platform. A moment later, his face appeared over the edge.

"River, are you coming?" he whispered, waving me forward.

I took a deep breath, grappling with the strange sensation that had overcome me. I wasn't aware of ever having been afraid of heights, but the rooftops of Avenston weren't like this. If I fell from a rooftop, I could easily survive. I was agile, strong. I could catch myself. I could do a million different things to make sure I wouldn't get hurt. This was different.

I turned my gaze sideways, staring out at the sharp patterns of the mountains silhouetted against the sky. The lights of the ship burned in my peripheral vision and the wind hammered at my face, rocking me back and forth, forcing tears into my eyes. The entire world stretched out beneath me like an endless black abyss. I trembled, shivering with cold and some sort of primal fear that I'd never known before. I gasped against the icy wind, blinking the tears away, my entire will focused on hanging onto those ropes.

"River, hurry!"

I blinked, trying not to look up at Crow. I felt foolish, angry with myself, yet at the same time terrified. I knew that if I let go of that webbing, something would go wrong. A gust of wind would catch me and blow me right out of the sky. Or a rope would break, or my hand would slip...

Then I saw something: a distant glow at the edge of the Blackrock Mountains, like a halo in the sky. I stared at it, momentarily perplexed, and suddenly realized what it was. I was seeing the light of the slave mines. Suddenly it all came into focus. That was where the Vangars had taken Kale. I was supposed to be there. All of this had happened because I was trying to get there, trying to help him escape before something horrible happened. All of this had happened because I had wanted to do things my way, but my plan had failed. There was no one to blame for my situation but me.

My mind had been reeling with images of falling, with visions of my body crashing into the city below, or rushing past it to slam into the hard, barren earth of the eastern plains. I could see myself dropping into that yawning darkness. I could even imagine the hard barren ground rushing up to meet me as I fell. Then my focus changed. As I thought of Kale, tortured and malnourished, slowly succumbing to the inevitable death that waited in those cold dark mines, I regained my sense of purpose.

I took a deep breath and released my grip with one hand. Slowly, deliberately, I moved it up to the next link of webbing. I latched on with a white-knuckled grip and forced my second hand to do the same. And then my feet. One step at a time, one inch at a time, I crawled the rest of the way to the platform. The queasy churning in my gut never went away, but the shaking of my hands diminished somewhat as I began to move. I latched onto the next section of webbing, took one cautious step, and then did it again. And again.

At last I reached the edge of the platform, only to realize that somehow I had to get around the thing. I'd have to let go of the ropes, grab onto the platform, and swing myself up. It was a simple task, really. Something I could have done with my eyes closed if I'd been closer to the ground. Somehow, hanging off that ledge thousands of feet in the air was different. I couldn't do it. I just couldn't.

But I had to try, I thought, glancing at that light on the horizon. If I died, at least I would know I had given everything I could in the effort to rescue Kale. *Better to die free than to live as a slave,* I reminded myself. I bit my lower lip, forcing one hand out to the ledge. I latched onto it, felt my grip close around the thin metal railing, and my heart skipped a beat.

I was going to fall. I knew it. Something was going to go wrong. The metal frame wasn't strong enough, or perhaps there was a loose bolt somewhere. Or the rope would catch my leg just as I jumped and pull me down, hurtling me to the earth. *Something* was going to go wrong.

Then I felt Crow's warm grip on my hand. It was like the warmth of a fire on a cold day, and the sensation instantly spread throughout the rest of my

121

body. Immediately, the shaking stopped. I took a deep breath and felt the warmth move into my lungs. A strange, calm feeling washed over me. Suddenly, I knew everything would be okay.

Almost casually, I threw my other arm up over the ledge and started climbing. Crow caught me by the shoulders and dragged me up. A moment later, I was standing on the platform, staring out at the endless black landscape. I glanced at Crow and saw him staring at me, and for a moment I felt ashamed. I knew what he had done for me. I knew that somehow he had used his powers to calm my fears and help me get over that ledge.

Thankfully, he didn't mention it, and I didn't have to humiliate myself by thanking him. At least he understood that much about me. I looked over the edge and saw the city below us, and quickly stepped back.

"What now?" I said, fixing my gaze on the burner at the center of the platform. The structure itself was fairly large, about eight feet tall and four in diameter. Large enough to hold several tanks of fuel, which I noticed the workers had stored inside. I assumed they kept the fuel tanks in a constant rotation, probably lowering the empty containers down to the city using ropes and pulleys.

"Hang on," Crow said. He reached under his cloak and one of those shiny daggers appeared in his hand. He stepped up to the ledge and methodically began slicing the tethers. The ropes were as thick as a Vangar's arm, but his blade sliced through them like warm butter.

As he cut the first rope, the platform rose to one side, threatening to dump us over the edge. I moved to the center and latched onto a handrail. Crow deftly leapt to the other side of the platform and cut another rope, balancing the weight. I took a deep breath as the platform righted itself. Crow went to work on another rope. In this manner he cut us loose, one rope at a time, zigzagging back and forth across the platform until at last we broke free.

Crow joined me at the center of the platform as the balloon lifted gently into the air, no longer tethered to the city. We rocked back and forth as we made our ascent, and our aircraft made a gliding sound as it brushed past the other balloons. I had the terrifying thought that we might get caught on one of the other balloons, but then we slid past them and suddenly we were drifting up towards an ocean of clear, bright stars. The city shrank to little more than a bright spot against the darkness below us.

A breeze caught our makeshift aircraft, and we began drifting to the east, towards the edge of the Blackrock Mountains. I pressed up against the structure, trying to ignore the cold wind whipping my hair and stinging my skin. "At least we're going the right way," I said.

"The wind currents from the ocean," Crow explained. "Mother told me all about them. A good pilot can use the air currents to speed his flight."

I considered that. I had always known that my mother had been a pilot, but I'd never given it much thought. Looking back, I wondered if the story of her death had somehow influenced my fear of heights. I could imagine hearing as a child the story about how my mother had flown over the mountains and crashed her plane. Small wonder that I had such terror built up in my subconscious mind.

I wondered if knowing that would somehow alleviate the problem. I took a step away from the burner, leaning towards the edge of the platform, and saw the vast black world spreading out below. I nervously danced back and latched on to the rail. "So much for that theory," I murmured.

"I wonder how close we can get to the mines?" I said. "We're at the mercy of the wind. Didn't Raehl say the Vangars race these things? How is that possible?"

"The air currents move in different speeds and directions. A person might go anywhere with a balloon like this, with the right equipment."

"I see. So how do we change direction?"

"Well, that's the trick," he said, looking upward. "If we cut the fuel, the air in the balloon cools and we drop. If we turn up the fire, we rise. It's just a matter of reaching the right altitude to find the wind we want."

I watched the mountains growing closer and noted that our flight path was taking us a good distance north of the mines. "Perhaps we should try a different altitude then," I said. "We need to fly further south."

"If only it were that easy," Crow said.

I looked at him sharply. "I don't understand... didn't you just say we could control the direction we fly?"

"I said we *could* if we had better controls. The balloons that the Vangars race have modified control systems to adjust the fuel supply. We can't control the fuel on this balloon. We can only turn it on and off."

I groaned. "I suppose we should cut the fuel now, then," I said. "If we land too far into the mountains, it could take days to get back."

"For you, perhaps," he said, grinning from ear to ear. "I however, can fly." With that, he spread his cloak and leapt off the platform. An involuntary scream escaped my lips as he vanished over the edge. A moment later, he reappeared a dozen yards to the north. I had almost forgotten about his stupid cloak.

"Fear not, big sister," he called over the hissing noise of his wing jets. "I'm your pilot today!"

Crow vanished into the sky overhead and everything went silent for a moment. Then I noticed a faint tugging sensation coming from up above, and the balloon slowly changed direction. A few seconds later, we were moving south at a rapid pace, on a direct course for the camp. Crow rejoined me on the platform.

"That should get us going," he said. "I'll do that again if we change course. We won't have to walk far at all."

I stared at him, baffled by his fearlessness. "Does our mother have one of those things?" I said, nodding at his cloak.

"Absolutely not. She's terrified of them. She believes people were meant to fly with a machine wrapped around them, where it's safe."

I laughed at that, and he joined in. "Perhaps you should try flying her way someday," he added. "It might suit you."

"If it's all the same, I think I'll stay on the ground from now on," I said. "The sky is for birds."

An hour from the time we cut loose, we settled our balloon down on the prairie at the edge of the Blackrock Mountains just a few miles northwest of the mines. We had very little control of the thing as it plummeted towards the ground, and though it was going at a smooth angle relative to the earth, it was going quite fast. Rather than risk breaking my neck in

125

the crash, I leapt off and tumbled as I hit the ground. Crow simply flew into the air and then landed next to me as I was brushing off the dust.

I took off running in the direction of the mines. "This way," I called over my shoulder. Crow leapt into the air and flew up next to me, hovering just off to my right.

"Tell me, why didn't we just do this in the first place?"

"What?" I said between breaths. I was a little annoyed that he could just fly along next to me like that.

"Why didn't we just come here first, rather than getting you captured?"

"You'll see," I said breathlessly

True to my word, an hour later, he understood. We stood on a bluff overlooking the mines, watching the thousands of workers and Vangar slave drivers. The hole in the earth was an abyss at least two miles wide. We couldn't even see the bottom. A steady stream of ore cars moved in and out of the mines, some of them hand-drawn by slaves, others carted up the slope to the crusher by steam-powered machines.

After the crusher, a series of conveyor belts carried the raw materials off to the smelting furnaces. Just beyond that, a steam locomotive idled on the rails as the slaves loaded the cars with refined steel and freshly hewn timber. I also noticed a number of heavy machines, such as the earthmovers that I would later learn to call "steamshovels," and the plows that formed the roads and reinforced the earth as the workers dug ever deeper into the ground.

"Sentinel," I said, pointing. Several sentinels were walking across a massive bridge that connected two sections of land on either side of the mines. A sharp cliff cut into the mountain at the edge of the ravine next to the bridge, making it otherwise impassible. Without the bridge, the only other way around was to walk the entire perimeter of the mines. Even from that distance, we could hear the sentinel's heavy thudding footsteps.

"What are they?" Crow said. He had never seen a sentinel up close before.

"The Vangars use Tal'mar magic to meld warriors' bodies with machinery. They are as strong as twenty men. They are the reason the uprising in Avenston will fail."

Crow nodded, taking it all in. "I understand now," he said. "This does complicate matters."

We withdrew from the bluff into the shelter of the trees to formulate our plan. Crow insisted that the best way to find Kale was from the air. "I won't recognize your friend, but I can easily teach you to use my wing," he said. "You can circle the area out of reach of their lights, and they'll be none the wiser."

"Not a chance," I said flatly. "There's got to be another way."

He considered this for a while. "I suppose I must do it then. But how will I be able to identify your friend among so many?"

"Look for his scar," I said. I explained about the boiler accident that had scarred Kale's cheek when he was young. Crow nodded.

"That might suffice," he said, opening his cloak. "I'll take a look. Wait for me here."

My heart skipped a beat as he leapt over the edge, swooped up into the heavens, and disappeared into the darkened sky. I took a deep breath. "I'll never get used to that," I mumbled.

I moved back to watch the camp from the safety of the shadows under the trees. While I waited, I quietly watched all the work going on in the mines. I hated the way the Vangars had leveled the mountains into empty craters and clear-cut the trees, but I couldn't help being somewhat awed. The Vangars had used their technological powers to create machines that could lift a ton of earth in a single scoop, and others that could crush and smelt the rock into pure ore in minutes. The Vangars' efficiency of industrialization was breathtaking, if not exactly friendly to the environment.

On the eastern end of the camp, the Vangars had built a sawmill into which they fed full-sized trees using a steamshovel fitted with some sort of grasping claw. As I watched, the machine lifted an entire tree from the back of a steamwagon and loaded it onto the mill. At the far end, another machine hoisted the sawn lumber onto the freight cars. From what I could tell, this process was nonstop, day and night. I could scarcely imagine where it all went.

That wasn't true, though. I knew that most of the materials the Vangars processed went straight into their dragon ships and back to their homeland across the sea. I had seen the ships coming and going for my entire life. The materials that didn't go offshore were processed by slaves and factory workers into usable goods like lumber, clothing, and weapons.

I truly understood the Vangars now. I had always known they were using our resources to sustain their kingdom, but now I could see the big picture. Eventually, when the trees were gone and the mountains had been mined away, they would move on to another kingdom, and then another until they had consumed everything that the world had to give. They were voracious, tireless. They truly were like locusts swarming across the world, so fast that we couldn't stop them no matter what we did.

This was due to the fact that their own land, by its very nature, was deprived of natural resources. So they set out in search of more and just happened to find us. It wasn't personal to them. They just happened to be very good at finding resources and consuming them. If it hadn't been the Vangars, I supposed it would have been someone else eventually. Even us, given enough time. How else could King Ryshan have continued to feed the needs of our quickly growing nation? In time, we might have become very much like the Vangars, if they hadn't come first.

That knowledge didn't make me feel any better, though. I didn't like the idea that no matter who won the war, we would all end up the same way. I had to believe that there was a better way if we could just find it. I couldn't examine the thought any further because Crow swooped down out of the sky and landed next to me. I nearly jumped out of my skin. I'd expected him to be gone for a while. It hadn't been fifteen minutes since he'd left my side.

"I found your friend," he said with a stone-faced look.

"I see. And what's the bad news?"

"I also found three sentinels within shouting distance. I'm sure we could overcome the Vangar guards, but the sentinels present a problem."

I moved forward, gazing out over the precipice. "Where?" I said. He pointed. Kale was at the far end of the mining encampment, near the loading platforms for the locomotives. "What's he doing?"

"If I'm not mistaken, he operates a machine that moves timber from the carts onto the locomotive train."

I blinked. "They captured him with stolen machine parts and then gave him a job running a steamshovel?" I said in disbelief.

Crow shrugged. "He seems to perform well. The guards weren't paying any attention to him at all."

I sighed. "All right. Show me how to get there. I want to see with my own eyes."

Crow gestured down the side of the mountain. "It won't be easy," he said. "They put the bridge there for a reason."

"Of course not," I muttered.

Chapter 9

With Crow's help, I managed to navigate my way down the mountain and around the southern end of the camp without being noticed. My eyes weren't as sharp as his, but at least I managed to make the journey without breaking my neck. When we came creeping up the hill behind the locomotive platform I could see the red light of dawn breaking across the eastern sky. I hoped it wasn't an omen.

Crow and I hid in a stand of quaky trees on the hillside behind the platform. I saw a handful of guards looking over the workers from the tops of the railcars, and a few more scattered around the area. I noticed that many of the Vangar guards were actually working alongside the other slaves. That surprised me. I hadn't witnessed this behavior before. In Avenston, the work was all done in factories and the Vangars lorded over the workers like tyrants. Here, they actually took part. It was another aspect of their culture that was completely strange to me.

"What shall we do?" Crow said after several minutes of watching them. "The sky is growing light already."

"We can't get to Kale without being noticed," I said. "We need to do something about those sentinels. We need a distraction."

He considered that. "I did see something that might help. I saw a cart of explosive charges going down into the mine when I was flying over the area. I believe they keep more in that building." He pointed to a wooden shack just beyond the lumber mill to the northeast.

"Can you get in without being seen?" I said, a smile playing across my features. I was getting an idea.

"I believe so. Do you have a plan?" I looked at him and suddenly had a change of heart.

"No, I suppose not."

"River, what aren't you telling me? What are you thinking?"

"I can't let you do it," I said. "You're my little brother. It's too dangerous. I'll figure something else out."

He placed his hand on my shoulder and stared into my eyes. "River, trust me. You know I can get past those guards. How do you think I got in and out of the sky city?"

I sighed. "It's too dangerous. Even if you get the explosives and manage to kill one or two of the sentinels, what about the rest? Every Vangar in the area will come running. They'll overwhelm us so fast-"

"Not if they can't," he said slyly.

I frowned. "What are you talking about?"

"Stay here, sister. I have a plan."

He rushed down the hillside behind the trees and leapt into the air. "Wait!" I called after him in a loud whisper. "What are you doing?"

"Keep watch," he said. "You'll know when it's time." He swooped up into the air over the eastern edge of camp and disappeared into the treetops.

I stomped back up the slope and knelt down under the trees, frustrated. It was bad enough knowing we were in a hopeless situation. Crow taking off on his own made me feel absolutely helpless.

I watched the shack intently, hoping to catch a glimpse of Crow so I'd know what he was up to. I never saw him. The workers came and went, the guards paced back and forth across the railcars. Then, a few minutes later, I heard a shout. I glanced up and saw one of the guards on the railcars pointing. He quickly climbed down and took off at a run. The others followed after him. As they gathered and began running to the north, I realized that was my signal.

I hunched down low, trying to blend in with the grass as I raced down the slope and across the clearing to the backside of the locomotive platform. I paused there, making sure I hadn't been noticed, and then quietly slipped into the shadows between two cars. From there, I could finally see what was happening.

To the north, I saw the guards chasing Crow across the camp and towards the bridge. He had a dozen of them on his tail, not counting the three sentinels that had pulled out ahead of the group. My heart nearly froze. What was he doing?

Trust him, I reminded myself. *Trust him and keep moving.*

I threw a glance around the area to make sure the guards were all gone, and then broke into a run towards Kale's steamshovel. The slaves had all stopped working to watch the excitement. A few of them noticed me as I raced across the clearing. "Hey!" one of them said, pointing at me. I ignored him.

"Kale!" I called out as I reached the shovel. "Hurry!"

133

He didn't hear me over the noise of the steamshovel, but he looked down as I came running up. His eyes went wide with recognition. He glanced around nervously, looking for the guards, and then realized that they were gone. He quickly jumped down to join me.

"River, what are you doing here?" he said, throwing his arms around me.

"There's no time to explain," I said. "We have to move before the Vangars notice you're gone."

He frowned, looking around nervously. "How? Did you bring horses or a steamwagon?"

I bit my lip. "Not exactly."

Kale looked at me like I was nuts. "River, how are we going to get away from a hundred angry Vangars?"

"I, uh... I don't know. I hadn't actually planned that far." I'd been hoping to sneak Kale out quietly under the cover of darkness, but that plan had proven impossible. Now that my brother had taken matters into his own hands and we had the Vangars' full attention, that wasn't going to happen. And it was nearly daylight. I suddenly realized we had a problem.

"Oh boy," Kale muttered, shaking his head. "Did you come here to get me out or to get us all killed?"

At that moment, I heard the hissing sound of Crow's wing in the distance. I jerked my head around to seem him flying into the air at the far end of the bridge. A sentinel leapt after him just as Crow soared just out of reach. He swerved around in midair and went soaring back across the bridge, over their heads. The Vangars tumbled into each other as they tried to reverse course.

Halfway across the bridge, Crow reached into his cloak and produced two cannon charges. He threw them down and swooped into the air before they exploded. The charges hit the wooden deck of the bridge just ahead of the Vangars. They exploded simultaneously with a walloping sound that got the attention of the entire camp.

Timbers flew apart, twisting into the sky, flames licking at them as they spiraled back down into the mines. The heavy frame of the bridge shuddered, swaying precariously back and forth. The initial explosion threw several Vangars off the bridge. They didn't even have time to scream as they disappeared into the abyss below. The rest of them turned to make a run for the northern embankment as the bridge rocked underneath them.

Crow landed just south of the bridge and turned back to survey his handiwork. Just then a sentinel came roaring through the flames, hurdling across the gap in the bridge. He cleared the breach and landed heavily on the far side, a few yards in front of Crow. The weight of the sentinel's landing was too much for the already stressed wooden beams. He took one step before the support beams snapped violently under his weight.

As the floor gave out, the sentinel reached out, clawing wildly at the collapsing timbers. He managed to grab onto a section of beam. For a moment, he seemed to have found a handhold. Then the entire bridge gave out beneath him with a groaning sound. The beams pulled out of the ground and tumbled inward as the bridge collapsed in on itself. The sentinel let out a scream as the burning structure went plummeting into the darkness, taking him along for the ride. Crow smiled and leapt into the air.

I pulled my gaze away from the scene, trying to clear my head. Crow had bought us some time by trapping the guards on the far side of the ravine, but what now? We couldn't make a run for it. Not in broad daylight. Kale was right. We need a steamwagon, or...

"The train!" I said to Kale. "Can you operate it?"

"I can figure it out," he said. "But I won't leave without Nena."

I blinked. "Who?"

"Nena... I'll explain later. He turned to run back towards the mine. I stared after him with an odd feeling in my gut.

Crow landed on the ground next to me. He shot me a perplexed look. "Where is your friend going?"

I shook my head. "Help him," I said, turning toward the locomotive.

"What are you doing?"

"The train," I said over my shoulder. "We're taking the train. Help Kale. Hurry!"

Crow leapt into the air and vanished into the mines. I broke into a full out run towards the train platform. The slave workers cheered as I ran by. They didn't know what I was up to, but they seemed to be under the impression that I was going to rescue them. I considered that as I reached the engine. I couldn't see any reason why not. The more of us, the better.

I caught the handrail and swung myself up onto the engineer's platform. I was standing on a grated metal floor in front of a large coal-fired furnace. I noted steel and copper pipes winding back and forth along the engine, connecting with the large boiler up front.

"Simple enough," I mumbled. I'd worked with enough steam engines to recognize how they worked. I located the pressure lever and closed it, allowing the boiler to build up enough pressure to operate the engine. Then I opened up the door to the furnace and saw a thick bed of deep red coals.

"Stand aside!" someone yelled behind me. I spun around and saw that one of the slaves had climbed on top of the coal car behind me. He was a tall, thin man, built a lot like Tinker had been, but he had a beard and a head of thinning gray hair. I moved to the side of the platform, and he threw a shovelful of coal into the burner. I crawled up next to him, snatched up a second shovel, and started helping.

Together, we quickly filled the burner to capacity. I watched the flames licking up through the coal and then closed the door, forcing the acrid smoke up the chimney. "It ain't gonna work," the man said, coming down next to me. "We won't build up pressure fast enough."

I craned my neck around, looking past the railcars and saw a horde of Vangar warriors making their way out of the pit. Ahead of them, dozens of slaves were piling onto the train, calling out for the others to join them. I looked at the man next to me. "What's your name?"

"Mal Tanner."

"Mal, is there any other fuel here? Oil or kerosene maybe? We need something to heat this fire up."

"Sure, we got lots of oil, but they keep it locked up in the shack," he said.

I clutched the handrail nervously, calculating the distance. The Vangars were getting closer by the moment. I could make it to the shack, but I doubted I'd make it back. Even if I somehow managed it, I knew the fire wouldn't heat up fast enough. Of course, there were explosives in that shack as well...

"No, that's crazy," I mumbled.

Just then, Crow came flying up out of the pit. He was carrying a young woman with dark hair. She was clinging to his back. The tattered remains of her dress revealed most of her smooth, olive-colored skin. Somehow, she seemed to have managed to keep the important parts covered, but that was about it.

The extra weight gave Crow a little trouble flying, but he managed. He *whooshed* over the Vangars' heads and landed next to the locomotive, setting her gently on the ground a few yards away.

"Go!" he shouted at me. "I'll be right back."

Mal swung around and pulled the lever to release the brakes. "Pressure valve's right here," he said, reaching out to twist it, forcing the boiler's energy into the engine. "With the brakes off, she'll start rolling." The massive pistons began to cycle, and the steam engine chugged slowly to life. Like a raft drifting across a slow-moving river, we began to move. "Easy as that," he said.

I spun around to get a look at Crow and found the girl standing behind me. I'd been too preoccupied to notice her climbing onto the platform. "I'm Nena," she said, smiling

"So you are," I said, arching an eyebrow. I looked her up and down, taking in the olive-dark skin and crystal blue eyes, the perfect thin waist and generous proportions. I decided she wasn't nearly as attractive as she looked.

I leaned past her and saw the Vangars flowing out of the mine to chase after us. Several of them caught up to the last car and climbed aboard as we rolled away from the platform. A group of slaves armed with shovels and picks went rushing back to the last car to fight them off. Crow appeared behind them. This time he had Kale with him.

As the train picked up speed down the hill, I realized that Crow was having a hard time keeping up. Kale was considerably heavier than Nena, and Crow's wing was having trouble supporting the extra weight. I resisted the urge to pull the brakes, knowing that if I did we'd have a hundred ruthless Vangars swarming over the train.

Crow passed over their heads, swerving left and right as he struggled with Kale's shifting weight. One of the Vangars noticed them. He stopped in his tracks and pulled a short-handled hatchet from his belt. "Look out!" I shouted, but they couldn't hear me. The Vangar drew his arm back, took aim, and let fly. My breath caught in my chest is the axe spiraled through the air with deadly perfect aim.

Crow's irregular flight pattern saved them, but just barely. As the hatchet found its target, the blade barely missed Kale's thigh. It sliced into Crow's cloak and made a clanging sound as it struck one of the steamjets. A wild burst of steam shot out and the two of them rocketed into the sky overhead. I could hardly watch as they spiraled out of control. Kale held on for all he was worth as the momentum spun his legs out sideways, until he was almost at a ninety-degree angle to Crow's body. Then the broken steamjet gave out with one final burst. It died and they went into a freefall.

Nena gasped next to me and I gripped the rail with both hands, helplessly watching them hurtle towards the ground. I saw Crow twisting and turning, trying to do something with his cloak. He shouted something but I could only hear broken pieces of his words. Kale couldn't do any more than hang on for dear life. At that point, he was probably wondering if it would be safer to let go. I assumed Crow was telling him not to.

I couldn't think or even breathe as I watched them fall.

Half a second before they hit the ground, Crow managed to spread the wings of his cloak and it caught air. They swooped down within an inch of the ground and then arced back up into the air. The momentum carried them high over the heads of the watching Vangars.

Crow angled himself into a slow dive, taking advantage of the extra speed he'd gained. He hurtled past the Vangars, easily catching up with the train. At the last second, he twisted, dropping his passenger to the top of the railcar. Kale landing right in the middle of the fight between the slaves and the Vangars who had climbed aboard the last car. He let out a lusty war cry as he took up the battle.

Crow had just enough inertia to make it to the front of the train. He rocketed up to the locomotive and landed awkwardly on the pile of coal. He stood up, covered in black dust. He brushed it off the best he could and jumped up to the platform next to us.

"You scared the life out of me," I said, throwing my arms around him.

He grinned. "I told you to trust me, didn't I?"

I glanced at Nena and saw her breathlessly watching the fight at the back of the train. Kale drove his fist into a Vangar's nose and Nena let out a cheer. I rolled my eyes.

Someone shouted and pointed back up the hill towards the camp. I looked up just in time to see a sentinel come plowing down the slope. He was bounding on all fours, like the ones who had chased me out of Avenston. I knew immediately that we only had seconds until he caught us. I gave Crow a look.

"We're in trouble," I said.

"Can't this thing go any faster?"

"It would if the engine was hotter," said Mal. "There wasn't enough time to get the fire going."

Crow reached into his cloak and pulled out another small vial of starfall. "Everyone get back," he said.

I gave him a look that said *"Are you sure?"* and he motioned for me to get out of the way. I leapt onto the coal car, motioning for Mal and Nena to join me. After he was sure they were safe, Crow opened the burner, threw in the vial, and slammed it shut.

I wasn't sure what would happen at first. A similar vial in the boneshaker had simply burned like a piece of wood. Crow had assured me that the vial would safely and reliably burn for years that way. It didn't seem like that would be much help. To my surprise, the solution reacted in an entirely different way to the intense heat inside the locomotive's furnace.

There was a roar like the sound of an explosion, and the pressure inside the furnace started building so fast that it nearly separated at the welds. I saw blue and green flames licking out around the corners and at the edges of the door, and the steel bowed outward as if it might explode. I jumped to open the valve, allowing the extra pressure out of the boiler. The effect was instant.

The power went straight to the wheels. The locomotive put on a burst of speed so fast that it nearly threw us off the car. An ear-shattering squeal erupted from the rails beneath us and I realized that the wheels were spinning, trying to push the train faster than it could accelerate. The wheels were spinning so fast that it was conceivable they could burn through the track.

Or, the axle could break. Or a hub could come loose. If any of those things happened, the wheels might come completely off the rails. The train would jump the tracks and probably kill every one of us on board in the ensuing crash. I shot Crow a worried look.

"What is that noise?" he shouted.

"The wheels are spinning. We've got to slow it down."

I latched onto the pressure-release valve, trying to release some of the energy from the engine. I cried out as my hands burned at the metal's touch. The heat from the furnace washed over me in waves. I fought my instinctive reaction to let go. I forced my fingers around the valve. It resisted for a moment and then broke loose. A burst of steam went up the smokestack as the valve opened.

As the engine lost pressure, the wheels immediately regained contact with the surface of the tracks. The train lurched forward and then smoothed out, once again accelerating at a steady pace. I twisted the valve, carefully returning some of the pressure back to the engine.

I stepped away from the furnace, glancing at the blisters appearing on my hand. Crow reached out to touch me, and I immediately felt a cooling sensation move across my skin. I fought the urge to pull away from him. I wasn't entirely comfortable with his gift yet. I knew that he was just trying to help his big sister and didn't mean anything by it. Thankfully, it was all over in just a few seconds. The blisters on my hands vanished and the cooling sensation dissipated.

The sound of wrenching metal and a scream came from behind us. I twisted around to see what had happened. A shockwave rolled up the train, rattling the platform under my feet. I stepped past my companions and climbed to the top of the coal pile. I reached the top just in time to see a sentinel pulling himself up over the back railcar. The slaves scattered in front of him and he leapt forward, pouncing on the nearest person. The poor man fell hard, smashing his head against the roof of the railcar. I couldn't tell if the fall had killed him, but the sentinel raised his fist to finish the man off.

Kale appeared out of nowhere brandishing a flat-nosed shovel. He hauled off, swinging it with such force that when it hit the sentinel on the side of the helmet, we heard the *klang* all the way at the engine. The sentinel dropped back on his rump, both hands going to his head as the steel vibrated like a tuning fork. Kale started to take another swing but then realized he'd broken off the end of his shovel.

The sentinel lashed out, taking a swing at him, but Kale danced back. The sentinel twisted awkwardly around to get back to his feet. "Run!" I shouted.

Kale must have heard me because he dropped the handle and broke into a sprint. He hurled himself across the gap between two railcars and landed on the next one still running. Behind him, the sentinel crawled to his feet and started chasing after him. Nena screamed.

"That's not helping," I muttered.

I stepped back onto the platform and scanned the engine room, looking for something to use as a weapon. We had more shovels, but I knew they wouldn't do me any good. I needed something else. Something that could kill a sentinel. *Unlikely,* I thought.

I spied a lantern hanging from the ceiling in the corner and a grim smile broke out on my lips. My first

143

encounter with the sentinels came to mind, and I thought of the hot oil spurting out of that hydraulic pipe. I wondered what would happen if those pipes got hot enough to melt. I snatched the lantern off the hook and handed it to Crow.

"Hit him with this," I ordered. "Don't miss!"

Crow leapt across the bed of coal, racing back towards the sentinel. I watched as the slaves parted to make way for him. They were terrified. It was inconceivable to them that we might actually beat this creature. I set my jaw, determined to show them that it was possible.

Kale and Crow met halfway down the train. I heard Crow yell at Kale to keep moving. Kale did so, brushing past Crow with a confused look on his face. Kale joined us at the front, giving me a perplexed look as he arrived. "What is he doing?" he said. "That lantern's not even burning."

"Not yet," I said.

We all turned to watch Crow confront the sentinel. I felt a little nervous as I saw him running towards that giant. I had just begun getting used to the fact that I had a little brother. I didn't think I'd ever get used to seeing him in that kind of danger. To make matters worse, Crow pushed his luck farther than he should have. He ran right up to the sentinel and then threw the lantern as hard as he could. It smashed into a million pieces all over the sentinel's chest, spraying him with kerosene. The sentinel laughed and took a swing at him.

Crow tumbled backwards, narrowly dodging the blow. He agilely leapt to his feet and broke into a run towards the front of the train. The sentinel dropped to all fours and pounced after him.

There was no time to warn Crow of the danger. I spun around, flinging open the door to the furnace, and reached for a shovel. I snatched up a load of fiery coals. The others made way for me as I climbed to the far end of the coal car. I could see the worry on Crow's face as he raced toward me, leaping from car to car with the agility of a panther. Behind him, the Vangar bounded forward, the railcar roofs crushing under his weight every time he landed.

The freed slaves scattered, some climbing down the sides of the cars, others rushing forward, trying to get out of the sentinel's path. I took a few steps and leapt onto the next car, shovel still in hand. Crow immediately saw what I was up to. He leapt in the air, vaulting over the space between two cars and then landed gracefully on the car behind me. I hauled back and let loose with my shovelful of embers.

The sentinel was in midair as I threw it, and he landed on the railcar behind us with a heavy crunch. The embers splashed over the sentinel's armor as he landed, and the kerosene immediately burst into flames. The wind quickly whipped up the fire.

The sentinel twisted awkwardly as he rose to his feet, suddenly realizing the trouble he was in. He wrestled around, struggling to pat out the flames, stumbling erratically. He was so distressed that he lost his footing on the train and fell sideways over the edge of the roof.

As he fell, the sentinel reached out to catch himself and latched onto something near the bottom of the car. The train lurched for a second and I heard a snapping sound. Then the sentinel lost his grip and went tumbling away from the train, smoke and dust rising in a cloud around him. The train raced forward, still gaining speed as he disappeared behind us.

Nena threw her arms around Kale, squealing about how brave he was. Or something like that. I really wasn't listening. The slaves climbed back onto the railcar roofs and began cheering.

Once I was sure we were safe, I climbed back down to the platform and turned the pressure valve down to make sure the boiler wouldn't burst. The pressure gauge dropped, but only slightly out of the danger zone. Crow joined me, putting his arm over my shoulder.

"We did it," he said, grinning.

"We did," I said, glancing at Kale and Nena locked in a tight embrace a few feet away.

"You don't seem very happy. Is *something* bothering you?"

I knew he was referring to Nena, but I ignored his comment. "We have a problem," I said. "I can't cool the engine down, and it's not losing pressure."

He frowned, and thumped the pressure gauge with his knuckle. "It's not going to blow up is it?"

"I don't think so. We're safe for now."

"Then what's the problem?"

I reached for the brake handle and it flopped loosely in my hand. "We have no brakes," I said. "The sentinel snapped the lines when he fell. And we're still gaining speed."

Crow shot me a nervous glance and then leaned over to look up the tracks. "What's ahead?" he said.

"Avenston."

"I see. And then what?"

"The end of the line. We're going to crash."

Chapter 10

After mashing lips with Nena for a minute, Kale joined us on the platform. He threw his arms around me, lifting me off the ground. "I can't believe you came after me, River. You're insane."

"You may be right," I said. "Put me down."

He set me gently on the platform, noting my grim expression. "What's wrong?"

I quickly explained the situation. There was no delicate way to explain that we were all about to crash and die horribly. His smile vanished as I spoke. "Maybe we could jump off the train," he said.

"We're already going too fast. We'd all break our necks."

We turned to look at the slaves laughing, clapping each other on the backs, jubilant about their escape. They were completely unaware of our true situation. "What about the river?" Nena said. "The train goes right over the river outside of Avenston. Could we jump in the water?"

"That's not a bad idea," Kale said.

I regarded the two of them, trying not to dismiss Nena's idea just because it was hers. "That might work," I said, "but we still have a few problems. The first is that we don't know what's waiting for us in Avenston. The last I heard, there was a full-scale uprising going on, and the overseer went there personally with two hundred soldiers."

"Then we won't go to Avenston," Kale said. "We go north, make a run for the mountains."

"Perhaps," I said, glancing at Crow. "That does fit nicely with our original plan, doesn't it?" He nodded quietly.

"What plan?" Kale said. "What are you talking about?"

"I'll explain later," I said. "Right now we need to worry about this train. The sun's already up so that means the factories will be full of workers when it pulls into Avenston. If we don't give them some kind of warning, people will die."

"We could blow the whistle," Kale said helpfully and then added, "If we're still on the train, that is."

"I might be able to rig it open," I said. "Let it blast all the way into town. That would at least give them some warning. I'm not sure it would be enough, though."

"I could fly ahead and warn them," Crow said, "if my wing wasn't damaged." He took off his cloak and flipped it around, showing me the busted steamjet under the fabric. I examined it.

"When the axe hit this and it broke, you shot up in the sky," I said.

"Yes, it released the entire system's pressure all at once. I can replenish the steam easily enough, but with no pressure I still can't get off the ground."

"What if we close off the damaged jet?" I said. "Will the others still work?"

"I suppose. But we'd need a smithy for that, or at least a good vice."

I grinned. "How about a forge and a few shovels?"

He looked skeptical. "You mean the furnace? I can't see how it will work, but I can't think of anything better."

"It's worth a shot," Kale said.

"Let's do it," I said. "Give it to me."

As we readied for our experiment, I found a toolbox in the front corner that had a hammer in it. I held it up triumphantly. "Now we just need to heat the metal and bend it shut," I said.

I handed the hammer to Kale and opened the furnace, grabbing Crow's cloak. He winced as I pressed the edge of the wing into the furnace and the fabric immediately caught fire. I pulled it out, stomping out the flames.

Kale quickly struck the heated metal before it had a chance to cool. The tube collapsed partway.

"That's not enough," I said. "That stuff is stronger than normal copper. We'll have to try again."

"Try not to burn it," Crow said anxiously.

I thrust the end back into the fire, let it rest for a few seconds, and withdrew it. Once again, I had to stomp out the flames. Before the metal cooled, Kale hammered the jet solidly shut. He stood back admiring his handiwork. After it cooled, I handed the cloak back to Crow and he woefully examined it. A few inches of material had burned away, but the rest of the cloak was intact.

"Either it's fixed or I'll crash straight into the ground and you won't have to worry about me anymore," he said skeptically.

"It's not burned that bad," I said. "I hope. Do you think you can still steer it?"

"There's only one way to be sure."

He donned the cloak, reattaching the fittings to his arms and legs, and then refilled the long pipe-like tanks with water from the train's boiler supply. With his tanks filled, Crow activated the condenser, a device he said helped to compress the steam. After a few minutes, he said the cloak was ready. He test fired the jets, lifting himself a few inches off the platform, and gave me a satisfied look.

"That's it then," he said. "I'll follow the tracks into the city. I'll warn everyone I can."

"Do your best," I said. "And watch out for Vangars."

Crow leapt off the platform and shot into the air. I watched him for a few seconds and noticed that he did seem to have some trouble controlling his direction. His flight wasn't nearly as straight as before, nor as elegant. It didn't take him long to adjust, though. He changed his posture, compensating for the change in thrust, and took off. Less than a minute later, he was out of sight.

I pulled my attention back to the train and found Kale and Nena staring at me. "I'd better warn the others," I said. "At this speed, it won't be long before we hit Avenston."

"I'll help," Kale said. "Nena, you stay here. I don't want you to risk climbing back and forth on the train."

I climbed over the coal to the next car and Kale joined me. I glanced over my shoulder at Nena. "So how did you two meet?" I said casually.

"There weren't many women at the mines," he said with a grin. "I made it a point to meet them all."

"I bet you did," I said cynically.

"I know what you're thinking but it's not like that. One of the Vangars tried to rape Nena but she stabbed him in the eye with his own dagger. Dropped dead on the spot. That's why they sent her to the mines. I guess nobody else wanted to chance it."

My eyebrows went up. "I didn't know she had it in her," I said.

"You'd be surprised," he said with a wink.

I rolled my eyes and turned my attention to the group that had gathered nearby. "Listen up!" I shouted. "We've got a situation."

I explained about the brakes and about our plan to jump into the river. I asked them to pass word along to the others who weren't in earshot. "Anyone who doesn't jump will die," I said, turning away. "You must jump when we say it's time."

I didn't bother telling them they might die anyway. At the speed we were going, I wasn't sure the river would make such an easy target. Even if we all managed to make it past the riverbank and hit the water, there was no telling how shallow it might be. The river always runs low in late summer. It's also well known that the river bottom is covered in sharp rocks. Every year when it floods, the river changes course, pulling earth and rocks along with it. Assuming everything else went right, those rocks could still kill us.

It wasn't long before we saw the ever present smoke in the sky over Avenston. There was no cheering at that point, no more jubilation. We all knew what was coming, and it didn't take a genius to figure out the odds. As the city grew visible in the distance, I noticed a speck on the horizon. It was Crow. Less than a minute later, he landed on the train.

"The workers are spreading the word," he said. "They'll be watching for the train. I couldn't do more than that with the Vangars watching over them."

"It'll have to do then," I said. "What else did you see?"

"There was fighting, but not much. I saw fires near the northern end of the city."

"The rebels have probably gotten themselves backed into a corner," I said. I looked down the rails and noticed that the sky had grown considerably darker. We were moving into the smoke. We only had minutes until we reached the river.

I climbed to the top of the coal and called for everyone's attention. "It's not safe to go into Avenston," I said. "The overseer is there, and the sentinels are watching for us. After we jump off the train, follow Kale. He will guide you all into the mountains, to a safe place."

I climbed back down to the engine platform and Kale whispered, "You want them to follow me, that's the plan? What about you?"

"I have to get the overseer's attention," I said. "I need to pull his fighters away from the others, or they'll all be killed."

His eyes widened. "You're using yourself as bait?"

"Something like that," I said. "They need our help. They wouldn't be in this situation if it wasn't for us. They risked their lives so that Crow and I could get to you. I have to try to help them. I owe them that much."

He took a deep breath, swelling his massive chest and then released it slowly. "I don't suppose I can talk you out of this."

"Not a chance."

"Fine. Say it works. You get their attention and you draw the Vangars away from the fight. Then what?"

"If my plan works, I'll meet up with you tomorrow."

"Meet up with us?" he whispered. "What if the Vangars follow you? Look around you, River, these people can't fight. They're half-starved. They'll be destroyed."

"We're not going to fight. Crow and I will make sure that doesn't happen. We just want the Vangars to follow us, not to catch us. I need you to take the others and move north as fast as you can. I'll give you until nightfall."

"And then what?"

"And then the Vangars will be on your trail. You've got to move fast. Steal some steamwagons or horses, whatever you can manage. Just get moving and don't look back. Along the way, leave tracks. Make fires. Make sure the Vangars can follow your trail."

"All right," he said reluctantly. "I hope you know what you're doing. Where will we meet?"

"I'll find you."

I turned my attention to Crow. "I can get back into the city and get Rutherford's attention, but once I have it, I'll need your help."

"I understand. What do you want me to do?"

"There's an old abandoned factory south of Dockside. Inside you'll find ammunition and explosives..."

The sleepwalkers had been hoarding supplies for years, waiting for the chance to use them against the Vangars. I couldn't think of a better time than the present. I told Crow how to find the supplies, and how to avoid the sentinels on the way there.

"Wait until sunset before you move," I warned him. "That will give Kale and the others the time to get away from the city. If our plan is going to work, we have to time things perfectly."

"Sunset then," he repeated. "And what of you?"

"I'll move at the same time. Rutherford won't have any idea what hit him."

Crow smiled as he stepped off the platform. He rocketed ahead of the train and disappeared into the west. The rest of us climbed up along the ledges of the railcars, watching the horizon as the bridge appeared in the distance. We were moving fast, and it was growing larger by the second. In my mind, I calculated the speed of the locomotive and the width of the river, trying to time my signal so that no one would be hurt.

I glanced at the ground flying by, fixing my gaze on a large rock as we hurtled past. I picked out another, and then another. I had no idea what speed we were actually going, but I knew that we'd have to jump before the train hit the bridge. If I was right and luck was on our side, the momentum would carry us to safety.

As we grew closer I saw that the river was still running wide, but the waters were low. That wasn't a good sign. I glanced at the others and saw the worried looks on their faces. "Watch me," I shouted towards the others. "Jump at exactly the same spot!"

I closed my eyes and took a deep breath. In my mind's eye, I took it all in: the river, the bridge, the low sloping angle of the embankment. I could see us hurtling along the tracks at more than one hundred miles per hour. I could see the bridge looming in the distance, the deep blue water rolling by below. I saw the boulders and sage bushes flashing by, the light dancing across my eyelids. I could hear the roar of the steam engine; feel the pumping movement against the heels of my boots. And then, instinctively, I knew we were there. I opened my eyes just as we reached the embankment, and yelled for everyone to jump.

I experienced a moment of breathless terror as I leapt off the train and saw the hillside and riverbanks spanning the view below me. With crystal clarity, I took it all in: the hard-packed, rust-stained earth, the scrub brush and sage, the gravel along the banks and the large rocks scattered here and there along the water's edge. Then I could see the water, deep blue and sparkling like the sky at midnight. And suddenly, I could see everything under the surface.

I could see the boulders lying submerged, almost perfectly placed to break the bones of unsuspecting divers. I could see shadows of the banks stretched out here and there, the glint of the sharp stones at the bottom of the river. In one long sweep, I passed it over, and suddenly the deep blue water filled my vision.

I hit the river going fast. It felt like going through a wall. I was instantly submerged, sinking into the icy cold depths, my body reeling with shock from the impact and the cold. For a few moments the darkness closed in around me and I couldn't tell which way was up. Then I felt my feet pressing against the stony river bottom, and I pushed away from it. My ears popped painfully as I rose toward the surface.

I broke through and sucked in a deep, gasping breath, water splashing out around me in a broad circle. I turned slowly, treading water as I scanned the surface for the others, ignoring the shivering cold and sharp pain. One by one, they began to appear, bobbing up and down in the waves, calling out to one another as they surfaced.

Satisfied, I turned against the current and swam to the far bank on the west side of the river. As I climbed out of the water, I heard Kale calling out to me from the other side: "Be careful, River!"

I waved. "Move fast!" I shouted. "You have until sunset." As I turned away, I heard the rumble of thunder in the west. A breeze washed over my wet body, and a shiver crawled up my spine.

The train was already a mile down the tracks by the time I got up the embankment and started walking. In the next few minutes, it completely vanished from sight. Ten minutes later, I heard the crash. I was too far from the city to see it happen, but the sound echoed out across the plains like a wagonload of cannon charges exploding all at once. I saw a column of smoke rising into the sky and I stared at it for the next two hours as I followed the tracks into Avenston.

The wind picked up as I walked. I leaned into it, blinking against the dust. I could smell the smoke of the city and the fires burning in Dockside, and I noted the acidic tinge of electricity in the air. Lightning arced across the western sky and a few seconds later, thunder rumbled across the plains. My clothes were dry by then, but the air had grown decidedly cold and a shiver swept over my body. With nothing else to do, I pressed on, moving towards the city.

I wasn't sure what to expect when I reached Avenston, so I took my time, carefully avoiding the busy streets and those I knew were frequented by Vangars and sentinels. Fortunately, time was on my side. I had told Crow not to make his move until dusk and that was still hours away.

I went down into Dockside first to get a look at the damage. It was spectacular. The train had continued accelerating all the way into the city. The depot at the end of the line was a large building filled with heavy steam-powered machines and empty railcars. When the train crashed, it hit the steamshovels first. The momentum of the train had pushed the railcars off the tracks and they scattered throughout the building, knocking down support beams and tearing down walls. A massive load of steel and timber scattered out along the tracks and spilled out into the streets beyond the depot.

Then came the fire. When the locomotive's furnace spilled its contents all over the ground the combination of lumber, coal, and the collapsed walls made quick kindling. The vial Crow had thrown into the mix probably exacerbated the problem. Between the massive crash and the ensuing fire, the damage was spread out over more than a quarter of a mile. Thankfully, Crow's warning had gone out fast enough that the pedestrians knew to get out of the way.

The unintended consequence of the crash was that Overseer Rutherford came into Dockside with several sentinels and fifty Vangar warriors. He was still screaming when I arrived, a full two hours after the crash. Rutherford wanted to get to the bottom of it. He wanted to know what had happened and why it happened. Naturally, the poor citizens didn't have a clue and wouldn't have told him if they did. That only served to aggravate Rutherford even more.

It was about that time that a Vangar pilot flew a gyro into the crash scene and landed next to the wreckage. He leapt out of the seat and raced up to Rutherford. "What happened?" the overseer screamed at him.

"There was an uprising in the mines," the pilot explained nervously. "Two dozen slaves escaped. They stole the train-"

"And you couldn't stop them?" Rutherford shouted. "Not one sentinel could catch the train before this happened? Do you know how much this wreck is going to cost me?"

"I'm sorry, sir. I don't know-"

Rutherford silenced the man with a punch to the face. Unfortunately, the overseer's anger got the best of him and he struck the pilot so hard that it crushed the poor man's skull. He dropped to the ground, dead as a doornail. I saw the other Vangars exchanging dark looks as this happened, and I realized that they were running out of patience with Rutherford. I wondered how much more it would take before they turned on him. Rutherford didn't seem to notice.

"Clean this mess up!" he shouted. "Get those fires out, you worthless wretches!"

The Vangars went back to work, muttering quietly amongst themselves. Rutherford stomped back across the tracks to where his carriage was parked. It was a gorgeous steamcoach, finer than any I had ever seen before. The carriage itself was made of elegant hand-carved hardwood and decorated judiciously with brass fittings and gold filigree inlays. Like a traditional coach, this one had a driver's seat located at the front, but the reins had been replaced with steering controls and the cargo area to the rear of the coach now held the large steam-powered engine.

A Vangar driver in a suit of dark blue and gold waited patiently at the controls. Rutherford crawled inside and ordered the driver to take him back to the fighting. After he left, I heard several Vangars start plotting to kill him. I snuck away with a smile on my face.

I patiently made my way north, hoping that the train crash had given the rebels some breathing room. What I found didn't leave me with a lot of hope. I climbed the roof of a building near the fighting and saw the rebels occupying the narrow stretch of plateau on the far side of the city wall. The wall itself had provided them with a barrier, but they were holding back a tide of well-armed Vangars.

I saw sentinels there too, at least five of them, though they seemed to be staying out of the fight. That was probably for safety's sake. The sentinels' destructive tendencies often do more harm than good. It only took a few moments to confirm my worst fears. The rebels' situation was hopeless. The Vangars outnumbered them ten to one, and they were armed to the teeth. When the time came, the rebels would have to choose between leaping over the cliff into the sea or face a slow death at the hands of the Vangars. That time didn't look too far off. It was a miracle that they'd managed to hold the Vangars off as long as they had.

I silently cursed myself for telling the Woodcarvers about my plan. If I hadn't gone to them, if I hadn't given them some hope, this might never have happened. And Crow wouldn't have gone to them and incited this unlikely scheme in the first place. What on earth had I been thinking? If they died because of me, I'd never forgive myself.

I rolled away from the ledge, lying on my back to stare up at the churning, smoky sky. *Just a few more hours,* I thought. *Hang on just a few more hours.*

As I lay there, the sky broke open and rain came pouring down in a torrent. I climbed back down from the rooftop and hurried back to the footbridge where I'd left the boneshaker. I was dripping wet by the time I got there, and I had to keep wiping the rain out of my eyes to keep my vision clear. I felt a nervous fluttering in my stomach as I approached the hiding spot, and I couldn't help but fear for the worst.

What if someone had found it? What if the boneshaker had been damaged, or stolen? What if the Vangars had discovered it and they were hiding there now, patiently waiting for my return? I threw a quick glance up and down the street before I slipped down the side of the bridge and disappeared into the shadows below. I pulled back the branches and cautiously stepped inside.

There she was, waiting for me just as I'd left her. Not a soul had been under that bridge. I shook the rain out of my hair and off my arms. It was still pouring outside, but at least I could dry off under the bridge for a few hours.

I picked up my revolver, examining the barrel and fittings for signs of rust or other damage, and found it good as new. I spun the cylinder, counting how many shots I had left. Ten. I silently berated myself for not bringing an ammo bag, though I don't know where I would have found one.

The boneshaker's burner was still warm, thanks to Crow's vial, but the boiler was empty. The stream under the bridge might have provided an ample water source earlier in the year, but it had gone dry under the late summer heat. I was going to have to sneak to the nearest well and collect a pail of water. It was too early for that, though, too bright. I was going to have to wait a while. I didn't feel like going back out into the rain yet anyway.

I settled onto the seat and saw my face reflected in the brass and copper plumbing. I couldn't help but think of Tinker. The boneshaker had been his last great invention. Just like the plane he'd made for my mother, this was something that might have changed the world. The boneshaker was a cheap and efficient method of travel that anyone could appreciate. All of that notwithstanding, I almost felt like he'd designed the boneshaker *just for me*. I wondered if my mother had felt the same way about her plane. Perhaps someday I would get to ask her.

I had too many things on my mind. I had too many emotions trying to surface about my mother and Crow, about the death of Tinker, even the somewhat unexpected tinge of jealousy I'd gotten from seeing Kale and Nena together. Most of all, I was tired. I wanted to sleep. My body *craved* sleep. I decided it wouldn't hurt to take a quick nap. I couldn't do anything else until sunset.

I crawled off the boneshaker and stretched out on the ground, trying to get into a reasonably comfortable position. I didn't really manage it, but I quickly fell asleep anyway. I don't remember what I dreamed, but I woke with a feeling of despair and the certainty that I had forgotten something important.

The rain had stopped and the first thing I became conscious of was the steady dripping sound of water falling at the edges of the bridge. It was quite dark under the bridge, and I immediately thought I had overslept. I heard the distant crack of muskets and explosions to the north, and felt panic rising inside me. I slipped out between the lilac bushes and found to my relief that the sun had just set. I hadn't overslept by much, but I had to move fast.

I made my way to the nearest well and found the usual group of women there, finishing up the day's laundry and filling their cooking kettles with the water they'd need to get through the night. They were running late because of the rain. Otherwise, they would have headed home already.

There was no avoiding them, so I snatched up one of the many wooden pails lined up and down the boardwalk and hurried over to the well. The women looked me up and down in the same way that they always had. I heard a few of them muttering unkind words under their breath, but none made a move to stop me. To them, I was a streetwalker. I was a miscreant, a rogue, possibly even a prostitute. It probably didn't help that my leathers were stained with coal and my body was bruised from the overseer's beatings. I suppose it didn't help that I still had Rutherford's slave collar around my throat, either. I hadn't bothered trying to get the thing off yet. I'd heard stories, and I knew it would take the work of an accomplished locksmith or at least a blacksmith with a delicate touch. I didn't have the slightest idea where to find either one.

I felt cold stares on my back as I lowered the bucket into the well and then cranked the pulley to retrieve it. As I poured the water into the pail, I heard quiet murmuring and snickering sounds behind my back. I lifted my pail, turning to leave, and found myself standing face to face with a hard-faced shrew in her early thirties. She was large, slightly taller than I was and a good fifty pounds heavier, and she had an icy look in her eyes.

"What've we got here, girls?" she said. Her voice was unnaturally high-pitched for a woman of her size. "Vangars sendin' their whores out for water now?"

A few of the other women laughed, the rest just stared at me with ice-cold glares. I turned aside to walk past her, but the woman reached out and caught me by the arm. "Where you think you're goin'? We don't share water with Vangar whores 'round here."

I looked up into her face and then over her shoulder at the others. They were glaring, sneering. They'd already decided I was beaten. After all, how could a small thing like me stand up to that shrew? Or the rest of them for that matter... there were at least twenty of them.

"Take your hand off me," I said, twisting away. She tightened her grip, wrenching my arm so that the pail spilled half its contents. I pulled back, but her left hand flashed out, brandishing a dagger that she'd hidden under her bodice.

"Drop that pail, whore," she said, aiming the blade at my rib cage.

"That's enough," I said. I jerked forward, pulling her into me. I gave her a solid head-butt, slamming my forehead right into the bridge of her nose. She stumbled back, startled, and a shriek escaped her lips. She released the bucket and dropped the dagger as both hands went to her face. Blood gushed out between her fingers.

I dropped the pail, locking my hand into a fist and raised it as if to strike her. She jumped back, tripping over the edge of the boardwalk, and landed hard on her rump. I threw my glance back and forth and saw that nobody else was moving. I retrieved the dagger and examined it, appreciating the balance and craftsmanship. It wasn't half-bad. I was tempted to keep it. I raised my eyes to glower at the rest of the group.

"Anybody else?" I said with a crooked smile. They averted their eyes.

With practiced efficiency, I spun around and threw the dagger at the bucket dangling over the well. It pierced the slats, embedding itself right up to the hilt. The rope made a creaking sound as the bucket swayed back and forth. I smiled. I turned back to face the shrew and she flinched as I reached out to take her pail of water. I snatched it up and left without another word.

I ducked into a nearby alley and made my way back to the boneshaker, checking frequently to be sure I wasn't followed. As I reached the bridge, I realized that time had gotten away from me. Thanks to the scene at the well, it was now dark and I was behind schedule. I was lucky that Crow hadn't made his move yet. That thought set me to worrying that perhaps he had failed in his task; that he had been caught, or something else had gone wrong.

I hurried to fill the boiler on the boneshaker. I cranked up the pressure valve. While I waited for it to build up steam, I pushed the boneshaker out from under the bridge, leaving it just barely concealed in the shadows at the edge of the bushes. As luck would have it, a sentinel appeared while I was waiting.

I was sitting on the boneshaker with my eyes on the pressure gauge when I heard the familiar *kachunk-kachunk* and the sound of whirring of gears coming down the street. The sentinel was a hundred yards away. For the moment, he seemed completely unaware of me. I knelt down against the handlebars, trying to cover as much of the shiny reflective metal as I could. I bit my lower lip, praying he'd move on to the next street.

Naturally, he turned to face me and started walking. I glanced at the gauge, moving slowly so as not to attract his attention. *Halfway,* I thought. Crow's vial was working nicely, but it still wasn't fast enough. I needed another minute at least. I held my breath, my right hand slowly going to my revolver.

The sentinel strode forward, turning his head slowly from side to side as he walked. He passed an alley, pausing momentarily to look inside. Finding nothing of interest, he moved on. Then, twenty yards ahead, he sensed something. He froze in the middle of the street and pulled his gaze away from the surrounding buildings. Slowly, deliberately, he looked straight at me.

He doesn't see me, I thought. *Not yet.*

Perhaps I was right, but he certainly saw *something.* Was it a reflection of light? Was it the odd shape of the boneshaker against the shadowy backdrop of the bushes? *Was it me?*

A chill crawled up and down my spine as he stood there motionless, his gaze moving back and forth over me. I froze, not even daring to breathe as my heart thudded in my chest. *Just a few more seconds...*

The sentinel fixed his gaze on me and started walking. I knew I was out of luck. My hand closed on the grip of my revolver. I was prepared to do whatever I must to get around that sentinel. Crow was counting on me, and so were a hundred others.

I heard a *whooshing* sound overhead and raised my gaze to see Crow slicing through the sky over the city. The noise caught the sentinel's attention, too. He twisted his upper body, turning to catch a glimpse of the source of that noise. His hands flexed into fists as he saw Crow. The sentinel broke into a run down the street, his gaze bouncing back and forth between Crow and the road ahead. I relaxed my grip and sat upright, checking the pressure gauge one last time. Then I revved up the throttle, slammed the boneshaker into gear, and burst onto the street in an explosion of leaves and thundering exhaust.

The sound of the boneshaker's engine filled my ears, echoing back and forth between the tall stone and brick buildings, almost as noisy as the old combustion engine had been. I purposely revved the throttle, not just because the wind felt so good on my face, but because I wanted to achieve that smooth, flawless ride I had experienced before. Unfortunately, I had to make a turn, and then another and another. There was no way to achieve open throttle inside the city. Not outside Main Street, anyway.

I clenched my teeth to keep them from rattling out of my head as I zigzagged towards the north end of the city. I caught glimpses here and there of the sentinel on parallel streets. I had taken a different route on purpose, but I still managed to capture his attention. I didn't want to get cornered so I revved up the engine and took a side street, coming out just ahead of him.

The sentinel put on a burst of speed as he recognized me, but I had an advantage in navigating the city's tight corners. I had brakes. With very little practice, I had become quite adept at slowing just enough to skid around the corners without stopping. I rounded a tight curve and gunned the throttle on the way out, breaking into a wide open sprint. The distance between us grew. Then the sentinel found his pace and started gaining on me.

Every time the sentinel began to close the distance between us, I took a sharp corner and put him another twenty yards back. No matter how he tried, he couldn't catch me. As I climbed the hill towards the palace, I saw Crow circling in the sky overhead. The Vangars had opened fire on him with everything they had, but their firearms weren't accurate enough to be a real threat. Crow swooped through the air making circles and figure eights, twisting, dropping into a freefall only to recover just beyond their reach. His movement was so unpredictable that I could hardly even follow him with my eyes.

I took Crow's playfulness as a good sign. His goal had been to deliver all the ammunition that he could carry to the rebels. The fact that he was toying with the Vangars must have meant that he'd accomplished his mission.

I gunned the throttle as I roared up the hill, deliberately making a spectacle of myself. Crow noticed me right away. He gave me a wave and then flew over my head, flying back towards the center of the city. I hit the brakes and skidded sideways; pausing for just a moment to make sure the Vangars got a good look at me.

I was several seconds ahead of the sentinel that had been chasing me, so I sat there for a moment, revving the throttle. The Vangars had overturned several steamwagons to use as protection from the rebels. Off to the side, I saw Overseer Rutherford's fancy gilded steamcoach idling at the edge of a building. I revved the throttle a couple more times, making sure he noticed me. Sure enough, Rutherford's face appeared in the window and he instantly started screaming.

The sentinel that had been chasing me flew around the corner at just that moment. He ran right past me. He reached out for me as he flew by, but he was going too fast. I ducked as he flew past, and his momentum carried him into the side of one of the wagons.

I laughed. I hammered the boneshaker into gear and tore off down the street. I didn't need to look back to know they were after me. Every single one of them. At least I had succeeded in taking the heat off the rebels. Now I just had to stay alive.

Chapter 11

I was more confident this time as I led the sentinels on a high-speed chase down the winding streets of Avenston. I'd been there before. I knew my machine in a way now that made it almost an extension of my own body. I could feel it moving into the curves, could feel the drag of the air around me and the momentum of the boneshaker's weight. I could almost sense the bumps and waves in the road before I could even see them, as if I could reach out and touch the earth itself with my mind.

This is why my mother flies, I thought. *This is what she feels.*

That was an encouraging thought. It made me want to go even faster. I tightened the throttle and flew towards Main Street, thoughts of my first escape fresh in my memory. I already knew the best way out of the city. I just had to do it again. As I flew around a corner and accelerated into Main, I felt the street go smooth under my tires.

Waves of adrenaline washed over me and I felt a surge of satisfaction. For a few brief seconds I forgot about the sentinels and everything else, and allowed the moment to take me. Then I glanced ahead and realized that the sentinels had cut off my path. My heart skipped a beat as I saw three of them gathering at the city gate. I glanced over my shoulder and saw half a dozen more converging on the street behind me. I was trapped.

I threw my gaze left and right, searching for an escape. A few streets opened up to the west, but I couldn't go that way. That would lead me right back to the palace, and right into the arms of the Vangars. There were no streets to the east. The north end of Main was a solid wall of bakeries, butchers, and storefronts. All I had was a straight shot, right into those sentinels.

I set my jaw, my left hand snaking around to grab my revolver as I gripped the throttle in my right. I raised my weapon, glanced down the sights, and fired. My first shot was high, setting off a spark as it ricocheted off the gate ten feet over their heads. That gave the sentinels a warning. They spread out and dropped to all fours, making themselves harder targets.

I fired another round and then a third, hoping that if nothing else I could keep them scattered enough to break through. That was silly, though. I knew in my heart that I'd never get past them. The sentinels were too fast, and too well protected in their suits of heavy steel armor. All they had to do was jump in front of me, and I'd be dead.

A shadow flew overhead and Crow appeared in my vision. He must have been watching me from above. I frowned, wondering if he was trying to draw their attention. As Crow approached the gates, I saw something fall. Something small and dark against the blackness of the sky... *Kaboom!*

A cannon charge hit the road, right in the midst of the three sentinels. The explosion sent two of them flying backwards across the street. The one on the right hit the window of a store and disappeared inside with a crash. The other smashed into the side of a brick wall and went halfway through.

The explosion knocked the third sentinel off his feet, but he quickly recovered. Rather than waiting for another attack, he leapt into action. He dropped to all fours and rushed me.

I knew immediately that I was in trouble. Crow couldn't help me now. He couldn't throw another bomb for fear of hurting me. I couldn't fire at the sentinel without fear of shooting Crow. I jammed the revolver into my belt and hit the throttle.

Cobblestones shattered as the sentinel pounced and then rebounded into the air. He split the distance between us in one great leap. I hit the brakes, skidding sideways as I tried to avoid him. I was going too fast for such a maneuver, and the streets were still slick from the rain. The Boneshaker's rear wheel slid forward and the entire machine went down.

I managed to pull my leg out from under the boneshaker as it hit the ground. Half a second slower and it would have been a meat grinder. I balanced precariously on top of the machine, hanging on for dear life as it skidded sideways down the street, sparks fountaining up around me.

The sentinel leapt into the air and landed safely behind me. I scanned the street, looking for somewhere I might leap to safety. As I was searching, the handlebars caught a cobblestone. The momentum threw the boneshaker into the air, and me along with it. As I somersaulted into the sky, I tried to push away from the machine. If it landed on top of me, I knew it would probably kill me.

I managed get clear of the boneshaker but I couldn't recover before I hit the ground. I landed on my side, my left leg twisting underneath me. I felt my ribs cracking, driving the breath from my lungs. I rolled, bouncing jarringly across the stones as the boneshaker hit the street ahead of me. The sound of grinding metal and hissing steam filled my ears.

Something caught the cobblestones again, a handlebar or piece of pipe, and the boneshaker flipped end over end. It finished spectacularly by smashing into the city wall with a groaning sound. I rolled to a stop just a few feet away.

My breath came in brief, painful gasps. I couldn't seem to suck air into my lungs. I tasted blood on my lips and knew that something inside me had been damaged. I had broken bones. At least my ribs, but maybe more.

It should have been painful but it wasn't. Instead, a strange, tingling warmth had washed over me. I clawed at the ground, trying to suck air into my lungs, but it wouldn't come. My eyes went wide with terror as I heard faint gurgling sounds in my chest. A shadow fell over me. I glanced up and saw Crow's face looking down. He reached out to touch me and darkness closed in. I lost consciousness.

I came to briefly, but I couldn't make sense of anything. My body was warm but the wind on my face was cold. I felt like I was floating. As my eyes rolled back in my head, I caught a glimpse of stars. My last receding thought was that somehow the boneshaker had survived the crash, and that I was riding it out across the plains. That of course, was nonsense.

When I next awoke, I was lying on Analyn's cot. I pushed myself upright, fighting the thudding pain in my ribs, and saw Analyn sitting in her rocker by the fire. "What happened?" I said, though I could have put it together myself if I'd been thinking clearly.

"You were nearly killed."

I glanced around the cave. "Where's Crow?"

"He left. He went to make sure the sentinels didn't catch up with the others."

"How long ago did he leave?"

"Half an hour."

I closed my eyes, trying to think clearly. Crow had saved me from the clutches of the sentinels and then flown directly to the ruins of Anora. He had healed me. I was fairly certain that I would have been dead if not for him. I wondered how much time that had taken. I wondered how fast he had traveled, and how far the sentinels were behind him. I had seen them run on the open plains. I knew how fast they were capable of running.

"Crow can't stop them alone," I said.

"Don't underestimate him," she said. "He saved you, didn't he?"

I crawled to my feet, fighting the queasy sensation in my gut. I leaned against the post next to the cot. "He saved me," I mumbled in agreement, "but who's gonna save him?"

"It's not your battle anymore," Analyn said. "The others have gone into the mountains. We can only hope they make it to Sanctuary, according to our plan. The sentinels might catch them or they might not. There's nothing you can do about it, either way."

"Yes there is," I said. I walked up to the fireplace and snatched her rifle off the mantle. I blew the layer of dust away and examined it. "Where's your ammo kit?"

"Sometimes you're just like your mother," Analyn said without looking up.

"Then you know you can't stop me."

She snorted, shaking her head. "Check the drawer by the table."

I did, and found it there. I spread it out on the table, quickly loaded the rifle, and then filled a bag with as many charges as I could carry.

Analyn was shaking her head in frustration as I charged down the tunnel and made my way to the trap door entrance. A wave of fresh cold air hit me as I climbed out of the tunnel and found myself standing among the ruins. Brilliant starlight cascaded down over the city, casting long black shadows all around me. I leapt over the foundation of the fallen building and went running down the street toward the city gates.

I ran slowly at first, testing my body. I felt pain in my right leg and in my ribs, but not the sharp, jarring pain of an acute injury. This was the dull ache of an old wound, of an injury that's healed, or nearly so. I treated it as such and pressed on, clutching Analyn's long rifle as I tore through the weed-grown streets. As I approached the remnants of the city gates, I locked my eyes on the prairie, scanning ahead for any sign of life in the distance. That was when the sentinel hit me.

He appeared out of nowhere, a flash of color and movement, a massive fist ramming into my chest hard enough that it would have killed me if I hadn't twisted aside at the last moment. My legs went out from under me and I somersaulted backwards, landing facedown on the crumbling cobblestone street. The rifle whirled into the air, making a *clanking* sound as it struck the ground somewhere behind me.

The sentinel loomed over me. In a daze, I pushed back to my feet and Overseer Rutherford appeared behind him. "This is the one?" the sentinel said in a booming voice.

Rutherford smiled. "Yes, she's the one."

"I told you it was her."

"You will be rewarded, Wulvar. Kill her."

Wulvar. Somehow I knew this was Wulvine's brother. My suspicion was confirmed when I saw the look in his eyes as he stepped forward, reaching out to take me by the throat. As that cold mechanical hand closed around my throat and lifted me off my feet, I saw his brother's eyes staring back at me.

It sent a shiver down my spine, seeing life in those eyes again. The last time I'd seen Wulvine, he'd been wearing the wide-eyed, hazy stare of a man gone to the next world. I clutched at Wulvar's arm, trying to hold my weight so my neck wouldn't snap. I managed to cough out the words: "You look like someone I used to know."

Wulvar didn't seem to appreciate my dark humor. He threw me backwards. Once again, the sky and earth spun through my vision as I somersaulted down the street. I landed hard, but this time I was ready. I caught myself on the way down, my limbs absorbing the impact as I dropped to all fours. I stopped inches from the ground, muscles coiled, my reflexes like a panther ready to spring.

I glanced back and forth between them, sharp, calculating... I pushed to my feet and ran the other way.

I knew better than to take on the two of them. I knew from years of experience that the only way to kill a sentinel was to outsmart him. That was what had worked in the past, and it was the only thing I could hope to do now. I turned and ran, focusing all of that energy and terror into an all-out sprint. I was a dozen yards away before either of them could even react.

"Go!" Rutherford shouted as I vanished into the shadows. "Get her!"

A smiled tugged at the corners of my mouth as I leapt over the crumbling walls and foundations, my mind easily recalling the paths I'd walked when searching for parts to repair the boneshaker. I knew this place.

No, it was more than that. It was more than my own memory, it was the memory of the ghosts that surrounded me. It was the thousands of victims of the Vangar horde guiding me. The ruins of Anora had always had a sense of cold isolation about them, a somberness like that of a graveyard under the full moon, but suddenly all that changed. Suddenly, it seemed I knew these streets as if I had lived there. I knew the buildings, the alleys, the dark secret passages that time had forgotten. And I knew exactly where to lead the sentinel.

A strange sound filled my ears like the roar of a crowd, like the sound of a thousand ancestors calling out to me at once. I followed, for there was nothing else I could do. I led the sentinel deeper into the city, through dark crumbling alleyways and past abrupt, tilted walls. I led him across the broken foundations and rotten timbers, through the scattered ruins of all the lives that his kind had destroyed. Somehow, without even knowing where I was going, I led him to an ancient factory.

I faltered as I entered that old building. It was a dark, dreary place. A cold chill crawled across my skin as I stepped through the open doorframe and saw cobwebs dangling like sheets from the rotten timbers, glistening gray in the broken starlight that filtered down through the holes in the roof. Old pieces of rust-covered machinery rose like monsters out of the inky blackness. I felt my chest tighten and the sound in my ears faded, leaving only the heavy drumming of my heartbeat.

I moved through the machinery, trying to find a way through the back of the building to make my escape. Spider webs tugged at my face, clinging to my hair and my skin. I pulled at them, shivering as they stuck to me. Behind me, I heard the heavy thudding footsteps of the sentinel approaching the doorway. Finding no escape and no decent place to hide, I dropped to my knees behind an old lathe.

I watched the sentinel's shadowy form as he moved into the building. It may have been my imagination, but I thought I sensed a hesitation to his movements. I wondered if he too, felt the presence of all those ghosts.

A light came on. The sentinel had activated some sort of lantern built into the machinery of his body. The beam cut through the darkness like a single golden ray of sunlight. It moved back and forth, flashing across the old broken machines and the fallen sections of roof, illuminating the slow-moving motes of dust in the air as if they were hovering there, waiting for the light to put them on display.

And my tracks, I thought, wincing. If there was that much dust in the place, then I had left tracks. And the sentinel would easily follow them right to me. I almost sensed him smiling as he tilted his head, gazing at the footprints leading across the floor. I could imagine what he must have been thinking. This girl, this stupid human had led him right into her hiding place. Worse yet, I'd chosen a hiding place with no way to escape!

He took a step, and then another, and I shrank as I realized he was coming straight for me. My eyes were wide with fear, glistening with moisture as I searched the back wall. There was no door, no window, not even a ventilation hatch. I was trapped in that dark and dreary corner. I craned my neck around the lathe, stealing a glimpse at the sentinel. What I saw, I'll never forget.

As I moved, a sudden cacophony of noise filled my ears. It was the sound of band saws and drill presses, of lathes and anvils and saws coming to life all at once. The light of the sentinel's lantern flickered, strobing, flashing back and forth erratically. In the moments that followed, I still can't be sure exactly what it was that I witnessed. It seemed to me that the machinery itself came alive, that pipes and wires whipped out, tugging at the sentinel's limbs. I saw him falling to the ground. Perhaps I even saw something dragging him forward, hauling this massive abomination of flesh and machine deeper into the factory.

Regardless of what I saw or thought I saw, I will never forget the sound of his screams as the machinery began chewing through his armor. I saw flashes of light, sparks thrown from a saw blade. I heard the unmistakable sound of a large drill press, and I heard the sentinel screaming like a man suddenly confronted by the darkest nightmares of his deepest fever dreams.

I didn't wait to see the end result. I leapt to my feet and broke into a run, the danger of exposure forgotten. I've never moved so fast in my life. I flew past the machines, my heart thudding in my ears as the light flickered against the walls. I burst through the doorway, leaping into the street, and ran to the far corner before I found the courage to stop and turn around.

It was over. I was outside, safe. The light was gone, the screaming nothing more than an echo in my mind. I saw nothing inside that doorway except an impenetrable wall of darkness.

I stood there a moment catching my breath, trying to banish the terrifying screams and visions from my mind. Then I heard a noise behind me, and it was every bit as horrifying as the sound of the sentinel's screams: *Click, whir, thump!*

I twisted around and saw Rutherford standing in the shadows along the edge of the street. His face twisted into a crooked smile and I saw starlight glinting on the machinery that allowed him to speak. "I gave Wulvar his chance," he said. "Now it's my turn."

I turned and ran. Whatever had happened in that building was forgotten as I flew down the street and turned the corner, my eyes roving the darkness for some safe place to hide. "I've missed you, River," the overseer called out behind me. "Don't you remember the wonderful times we had?"

I heard the strain in his voice, the thump of his footsteps as he tried to match my pace. The overseer was gifted with strength, but only on one side of his body. His mortal weakness remained, and he was no sentinel. He couldn't keep up with me.

This knowledge did little to comfort me as I turned another corner and raced back towards the center of the city. Part of me thought of the factory, and I wondered if I should lead Rutherford back there. Were the ghosts still there? Would they do to him what they had done to the sentinel? No, I didn't think so.

Somehow I had a feeling that their bloodlust had been sated, at least for tonight. It didn't matter anyway. I wouldn't go back there for all the Blackrock steel in the kingdom.

I turned another corner and broke into a run down a long straight street. Bright starlight fell down on the rooftops, glistening in the moisture on the tiles and moss. Dark shadows cut across the street, frost glinting at the edges of the walls and shadowy corners.

Suddenly, I found myself somewhere familiar, some place that I knew. I was standing over the trap door that led into the tunnels. I wasn't sure how exactly I had gotten there.

My mind flashed back to the night of Tinker's death. Nausea gripped me. This was exactly how it had happened. I'd led the sentinels right to him. Somehow, I had repeated that same foolish mistake with Analyn.

I threw my gaze around, mystified. How had I gotten there? I couldn't recall. Some part of my mind had taken over, some subconscious instinct that guided me back into safe territory. Only this wasn't safe. This was the way to our queen! My foolish mistake would cost her life just as surely as it had cost Tinker's.

Click, whir, thump.

Rutherford appeared on the street behind me. I heard his deep, rattling breath and his heavy, uneven steps. It was too late then to make a choice. I thrust open the trap door and leapt inside, dropping catlike to the floor of the tunnel. As soon as I felt the dirt under my boots, I broke into a run. Rutherford dropped heavily to the ground behind me.

"You think you can run?" he shouted. "You can't hide from me!"

I didn't respond. My instincts had taken over, and all I could do was flee. A panic gripped me, a memory of all the things Rutherford had done to me when I was his captive in Juntavar. I struggled to push those thoughts from my mind. I needed to *think*. I needed to find a way to stop him. Step by step, yard by yard I brought him closer to Analyn's tunnel. I saw the light growing in the distance, and I saw movement.

Analyn's shadowy silhouette appeared in front of me, and I reached for the lantern in her hand. "Put out the light!" I screamed. Then I turned and went racing down the tunnel, hoping to guide Rutherford away from her. Analyn must have obeyed my command, for I heard the overseer's heavy breathing as he pursued me deeper into the tunnels. He must have run right past her.

I pressed on, running just fast enough to stay out of Rutherford's reach, but not so fast that he might lose track of my light. When I came to a fork, I went to the left. When I came to another, I went left again.

At last, I found what I was looking for. I wasn't sure what to expect when I saw the blackness in the earth open up ahead, but I knew that there was no turning back. Instead of slowing, I put on a burst of speed. Then the ground unfolded in front of me and I leapt into the air, vaulting over the chasm. For one breathless moment I was airborne, with nothing between me and that gaping black chasm, and then I landed safely on the far side.

I paused there for a moment, holding the lantern. I looked back, waiting to see if Rutherford was still in pursuit. He was. Half a second later, he came around the corner. I broke into a run in the opposite direction.

I heard his laughter echoing up and down the tunnel around me.

"You can't run from me, River. I'm stronger than you. I'm stronger than your mother. I can chase you to the end of the-"

And then he found the end.

I stopped and turned to face him as Rutherford slid over the edge of the chasm. I saw the moment of surprise on his face, the cruel twisted smile that bled into terror as the ground vanished under his feet. He reached out and found no handhold as he tumbled forward and vanished.

I jogged closer, anxious to see if I had actually succeeded in killing him. As I stepped up to the ledge, I saw Rutherford hanging by the barest thread of a root clutched in his robotic arm. His human hand clawed desperately at the dirt walls, searching in vain for a more stable handhold. "Help!" he screamed as I looked down at him. "Help me!"

I looked into his face, thinking of the things he had done to me, letting the memories wash over me. I glanced at that metallic fist and remembered what it felt like crashing into my body. I locked eyes with him.

"Take back what you said," I said, still trying to catch my breath.

His eyes widened. "What?"

"I'm not weak. My mother isn't weak. We're stronger than you, Overseer."

He considered that for a second and then nodded emphatically. "Yes, you're strong. You're both strong. I'm the one who's weak. Now help me!"

I stared at him, frowning. "That's not enough."

He grimaced, the sad look on his face giving way to fury. "You stupid whore! When I get out of here, I'm going to kill you!"

I shook my head, giving him a pitiful look. "Rutherford, you're not getting out of there. Not ever."

His anger became blind rage. He lashed out, even though it was obvious he couldn't reach me from that distance. Failing that, he kicked and clawed at the dirt, trying to climb up out of the pit. He muttered and cursed under his breath, spittle dripping from his lips as he shouted. He kicked and twisted. The root holding his weight began to shift. It made a cracking sound, and his eyes widened. Suddenly, he became very still.

Slowly, Rutherford raised his eyes to look at me. He opened his mouth to speak, but no words came. *Click, whir, thump.* The root gave way, and he went tumbling backwards into the abyss. Darkness swallowed him. I watched him vanish, a multitude of emotions surfacing as he disappeared from sight.

I held the lantern out over the ledge, scanning the darkness for something. For anything. For a sign of whether he was truly gone or not. Five seconds passed. Ten. Fifteen. And suddenly, I heard the distant echoing crash of metal folding in upon itself. I heard the soft wheezing of a machine crushed under its own weight.

Click, whir... click...

And then silence. A smile broke out on my face. "I knew there was a bottom," I said into the darkness.

Chapter 12

I returned to Analyn's cave to be sure she was safe. She was rekindling the fire when I entered. I returned the lantern to its normal place on the table and stood a moment watching her. She didn't speak until I turned to leave, and she once again tried to stop me.

"Stay here," she said. "Let the rest of it play out. You've done your part."

"I'm not going to let them have all the fun."

"There's not going to be any fun," she said seriously. "If your friends make it across the mountains ahead of the Vangars, then they'll have to get through the Wastes also. They'll have to keep moving through ice and snow, day and night, with no food or shelter and only the clothes on their backs."

"You make it sound hopeless."

She didn't answer. She simply stared into the flames.

"You may be right," I said. "It doesn't matter. I'd rather die with them, knowing that I did what I could. I'd rather that, than live knowing I did nothing."

She sighed heavily as she settled into her rocker. "I understand. You couldn't live with yourself if you lost him."

"Crow is my brother," I said.

"I didn't mean Crow." She turned to give me a deliberate stare and I felt an uneasy fluttering in my stomach, as if she had just revealed my deepest secret.

"I don't know what you mean," I said.

She laughed quietly. "Of course not. It has nothing to do with Kale then, I suppose."

"Of course it does! He's my oldest friend."

"Is he?" she said with a wily sparkle in her eyes. "And nothing more?"

"Of course not. He's like... like a brother to me."

Analyn laughed aloud. She leaned back in her rocker, shaking her head. "Just like your mother," she muttered. "Just like her."

"I don't have time for this."

"All right, then. I suppose I'd better tell you how to get back to the camp."

"The mountain camp? Where I was born?"

"The very same. I told Crow to bring the others there. I told him they would find weapons and shelter. That is where they will confront the sentinels."

I frowned. "Confront them? What do you mean by that? I thought the whole point was to lead the Vangars to Sanctuary."

"It was. Unfortunately, the sentinels are too fast. The rebels must meet the sentinels on their own terms. If the sentinels were to overtake them in the snow..." Her voice drifted off because she didn't need to describe what would happen. She was right. The slaves were a good fighting force, but they were tired and starved. They'd be lucky to make it through the Wastes on their own, much less pursued by a dozen or more sentinels.

"Can they do it?" I said. "Will they have what they need to fight off the sentinels?"

"At least in the mountains, they'll have a chance," Analyn said. "It's been many years and I don't know what supplies are left at the camp. It's their only hope."

"If this works and they do defeat the sentinels, our plan is still ruined. There will be no one to follow the rebels to Sanctuary."

"I don't think that will be a problem. No, if our little rebellion succeeds in this battle, we'll have the Vangars' full attention. They will keep coming. It will only be a matter of time until they reach Sanctuary. We simply must be sure the rebels reach it first."

I considered that. Perhaps Analyn was right. If we did successfully kill a dozen sentinels, the Vangars would be concerned -or more likely angry- enough to pursue us into the Wastes. "I almost believe it could work," I said absently.

"You'd better hope it does."

"I have to hurry," I said, turning away. "If I run, I might catch them before the sentinels attack."

"Before you leave, heed my words: Your mother waited to share herself with the man she loved, and then she lost him. They could have had many years together."

I rolled my eyes. "I'll keep that in mind," I muttered.

"May your ancestors guide your footsteps," she said quietly as I vanished down the hall.

On my way out of the city, I took a minute to gather up my revolver, the rifle, and the ammo bag I'd dropped when Rutherford attacked me. From what I could tell in the darkness, the rifle appeared to be undamaged. I put a fresh charge in the barrel and pressed the stock to my shoulder as I walked toward the gates, my finger resting on the trigger. The memory of Rutherford's attack was still fresh in my mind and I wasn't taking any chances. The next sentinel I saw was getting shot in the face.

I cautiously exited the city and turned in a slow circle, making sure I was alone. That was when I noticed the flickering light of a lantern a hundred yards away, just up the riverbank. I grinned as I recognized the silhouetted shape of Rutherford's steamcoach parked in a stand of trees along the river.

I found the carriage empty and the boiler still full of pressure. I shouldn't say the carriage was *empty*. Rutherford had left behind two high-quality rifles, a large ammo kit, and several days' worth of food. I wasted no time. I climbed into the driver's seat, propped Analyn's rifle up next to me within easy reach, and released the brake. Seconds later, I was flying along the plains as fast as I could.

It wasn't long before I saw the fires burning along the edge of the Blackrock Mountains. I had instructed Kale to set fires along the way so the Vangars could easily follow his path. Suddenly, I wished I hadn't. I cursed myself for not planning better. If anyone had known how fast the sentinels could travel, it should have been me. I should have known they would need more time. Crow must have realized this when he rescued me and brought me to Analyn. If not for that, the entire mission might have been doomed.

I felt like a fool. The fires had given the sentinels a path right to the rebels. In my effort to make sure the Vangars found Sanctuary, I had all but guaranteed they'd find the rebels first and kill them.

I saw a fire burning a few miles to the south, and another in the hills up ahead. I headed for the nearest one. The steamcoach's lanterns cast pale yellow circles across the path ahead, illuminating changes in the terrain that I barely had time to avoid. I pushed my luck by driving faster than I should have, and twice it nearly cost me. The first was a boulder that seemed to appear out of nowhere. I nearly crashed the coach, turning to avoid it. As I swerved, the rear end lost traction and the rear corner of the coach smashed into the boulder as I zoomed past. I glanced back and decided there wasn't any major damage. I pressed on.

The second near-fatal accident happened when the earth suddenly gave way in front of me. For a split-second, I thought I might have found another collapsed tunnel. Then, as the front end went out from under me and I found myself free-floating over the bench seat, the lanterns illuminated the bottom of an old dry creek bed. The coach hit the bottom, jarring the spring suspension to life. I came down as the bench seat rebounded. I landed so hard that the impact threw me in the air, up over the roof of the coach.

As I flipped over, I reached out and latched onto a luggage rail mounted to the roof. The carriage bounced beneath me, swinging me down hard against the roof. My knees hit first. As they slammed into the light wooden panels, the roof gave way and I suddenly found myself lying across the roof of the carriage with my legs stuck through the roof.

I stretched, reaching for the front bar, pulling myself forward. I had to twist and kick at the wooden panels before they would release me. By then, the carriage was already up the far embankment and heading out across the plains. Ignoring the bone-jarring ride and the deep painful scrapes across my midsection, I pulled myself over the front of the coach and dropped back onto the seat. I reached for the controls and realized that Analyn's rifle was gone. My revolver was lying on the floor. Sadly, I didn't have time to go back. I did however, reduce my speed somewhat.

The fire wasn't nearly so high in the mountains as I'd first thought. Kale had led the group up an old logging road that cut a broad, overgrown swath back and forth up the mountainside. Navigating the old road was a challenge, but even so I could still travel faster by steamcoach than foot, so I pressed on.

When I finally reached the fire, I locked the wheel brakes and walked the area on foot. My heart sank as I saw the deep imprints of the sentinels' steel boots in the bare earth, following the trail northeast into the mountains. Finding nothing else of interest, I climbed back onto the coach.

I followed their tracks for as long as I could. Eventually, the old logging trail gave way to impassable slopes and dense undergrowth and I had to abandon the vehicle to follow the narrow trail on foot. I loaded up with all that I could carry, taking the ammunition and rifles of course, and also a good store of food.

Shouldering my burden, I stepped away from the carriage and began my trek into the mountains. A few minutes later, as I turned to follow the trail up a steep slope, something in the sky to the south caught my attention. I froze, staring into the distance, gradually making out the shape of a dragon ship against the backdrop of stars. Then, behind it, I saw another, and then a third. My heart froze in my chest.

No, I thought as I stared at those dark masses hovering over the southern plains.

I realized then that despite everything, our plan had actually worked. As a matter of fact, it had work *too well*. My mother had expected us to get the Vangars' attention. Well, we had done that. Regardless of all the wonderful things I'd heard about Sanctuary, I doubted the Tal'mar would be ready to confront three dragon ships at once. I dropped everything, even the rifles. I broke into a run up the steep mountain trail.

I hadn't gone a mile when I heard the sounds of fighting up above. I put on a burst of speed, tearing through the underbrush, leaping fallen logs and stones that jutted out along the trail. I saw flashes of light to the north and I left the path, carving my own way up the mountainside. Tree limbs snapped painfully at my face and my arms as I ran. Tall ferns covered in dewy moisture slapped my skin, and in no time my leathers were soaking wet.

Analyn had described the place to me. I didn't remember much from the time I'd spent there in my youth, but I was surprised to notice a sense of familiarity with that mountain. I recognized the smell of moss-covered evergreens and wild jasmine, and the scent of dark, musty earth. There was something else, something familiar to me about the shape of the land and the view of the plains that stretched out behind me. Somehow, I knew exactly where I was going.

A sudden explosion at the top of the mountain lit up the night, shaking the entire mountainside. I stopped and felt the earth vibrate under my feet as I watched a pillar of light extend up into the heavens. A dark gray cloud formed, rising up like a mushroom into the sky. I noticed uneasily that there was a strange sort of blue luminescence to it. I though of Crow and his vials of starfall, and couldn't help but wonder if the sentinels had gotten hold of him.

I felt a sick churning in my stomach and I had the horrible thought that Crow might have sacrificed himself the way that Tinker had, and my father... I threw caution to the wind and put on a burst of speed, no longer concerned about how much noise I made on my way up the mountain.

As I reached the plateau, I found the mountaintop covered in a deep fog. I saw flashes of light here and there and realized they were from multiple fires around the encampment. I went forward with my revolver drawn, my senses alert, eyes scanning for any sign of life. I heard movement up ahead, heavy breathing and the sound of whirring gears. *Sentinel,* I thought. Cautiously, I moved forward.

The luminescent gray-blue fog drifted around me, and I saw a dark shape appear on the ground up ahead. It was too large to be a man. It was a sentinel, and he seemed to be wounded. I trained my sites on him, not making a sound as I cautiously approached.

"That's three!" someone said off to my right. I froze, my eyes searching the fog.

"Four here!"

I heard footsteps running toward me and I swung my revolver around, searching for a target. A man appeared, jogging out of the fog. His face was covered in smudges of ash and coal and his clothes were tattered. He came to a stumbling halt as he saw me. A second man appeared out of nowhere and ran right into him. They tumbled to the ground at my feet.

"River?" the second man said, looking up at me. It was Mal Tanner, the slave I'd met on the train.

I drew my gaze away, scanning the fog, listening intently for signs of trouble. "What happened here?" I said in a low voice.

Mal pushed himself upright and then helped his friend get back to his feet. "Crow set a trap," he said.

"I'll say," said his partner. "The mother of all traps! Nearly blew off the whole mountaintop."

Others came out of the fog then, apparently attracted by the sound of our voices. Kale was among them. "That's seven!" he called out triumphantly, staring at the sentinel at our feet. Then he noticed me standing among the others and threw his arms around me, lifting me into the air. I looked down at him, noticing his scarred cheek and his deep blue eyes, and felt an unfamiliar stirring deep in my chest. Suddenly, I couldn't be sure if I wanted to slap his face or kiss him.

I was dumbstruck by the feeling. I had been worried about Kale, but I didn't realize how much until that moment. When the mountain blew up my first thought had been of Kale. I was terrified that something had happened to him, that he had been killed in the explosion or captured by the sentinels. I took a deep breath.

"Put me down," I said quietly, trying not to let him hear the emotions rattling around inside me. He complied, but he couldn't resist giving me a peck on the cheek as I settled to the ground.

"Careful," I said. "Nena might see."

His jaw dropped and he stared at me, confused for a moment, as if he had completely forgotten about her. Then he stepped away, forcing a smile. "Right," he mumbled. "Of course."

"Eight!" someone called out at the north end of the camp.

"Are there more?" I said.

"We didn't get a count of them," Kale said. "They were chasing us up the mountainside in the dark. I don't think there were more than a dozen, though. If any survived, I don't think they'll come back for us."

"Two more to the west," Crow's voice said in the mist above us. He *whooshed* down to land next to me. "I saw a survivor headed south. I think there was another behind him, but I couldn't be sure."

"I don't understand," I said, glancing back and forth between the two of them. "You had all of this planned out?"

"Not until we got here," Kale said. "That was when we knew we'd have to fight."

"Analyn convinced me of that," Crow said. "And she was right. We wouldn't have even made it out of the mountains with those sentinels chasing us."

"That won't be a problem now," Kale said, clapping him on the back. "The bomb was your brother's idea. We set up one of the tents and made it look like we were hiding inside. It never even occurred to the Vangars that it was a trap."

"Well it seems to have worked," I said, "but I'm not sure it helped matters."

They both stared at me. "What are you talking about?" said Kale. "This is just what you planned. We can head straight into the Wastelands now without worrying about the Vangars."

I sighed. "When I came across the plains, I saw three airships headed this way. There might even be more. And we just turned this whole mountaintop into a torch, guiding them right to us."

They glanced at each other, both thinking the same thing. "Pack up!" Kale shouted, turning away.

"Everyone pack up. Take as much as you can carry. We have to move, *now!*"

Crow gave me a worried look. "Get them moving," he said. "I'll fly south and get a count of the airships."

"Be careful," I warned. "They're well armed."

"Don't worry, sister. They won't even see me."

He vanished into the fog and I found myself standing alone in the middle of the camp. I heard the sound of voices all around me, of the rebels hurrying to pick up whatever weapons or supplies they could find, of Kale pushing them to move faster, work harder. A frosty wind blew across the mountaintop, clearing the fog and kissing my face with the taste of ice and snow. I walked to the edge of the plateau and saw the peak of the next mountain and beyond it, the radiance of starlight reflected on snow.

"We're coming mother," I whispered under my breath. "I hope you're ready for us."

End: Part One

A brief interlude:

The City in the Wastes

1

(Breeze Tinkerman, many years earlier)

I dreamed of ice.

Winter in my mind: a maelstrom of snow, savage winds, and bitter, icy cold. In my dream I found myself in Tinker's little valley where I had lived and grown as a child. I was next to the stream behind his tiny cottage. I stood alongside the frozen banks, staring down at the falls where the water had frozen into a perfect cascade of rippling icicles filled with color and dancing light, the water beneath sliding quietly by, tempting, beckoning.

I stepped closer, kneeling down, dragging my fingertips across the smooth glistening surface. The icy cold bit into my flesh, numbness spreading across my hands with the slow menacing inescapability of a poison. I watched the light and colors dancing hypnotically just beneath the surface, luring me in, hypnotizing me.

I heard a voice in the distance, low and muffled by the wind, and I wondered at the sound. I knew somehow that it must be Tinker. I struggled to pull my

195

gaze away from that ice, but I couldn't. It held me spellbound, lost, trapped in a prison as clear as glass.

My mind reached out to him, searching. I heard Tinker's voice like a whisper on the wind, calling out to me. *Breeze, where are you? Come back!*

Cold, I said in my mind. *Tinker, I'm so cold!*

Keep moving, child. Keep moving!

And my eyelids fluttered open.

2

I woke shivering, blinking against the brilliant white light of morning. I was lying on the ground, my body covered in a layer of fresh powdery snow. My mind was a haze of fleeting images and sharp, painful cold. As I moved, my body cried out. The memories came flooding back to me.

The crash had broken my leg. I'd spent several excruciating hours struggling to reunite the shattered pieces of bone and mend them sufficiently to support my weight. I had lost consciousness several times during this process and succumbed to the cold a bit more each time. When at last I could move, I had slowly crawled to my feet and dragged myself back to the wreckage of my plane.

My teeth were chattering like gears in one of Tinker's windup toys and my body shook in a strange frightful way that I could watch like an impartial observer, but I couldn't make it stop. A howling, frigid wind came roaring across the Wastes, growing in intensity until I thought it might bury me in snow. I was cold, numb enough that I almost wished that it would. I was ready to die, or so I thought.

As I lay there, waiting for the numbness to spread to the rest of my body, I thought of my daughter. I saw her face, the light dancing in her eyes as her carefree expression suddenly became serious. *No, mother!* she seemed to say.

That was my River, placid and serene one moment, a raging torrent the next. Her mood could change in a heartbeat, and she was so strong. Willful and fearless, too. Her courage was like nothing I'd ever seen in a child.

I suddenly felt ashamed for being so weak, so ready to give in. I owed River more than that. I had promised to come back to her; had promised I wouldn't be gone long. What did she think of me now, I wondered.

I pushed myself upright, mumbling incoherent words that may have made sense to me at the time but almost certainly would have been a steady stream of nonsensical gibberish to anyone listening. I managed to gather an armload of the pieces of my wrecked plane. Slowly, methodically, I kindled a small fire. With numb and shaking hands, I doused the wood in lantern fuel and then located the flint in my pack. After several clumsy attempts, I finally managed a spark. Instantly, the wood was alight.

As the flames licked into the air, I stood over the fire, letting the warmth caress my shivering skin. The heat worked slowly through my jacket and my boots, warming my flesh and gradually raising the temperature of my body until at some point, I stopped shivering. I didn't notice it happen. The numbness in my limbs gave way to tingling, and then to deep, aching pain. Gradually, this too subsided.

I didn't realize I wasn't shivering anymore until I felt the first pang of hunger in my gut. I ignored it at first. I was too tired, too exhausted to get back to my feet and find some food. But the hunger persisted. It would not be denied. Eventually, when my discomfort grew disproportionate to my lethargy, I complied. I located the pack and rummaged through it, searching for the food Tinker had packed for me. I tore into it like a ravenous wolf.

My body was desperate for food. At some point after my crash, I had healed my broken leg, but the process had left me nutritionally starved. Looking back later, I realized that I'd nearly killed myself just as surely as the snow. I should have had the presence of mind to go for the food, to see to my material needs before trying to heal myself. In the end, I'd nearly sealed my own fate.

After filling my belly, I huddled up with my back pressed against the airframe, watching in silence as twilight deepened into night. The warmth of the fire washed over me, and I began to feel almost human again. I dozed off for a bit. When I woke, the fire had grown low. I made a slow circle around the crash site, gathering what wood I could hold, and brought it back to the fire with me. Satisfied that I'd make it through the night, I settled back into my place before the fire, picking at the food as the twilight deepened into gloom.

As night fell, the landscape became a glistening field of endless white, contrasting brilliantly with the blanket of darkness that fell over the world. Stars twinkled in the sky overhead and I found myself gazing up at them. I frowned, realizing it was the first time I had really *looked* at the stars. I'd spent my entire life in the sky and never really looked up. Why would I? There was nothing practical in the heavens. The stars were simply jewels that decorated the night. Or were they? Was it possible that they had some sort of reason, some pattern? I pondered this for some time.

As the night deepened around me, I listened apprehensively to the sounds of large creatures moving about in the darkness. I heard the unmistakable sound of claws against the ice, and snorting and growling in the distance. The noise drifted back and forth across the endless plain in such a way that I couldn't even guess in which direction it had originated.

I couldn't identify the creatures, but in my mind I could all too easily imagine the horrific disfigured monsters lurking just beyond the light of my fire, waiting patiently, building the courage to pounce on me the second I closed my eyes. More than once my hand strayed to my side, reaching for the hilt of my sword or the handle of my revolver, only to find that I had neither. I'd left them behind, in Tinker's care, to reduce the weight load on the old plane. I'd have given anything for them now.

I lapsed in and out of consciousness until dawn, and at some point finally fell into a deep sleep. As I blinked against the first warm rays of sunlight, they touched my skin and beckoned me into a deeper sleep, but I knew somehow that if I submitted I would never awaken.

I pushed awkwardly to my feet and cried out as jolts of pain shot up and down my body. My head spun with vertigo. For a brief time all I could do was lean against the wreckage, clinging onto consciousness. At last, when the vertigo faded and my senses began to return, I squinted against the light and cast my gaze back and forth across the wastes. The mountains were invisible to me now, but I remembered from the night before that they surrounded me in every direction.

I turned slowly, trying to retrace the last moments of the crash in my mind. Which way was north? I couldn't remember. I sensed a gentle tugging in the back of my mind, almost of something beckoning me forward. The practical, logical part of my mind told me I was hallucinating again. That was the reasonable answer. I was wounded, frozen nearly to death, and half-starved. I had every right to be hallucinating.

Even so, I decided to follow my gut instinct. What did I have to lose? At worst, I was simply trading a slow death at the plane for a quick one in the Wastes. I took a piece of wood from the wreckage, using it as a crutch to help me walk, and went lurching across the ice.

My boots made crunching noises in the snow, but the sound was strangely muted by that vast expanse of nothingness. I came across tall drifts in the snow here and there and had to walk around them, or attempt to climb over without breaking through. I had the small comfort of knowing that the snow was only a foot or two thick in most places and that it was supported by a thick layer of ice just below the surface, but that did little to allay my fears of what might lie beneath.

I could only surmise that I had landed in the middle of some sort of lake or ocean, though I didn't dare guess how deep it was or whether the entire thing was frozen through. I tried not to think about the possibility that I was crossing an ocean of churning, icy black waters that were just waiting for me to step in a crack.

It didn't take long to come across the tracks of the creatures I had been listening to in the night. I was not surprised to find both a fox trail and the messy path of a pack of wolves. I even came across the massive footprints of a bear, the size I which I could scarcely imagine. Not even in legends had I heard of a creature so large. I began casting worried glances back and forth across the snow to be sure the beast hadn't caught my scent and followed after me. Not that I could ever be sure. Not in that white, frozen waste.

Despite all of this, these creatures were not the greatest of my worries. It was the other prints that truly frightened me. They were shaped like some strange hybrid of man and animal, a creature that appeared to have appendages shaped like human hands but larger, and claw marks extended out from the prints.

I saw signs indicating that the creatures traveled in groups of twenty or more, and that they varied in size from as small as a housecat to at least as large as a man. Judging by the prints, I guessed some of the creatures weighed several hundred pounds.

These discoveries were truly disquieting, and if nothing else they spurred me to keep moving, causing me to travel at a rate of speed that wouldn't have been possible otherwise. Even so, as the sun passed overhead and began its slow descent toward the horizon, I knew that I had only a few hours left to live. The fabled city in the wastes, the object of my journey, was nowhere in sight. I was tired and starved and I knew I couldn't go on much longer. Deep down I knew that the sensible thing would have been to lie down in the snow and fall into a deep comfortable sleep, knowing full well that I'd never wake up. At least that way I would be dead before the wild animals discovered me and began feeding on my still warm corpse.

Somehow, I couldn't bring myself to do it. Instead, some inexplicable will to survive urged me on, pressing me to keep putting one foot in front of the other, trudging through that icy barren landscape even when I knew there was no hope for anything better than a quick death. Perhaps it was an instinct, an almost mechanical reaction to fear and death that continued pushing me forward even when I knew I should stop.

For a brief time during the day, I was able to confirm by the passage of the sun through the sky that I was in fact traveling north. Unfortunately, the span of daylight hours seemed incredibly short and with the inevitable return of twilight it occurred to me that I didn't know which direction I was traveling, and that I might have ended up walking in circles. The only small assurance I had that this was not so, was the fact that I hadn't crossed the same path twice. After all, there were no other markers in this icy void. There were no rocks, trees, or hills. Just a vast plain of sparkling white, marred here and there by the passage of the creatures who somehow thrived in that barren wasteland.

If I'd had more presence of mind I might have gleaned more information about my direction of travel from the movement of the stars, but even if I had, such knowledge would not have helped me. Changing direction at that point would have been a silly notion at best.

Later that evening, just before sunset, I found a new trail. It was so odd, so out of place that I froze in my tracks and stared at the ground, almost certain that this was another wild hallucination. It must have been, I reasoned. There was no other explanation. These were not the tracks of some wild animal, but *footprints*. Shoe prints. And I knew immediately from the size, shape, and design that they were the footprints of the Tal'mar.

3

I stared long and hard, pondering the meaning of those tracks. My thoughts were muddled with exhaustion, hunger, and cold. It was a wonder I could manage to recognize them at all. But I did, and after some reflection, I began to suspect that I knew who had made them.

When I'd last seen my grandmother, she and the other refugees from the isle of Tal'mar had been heading northeast through the Borderlands, toward the Wastes. It was there that they hoped to escape from the invading Vangars. Robie had been with me at the time.

The Tal'mar had not invited us to join them. Quite the opposite, in fact. Some of the elves were suspicious of me because I had a claim to the throne and being half-human, the Tal'mar naturally mistrusted me. It was decided that for my own safety, it was best I return to the humans. I wouldn't have stayed anyway, but it was a painful memory nonetheless. My grandmother was my only kin; my last living relative (before my daughter was born, of course).

These thoughts and memories slowly formed in my frozen mind, and I was stunned by the implications. How had the Tal'mar made it this far? Why had they traveled so deep into the Wastes? I didn't have the clarity to work it all out, but I did have enough sense to follow those tracks. I knew I was likely following them to my doom, but at least I might solve that one mystery before I died. If nothing else, I hoped to learn the fate of my grandmother.

I staggered on, my head lowered against the wind, my eyes fixed only on the tracks frozen in the snow. I leaned heavily on my makeshift crutch, lurching ahead one step at a time. I don't know how long I pressed on in this manner, only that night fell and the wind bore down on me, hammering icy crystals into my exposed skin, and I kept thinking to myself *I can't go on, can't go on...* Yet somehow, I did.

Eventually the night brightened around me and everything seemed cast in a deep blue hue. I told myself that I was imagining things. It was another feverish dream, that bright blue light, a trick of the mind so close to death. I did not even bother to raise my eyes. I pressed on, one step at a time. Then, suddenly, the trail vanished and I realized mid step that some sort of black abyss was yawning up before me. I swayed unsteadily, trying to catch myself before walking over the edge like a fool, but I had no sense of balance left. Before I knew what was happening, the ground gave way beneath me and I fell.

Any normal, healthy, sensible person would have panicked. They would have reached out for a handhold, twisting and turning, crying out in fear. Instead, my body went limp as I fell. I watched with a strange sort of detachment as the heavens disappeared through the hole in the ice overhead and that strange blue light swallowed me up. I remember feeling only a vague curiosity, and the thought that went rolling around in my head was: *Well, isn't this interesting.*

When I hit the water, it didn't even occur to me to swim. I saw a flash of blue as I sank beneath the surface and everything went blurry. I knew matter-of-factly that I was dying. I closed my eyes, savoring the odd sensation of the water as it filled my ears, my nostrils, my lungs. I had expected it to be cold, but oddly it wasn't. It was like a heated bath and it folded around me like a blanket, warming my body and sucking me even deeper into its embrace. I smiled, succumbing to the odd warmth, and died.

Or so I imagined.

4

I woke on the shore of a lake, lying under the shade of a gnarled old oak. Rays of soft golden sunlight filtered down through the treetops, kissing the deep blue waters. Upon waking, I instinctively reached out, clutching at the grass, and sucked in a deep, gasping breath. The air was fresh and cool, sweet like the forest on a warm summer day. I felt a surge of energy course through my body. It was the invigorating, intoxicating rush of energy a child feels before a party, and it was strange to me. I hadn't felt like a child in a long, long time.

I pushed to my feet and threw my gaze back and forth, trying to get my bearings. Thick woods surrounded the lake on all sides. I heard the sounds of creatures that I couldn't identify moving about in the treetops, but none close enough that I could see them. I turned my head slightly, gazing out across the lake, wondering at the strange blue light that seemed to emanate from everything around me. In a vague detached way I could remember falling, hitting the water, and being swallowed up by that strange blue light. There was something about it... in fact, there was something about the whole place that seemed almost familiar.

I turned my gaze heavenward and gasped as I saw the surreal, shimmering wall of ice looming over me. I turned in a slow circle, watching it rush down to meet the treetops in the distance. I knew then that I must have been in some sort of cavern under the lake of ice. But that didn't make any sense. I was surrounded by trees and plants. The temperature in the cavern was perfectly comfortable, and yet that icy wall showed no signs of thawing in the warmth. I frowned, considering. None of it made any sense.

Out of the corner of my eye, I saw the movement of some large creature under the surface of the choppy water. A chill ran down my spine as I observed the enormous shadow passing slowly by. I felt as if the unknown beast were watching me, waiting for me to get within reach. I stumbled back a few steps to the tree line, warily watching the movement under the waves, terrified that the thing might be able to reach out and grab me.

I heard a grunting noise behind me and spun around, my eyes searching for the source of the sound. I noted movement in the tall foliage a dozen yards to my left, and then again just a few yards closer. Cautiously, quietly, I pressed myself up against the trunk of the oak. I waited, hardly daring to breathe. I heard another low grunting sound, like that of a large human male lifting something heavy.

I stared into the dense green undergrowth, hardly daring to breathe. The creatures –whatever they were– seemed to be moving in my direction. I subconsciously reached out to the tree with my mind, preparing to leap up into the branches. It had always been my experience that trees help the Tal'mar. They bend their branches down to catch us, and move them around before us to create a path as we run. I didn't get such a response from this tree. Instead, I got the cold irritated sense that the tree wanted me to get off its roots.

I took an awkward step back, staring up into the branches. A chill ran down my spine as I noted that the branches had taken on the shape of a face, and that it glared down at me with a disapproving stare. Perplexed, I reached out to the tree again. I thought I might explain the situation and ask permission to use its branches. Instead, as I opened my mind, I felt an invisible hand give me a slap right across the face.

This all happened in my mind of course, and yet the stinging sensation on my cheek was so real that I let out a yelp as I reached up to massage it. This was a mistake, of course. My scream had attracted the attention of the unknown beasts and I immediately noticed that the creatures in the underbrush had stopped moving. I could almost see their grisly, misshapen features, heads turning, eyes searching, salivating jaws aching for my flesh.

I heard a thump as of something hard hitting the ground, followed by several loud grunts. The tops of the ferns and flowers waved and shuddered as the beasts came crashing in my direction. I turned and fled. I followed the shore around the edge of the lake. My heart lurched as I heard the creatures stampeding out of the woods behind me. The forest floor shook with their noise.

I risked a glance over my shoulder as I ran and saw the leader of the pack launch himself out of the undergrowth, crashing down on the beach. It was a fur-covered creature that I mistook for a wolf at first. Then the creature landed on all fours and threw its head back, sniffing the air. Strangely, the creature's fur was orange. Its body structure was closer to that of a human than any other beast I had ever seen. It had a horrific leathery face with dark eyes and broad, misshapen features. The others behind it were smaller but no less intimidating. Their fur ranged in color from orange and brown like the leader, to violet and deep, dark black.

The monster reared up on its hind legs, standing like a man, and let out a roar as it pounded on its chest. I put on a burst of speed, knowing full well that it had already seen me. My gaze danced back and forth, searching the trees as I ran. I reached out to them with my mind asking for help and protection, and my head rang with deep, hollow laughter. I noticed movement in the branches around me and realized that more of the monstrous creatures were up there. They alighted from branch to branch with the agility of squirrels, their harsh chattering noises confirming my worst fear: these creatures were communicating with each other. They were sharing my location with the others, guiding the predators to me, their prey.

As I swung my gaze back around, I noted a distant path rising out of the forest floor up ahead, leading up a slope and into the woods. I raised my gaze and noted tall rectangular shapes in the distance. I blinked, surprised. I had discovered man-made structures. Suddenly, I knew where I was. This was it. This was the city in the wastes. The city was real, and against all probability, I had stumbled upon it. My mind instantly equated civilization with safety and I put on a burst of speed, flying along the beach and into the darkened woods, heading for those massive buildings.

As I passed under the canopy, I noted movement and frightening sounds all around me. The hideous, furry creatures were still shrieking back and forth at each other. I seemed to be outrunning them but I dared not stop. I crested a hilltop and flew down the other side so fast that I nearly barreled into a deer at the bottom of the ravine. I was upon her before she even saw me. I had to leap into the air to avoid crashing into her. As I did, the doe let out a frightened bellow and dashed off into the woods.

I landed awkwardly on the embankment and the loose soil gave way beneath me. I lost my balance and dropped painfully to the ground. No sooner had I hit the ground than a massive beast dropped out of the trees overhead. It had the same overall appearance as the other creatures, except that it had sleek blue fur, dark as the midnight sky, and a patch of fur on the right side of its head had been ripped away to expose shining bronze metal.

It landed heavily on the ground in front of me, glaring at me with dark yellow bloodshot eyes that intimated a human-like intelligence. A scream escaped my lips.

"Quiet!" the beast said in a low, terrifyingly human voice. "Follow me, if you wish to survive."

For a split second, I was too terrified to do anything but stare. The missing patch of fur caught my eyes. I watched the impossibly tiny gears whirring inside the thing's head, the tiny pipes curling around, back and forth, connecting the internal machinery to a tiny smokestack. A trail of steam puffed out of the smokestack behind its ear. I glanced down and I saw more torn flesh and more exposed machinery on its right arm and other parts of the creature's body.

I stared, dumbfounded, trying to understand what this thing was. Was it a beast? No, it was clearly a machine, but it had obviously been modeled after the other creatures in the forest. That didn't make any sense, though. Who would model a machine after a wild animal? For what purpose? And not only that: the creature could speak!

I stared at it, frowning as it turned away and lumbered down the ravine and across the hillside on all fours. It paused to turn back and wave at me, urging me onward. I heard the chatter of the other creatures in the woods behind us and I pushed to my feet and ran.

5

The creature guided me to the edge of the forest and down a steep, grassy slope. We climbed over a small fence at the edge of the lawn and I found myself standing in the middle of a wide street paved with smooth stones. Massive structures rose up in front of me, buildings of unimaginable proportion that pressed right up to the sky. I stood staring at them, awe-stricken, the strange beast at my side nearly forgotten.

The buildings were incredibly tall, not five stories or even ten, but dozens. The glass was perfectly smooth, reflecting my image back at me like a mirror. Most of the buildings were rectangular in shape, but they had very differently shaped roofs. Some were like pyramids at the top, others like large discs or bulbs. A few had plain flat rooftops like those of Avenston. The walls were constructed out of some sort of concrete or brick, but the materials were far superior to anything I had ever seen. From a distance, the buildings had looked almost white, but up close I saw shades of violet, blue and red. The colors were the soft pastel hues of sunset.

I had never imagined construction like this. I gazed into the darkened windows. Until that day I had only seen handmade glass, full of surface imperfections and bubbles. This hardly seemed like the same material. At that moment, I couldn't be sure it was actually glass. I wanted to reach out and touch my reflection, but I didn't dare. I had no idea how the strange substance might react.

"You are safe here," the beast next to me said in a low rumble. I slowly turned my head to stare at him. After a moment, I found my manners.

"I... thank you," I said awkwardly.

"No need. I am created to serve."

I tilted my head, my gaze straying to the exposed metal and machinery on the creature's head. "Are you a machine?"

He bowed his head. "I am the greatest of all machines. I was created in my master's image."

I stared at him, wondering, hardly knowing where to begin. "Who created you?"

"The Creator," he said patiently.

I took that as meaning the creature had an inventor, an engineer who had designed and built him. "Can you take me to the Creator?"

He didn't respond, but instead turned away and began walking. I hurried to follow after him. "I'm Breeze," I said. "What's your name?"

"The Creator named me Socrates. I am the greatest of all machines."

"So you said."

Socrates maintained a brisk pace as he led me through the city, but I had to stop him several times. First, when a machine the size of a steamwagon came rolling down the street, spraying a mist of water in its path. I stopped in my tracks and stared in disbelief as I saw the wide brush turning underneath, cleaning the cobblestones, leaving them sparkling clean and damp in its wake. A large steam engine on the rear of the machine seemed to power it, but I saw no sign of a human operator. The thing appeared to be driving itself.

Socrates realized I had stopped, and he came back for me. "What is that thing?" I said.

"Street sweeper," he said, his tone implying that it should have been perfectly obvious.

"How does it drive?"

"The street sweeper is propelled by an eight cylinder fifty-two gallon external combustion steam engine," he said as if reciting the words out of a textbook.

"Yes, I understand... *but who's driving it?*"

"The street sweeper is," he said impatiently. He took off down the street and disappeared around the corner. I had to jog to catch up with him.

A few blocks later, we passed a toy store. My heart leapt as I heard the voices of children playing in the distance and I assumed that we had finally found some semblance of humanity. As we got closer, I realized that the children were in fact machines made of gleaming brass and copper. Half a dozen of them ran in and out of the toy store, chasing one another, playing with the shop's collection of toys. They were human in appearance, but with exaggerated proportions. They had large bulbous heads and no hair. A few of them had smooth gleaming metal for skin, others had exposed gears and springs. Some of them had windup keys attached to their backs, while others simply had an opening to attach a key or some other device.

I slowed down to stare at them as we passed by. They seemed to take no note of us. I glanced into the store windows and saw that there were no humans in sight. Only toys, many of them strange and seemingly intelligent like the children and like my companion

Socrates. I noted however, that the children didn't have Socrates' intelligence. Instead, they seemed programmed only to play games.

Despite my disappointment, I was enamored of the creatures and I desperately wanted to stop and examine them, to understand how these strange machinations worked. Socrates had no patience for that sort of thing. I had asked him to take me to the Creator, and he was determined to perform this task as quickly as possible. As he lumbered down the street ahead of me, I promised myself that I would come back to the store later, when I had more time.

We pressed deeper into the city, until at last we came to a large park in the footprint of several tall buildings. The lawn was perfectly manicured, surrounded on all sides by neatly clipped hedges and decorated with tastefully appointed flowerbeds and ivy-covered fountains. In the distance, I saw some sort of tall robotic creature shaped like a box with wheels trimming the hedges by driving over the top of them.

The place was thick with trees, mostly oaks and chestnuts and a few others I didn't recognize. In the center of it all, Socrates guided me to a tall marble obelisk bearing a statue of a Tal'mar man with long hair. There was an inscription carved into a bronze plaque, but I couldn't decipher the script. As we approached the monument, Socrates fell to one knee and bowed his head in quiet contemplation.

"This is the Creator?" I said, the disappointment clear in my voice.

Socrates nodded silently. I sighed. I had been searching the windows and doorways ever since we entered the city, desperately hoping for a sign of life. Now at last I had to accept that conclusion which at first had been obvious, had I not refused to accept it. There was no life here. No humans, no Tal'mar. Only the trees, the machines, and the strange creatures out in the woods. I was alone.

"Turn around slowly," said a voice behind us.

I spun around. Half a dozen Tal'mar warriors appeared, melting out of the shadows under the trees. I recognized a few of them and I smiled to see them, though they didn't seem happy to see me. Their bows were drawn, their faces dark and unreadable. The one who spoke was middle-aged with long, jet black hair streaked with violet. I glanced at him and then the others, noting that most of them weren't wearing traditional Tal'mar clothes. The Tal'mar prefer close-fitting leathers and light fiber fabrics, and they always dress in natural colors that blend with their environment. Instead, they wore long robes, many of them brightly colored.

"I'm Breeze Tinkerman," I said. "I'm unarmed."

"Shackle her," said the leader, "and take her to the prison."

"Wait!" I said. "Don't you remember me? Don't you know who I am?"

"Of course I do," he said, turning away. "I should kill you now and be done with it."

I was speechless. Socrates scratched his rump and wandered off into the trees as the warriors pulled my arms behind my back and locked them in shackles. "Thanks a lot," I called after him. He didn't seem to notice.

The Tal'mar led me through the park and into one of the adjacent buildings. To my surprise, the doors opened as we approached. We entered a broad lobby with doors and passages sprouting out in every direction. The walls were covered in smooth plaster, and ceramic tiles lined the floors. To my immediate right was a large room with an entire wall made of glass. Inside, I saw a long hardwood table surrounded by velvet-upholstered chairs made of wrought iron and carved wood.

I noted that the brass sconces that lined the walls were not gas lamps or lanterns, but were electrical lights like the one Tinker had shown me before I left. The old merchant had told the truth. He had actually been to the city in the Wastes, and he'd returned with one of those lights as proof. If not for that light, I might never have come.

The guards pushed me forward, and another set of doors opened in front of us. We stepped into a small room that turned out to be an elevator. I had never seen such a thing before. I was baffled until one of the Tal'mar twisted a dial on the wall and pulled a lever, and we began to descend. My legs nearly went out from under me and the Tal'mar guards smiled at my country simplicity.

When the doors opened, they shoved me out. I found myself in a massive subterranean chamber. "Wait!" I said as the door slid shut. "I must see the queen!"

I heard the whirring sound of the elevator ascending back up the shaft. I was alone. Instantly, my senses closed in and a claustrophobic sense of isolation washed over me. I recognized the feeling. I had been a Tal'mar prisoner before. They have a way of turning off one's senses, making it so that you can't reach out with your mind. I suppose for a normal human it would be similar to losing the senses of touch and smell. The world around you remains unchanged, but the way you perceive it is altered.

I turned slowly, studying my environment, trying to fight the panic rising inside of me. I was in a massive basement. The floors, walls, and ceiling were made of the same smooth concrete as the building's exterior. Pillars rose to support the heavy steel beams lining the roof. Here and there, every few yards, a dim light shown down. I could see them lined up as they stretched into the distance.

I forced myself to take slow, deliberate breaths. I knew that whatever spell the Tal'mar were using on me was temporary, but that knowledge did little to allay my fears. I opened and closed my fists, gripping my skirts, feeling a bit like I had just woken in a coffin to find myself buried alive. *Don't be distracted,* I told myself. *Find a way out!*

I started by trying to pry the elevator door open, to see if I might climb the shaft. I was unable to make it move. The perfectly machined metal didn't leave space for a fingernail between the door and the frame, much less something useful like a dagger (which I didn't have anyway). Failing that, I decided to test the rest of my prison. I started by examining the walls. I walked the entire perimeter, searching for an opening or vent of some sort that I might fit through. I found nothing. I scanned the darkened corners and the shadowy spaces behind the pillars and beams, all to no avail.

What I did find at last was a ventilation shaft that opened up in the ceiling in the middle of the room. It was fifteen feet in the air, well out of reach, and located far enough from the adjacent beams that I'd never be able to jump that far even if was I lucky enough to climb up there. My situation was futile.

If nothing else, the two hours I spent going from end to end of that massive basement served to exhaust me. My body was still repairing the injury I had suffered in the crash, and I was hungry and spent. My injuries and the cold had taken a toll on me. I curled up on the floor next to the elevator and immediately fell into a deep sleep.

I dreamed of my daughter. I saw her playing in a bright sunny meadow, smiling, waving. I watched as she ran through the tall grass, turning in circles, spinning until she fell dizzily to the soft, mossy ground. I smiled and she laughed. Her voice was like music drifting on the wind, sweet as honey to my ears. She pushed awkwardly to her feet and began spinning again, and a warm sense of pride rushed through me. She was so beautiful, so perfect. She was the greatest thing I had ever accomplished.

I noticed something in the woods behind the meadow, a shadow looming just beyond the tree line. I called out to River, warning her to get away, but she was caught up in her laughter and she couldn't hear me. The shadow crept closer, suddenly forming into a Vangar warrior with a broad-headed fighting axe and a collection of scalps dangling from his belt. A wicked smile turned up the corners of his mouth.

"River!" I screamed at the top of my lungs. "Run! Get away!"

I ran towards her, but the softy muddy earth clung to my boots making it nearly impossible to move. I cried out, thrashing as my legs sank into the mud, terror washing over me, gripping at my chest. The Vangar strode forward, grinning like a devil, fresh blood splatters painting his face.

"Run!" I screamed vainly, tears flooding my eyes as I watched River dance right into his waiting arms, and he raised the axe...

6

I woke on the cold bare floor and heard the sound of the elevator descending into the basement. I pushed up into a sitting position, waiting, staring at that heavy steel door. I had no idea what to expect. The last time we'd parted ways, my grandmother had made it clear to me that her loyalties lay with her subjects rather than her own kin. She had turned her back on me as easily as she would a complete stranger. She had also made it clear that some of those subjects might try to kill me, and that she would do nothing to stop it. Perhaps that was about to happen.

At last, the doors parted, and my jaw dropped open. "Tam?" I said in disbelief. He gave me a half-smile as he stepped out of the elevator. He held out his hand, offering to help me to my feet.

Tam was the sullen warrior who had fallen in love with me before I married Robie. For a brief time, it seemed the two of them might kill each other in their efforts to win my affection. Eventually, I had chosen Robie and sent Tam back to his people. It wasn't a pleasant parting. I didn't know what to think when I saw him there, staring down at me. For some reason it hadn't even occurred to me until that moment that he might be among the other Tal'mar.

I felt like I should say something; like I should tell him that I was sorry or that I had made a mistake, but those things weren't true. I had made my decision. It was Robie I had loved. Sending Tam away had been the best thing for both of us.

I accepted his hand and he pulled me to my feet. Socrates lumbered out of the elevator behind him. "I'm sorry for what they have done to you," Tam said in a quiet voice. "It was wrong. Socrates told me you were here, and I came as soon as I could. The others would have kept this a secret until they decided what to do with you. They may not have told me even then."

"I don't understand any of this," I said. "What are the Tal'mar doing here?"

"The same as you. We followed the legends. We passed through the Borderlands and made our way across the Wastes. Eventually, we found this place and knew the legends were true."

"Legends," I muttered. "The Tal'mar's ancestors truly came out of the Wastelands, then."

"Indeed. Not just the Tal'mar, though."

I stared at him frowning. "What do you mean?"

"I will explain it all later. For now, we must focus on keeping you alive."

"They plan to kill me, then?"

"Some do. When last we met, I warned you that they would."

"Will you help me escape?"

He took a deep breath. "Breeze, I will help you but you must make a promise: you must swear to me that you'll never try to leave the city."

"That's ridiculous," I said, shaking my head. "I won't be your captive here."

"You don't understand. I can keep you alive. I can protect you, but I won't go into the Wastes with you. If you try to leave, the others will know. Make no mistake, they will follow you into the wastes and kill you."

"Why?" I said. "Why won't they just let me go? I have a daughter, Tam! I must go back to her."

He sighed, drawing his gaze to the ceiling. "Breeze, the Tal'mar have claimed this city as their own. They won't endanger it by letting outsiders know about it. We are forbidden to leave the city, ever. None of us can ever leave, not even me."

Looking into Tam's face, I could see the truth of his words. And knowing my grandmother as I did, I had no reason to doubt what he said. The Tal'mar had always been isolationists. When the Vangars attacked, the Tal'mar chose to run into the Wastelands looking for refuge rather than fight with the rest of us. Now that they had found that refuge, they were going to protect it at any cost.

"Come," Tam said, stepping into the elevator. "We will discuss these matters later."

Socrates and I stepped in after him, and Tam activated the elevator. On the way up, he turned to me and in a serious voice said, "Remember this well, Breeze Tinkerman: I will protect you to the death. Socrates will as well. Other than the two of us, you must trust no one. There are nearly three hundred Tal'mar in this city, and any one of them would betray you on a whim. The goodness is gone from my people. When the Vangars attacked, they killed the best of us."

I listened quietly, nodding, thinking about all that he had told me. His oath of loyalty surprised me. After all that had happened between us, I had expected Tam to hate me. I stared into his eyes and the darkness I saw there brought me pain. What had become of the haughty young warrior who had stolen kisses from me right in the midst of battle? This was not the Tam I knew. This man seemed hollow. I couldn't help but feel that in some way, it was my fault. I turned away from him, not wanting to face my own feelings. I didn't know what to say.

When the elevator doors opened, I saw that the glass room in the lobby was now brightly lit and filled with people. My grandmother and a dozen others sat around the table, and at least as many more stood hovering around them. They were excited, arguing. I could tell even without hearing their words that they were deciding my fate. I glanced at Tam, wondering how we were going to sneak past them.

"Come," he said, stepping out of the elevator. He proceeded to walk directly towards them.

I caught my breath. "What are you doing?" I said in a whisper. It occurred to me that he had betrayed me, but I instantly dismissed the thought. I was already their prisoner. But what did Tam hope to prove by leading me out in front of them? It was insane.

"Come," he repeated impatiently, and continued walking. Reluctantly, I followed him. As we appeared in front of the glass, they all turned to look at us and their voices fell silent. Tam opened the door.

"Brothers and sisters," Tam said as we entered. He turned toward my grandmother, bowing his head. "My queen."

"What is the meaning of this?" said an older gentleman in fine clothing near the head of the table. I recognized him as Lydian, my grandmother's most trusted advisor.

"I have come to tell you that Breeze is now mine."

My mouth fell open. I was about to refute his statement, but he shot me a glare that said, *Keep quiet!* The Tal'mar started muttering amongst themselves and Tam turned his attention back to them.

"Breeze is mine and I accept full responsibility for her. If anyone wishes to challenge me, they may do so now, but be warned: *I will allow no harm to come to her.*" The tone of his voice was cold, threatening. I suddenly understood that he was tactfully telling them that if anyone tried to harm me, he would kill them. The room was quiet as he met their gazes. Lydian spoke:

"This is not for you to decide, Tam."

"And yet I have," he said flatly. "Are you challenging me, Lydian?"

Lydian held his hands out in a gesture of peace, indicating that he was not prepared to fight. A wise move. The older man knew better than to tangle with a fierce young warrior like Tam, but the look on his face told me this wasn't over. Lydian would be plotting my murder the moment we turned our backs.

I reached out, putting my hand on Tam's arm, urging him to leave. He cast one more defiant glance around the room and then turned to open the door. No one said a word as he escorted me out of the building. Only when the three of us got outside did I find myself able to breathe.

Tam started walking down the street and I fell in next to him. Socrates lumbered along behind us like a pet. "Why did you do that?" I said.

"I did what was necessary." He cast a sideways glance at me. "Do not think I meant anything by claiming you. You will remain free, of course. I have merely sworn to protect you."

"But why?" I said. "They will all turn against you now. Why have you done this?"

"Because I love you," he said. "How could you not know this?"

I faltered in my step. "Tam-"

"I understand," he said, cutting me off. "You have a family. A husband and child. I can't return you to them, but I swear to keep you safe. Perhaps someday, we will find a way..."

As his voice trailed off, I realized that Tam didn't know about Robie yet. He didn't know my mate had died. I opened my mouth to tell him and then clamped it shut. Somehow, it didn't seem like the right time.

7

Tam took me to a distant part of the city that the Tal'mar had designated the "Old Quarter." It was a strange place, quaint and antiquated, a far cry from the high rise buildings and broad streets of downtown. Architecturally, the buildings were more like Riverfork or Anora. They were constructed of heavy timbers and stone masonry. The sidewalk was a true boardwalk, with wrought iron lamps lining the narrow cobbled streets. The place felt oddly familiar.

"This is all so strange," I said, staring at the buildings around us. "These buildings, the whole city. It's nothing like Silverspire."

Silverspire had been the capital city of the Tal'mar, a city of shining towers and a sprawling palace. For centuries, it had been the home of the Tal'mar and their queen. The Vangars had all but destroyed Silverspire when they invaded the kingdom.

"The people who built this city weren't Tal'mar," Socrates said.

I frowned, glancing back and forth between the two of them. "Tam, you said this city was the origin of the Tal'mar."

"This city is the origin of everything," Tam said. "Everyone came from here, not just the Tal'mar. Humans, elves, even Kanters all share a common ancestor."

I laughed at first, thinking it was a joke. I glanced back and forth between the two of them, but they weren't smiling.

"The Old Quarter is where the founders first lived, before they built the city," Tam explained.

"Indeed," Socrates chimed in. "The first settlers numbered twelve hundred and twenty-seven. They came to Sanctuary with little more than crude hand tools. They quickly mastered their new environment and built this town. Over the next decade, their elected leaders proposed a plan to build Sanctuary, a city greater than any built before it. The construction of Sanctuary took nearly a century."

"But how?" I said. "How did they plan and build all of this? How did they go from hand tools and carpentry to street sweepers and machines like... well, like you?"

"Knowledge grows exponentially," Socrates said. "It is difficult to process ore into steel and to process steel into tools, but once you have the tools, the task becomes simplified. Once you have tools, you may process ore and steel faster, and then create even more tools. One cannot build without tools, but as a civilization masters new technologies, that civilization can grow and expand rapidly. This city grew from the wilderness in less than a century."

"But the city is empty now," I said. "Where did everyone go? Tam, you said that the Tal'mar came from here. You said: '*Sanctuary is the source of everything.*' What does that mean?"

"Ah," Socrates said with a strange grin. "Now you must learn the history."

They took turns explaining everything. Tam patiently revealed to me that our civilization was but the most recent of many, and that we had very little knowledge of what had come before. He taught me about the cataclysm, about the great stone that had fallen from the heavens, and the way it changed the world and its peoples forever. I learned about the rise of the Tal'mar and all of the other races in the wake of Sanctuary's massive ecological disaster. I asked questions here and there, but for the most part I was enrapt in their tale.

It all seemed so improbable, this idea that the giants of Kantraya might be distant cousins of the Tal'mar or that humans and Vangars were simply different branches on the same family tree.

"What about the animals?" I said at last, staring at Socrates. "The creatures in the forest."

"Like me?" he said slyly. "The forests under the ice are filled with creatures from the ancient past. They have been protected here, somewhat changed perhaps, but still thriving. As you can see, I was designed to look like the creatures near Lakewood. Upon his death, the creator left these creatures in my charge."

"Lakewood? That's the place where I fell through the ice?"

"Yes, that is the name of the forest. You will find many more like it, interspersed throughout the city and in the lands beyond."

"All under the ice?" I said. "How is that possible?"

"The lake that once filled this area has drained into the earth, creating this massive cavern. As you have observed it is warm here, but the heat escapes through holes in the ice like the one you fell through. Obviously, there is no ice over Sanctuary itself. You can see the sky."

"So the ice holds just enough heat in, but it doesn't melt?"

"Exactly. Or to be more accurate, the ice continually melts and then reforms. You will find the city grows quite cold at night, or so I'm told. I have no sense of such things."

"We have so much more to learn," Tam said. "The city has libraries, tens of thousands of volumes of history and knowledge. But it will take time."

"*Time*," I mumbled. "The only thing I have and yet can't bear to waste. How will I get back to her, Tam? How will I get back to my daughter?"

He fell silent.

A few minutes later, an old tavern rose up on our right with a wooden sign hanging from the rafters over the front steps, displaying the name *The Black Rose*. "This should do," Tam said. "We'll find adequate accommodations inside, and the location is reasonably defensible."

I sighed, wondering what I'd gotten myself into.

We moved into the Black Rose and took up residence as if it had always been our home. I chose a room at the front of the building with a view of the street and the glistening towers in the distance. I didn't care much for the towers, but I wanted to see them every day to remind me where I was. I wanted to look out that window every morning and know that someday soon I would escape. I didn't care about the Vangars anymore. I didn't care about the war. I just wanted to be home with my little girl.

Tam took the room next to me. Socrates didn't choose a room, but seemed to wander from one to another as if his home was wherever he settled for the time. He didn't actually sleep, though, but he did disappear from time to time for maintenance. I shouldn't have been surprised to learn that special machines and robots in the city were designed specifically for that purpose. The machines actually repaired each other!

When Socrates was around, he made excellent company. He was a brilliant conversationalist with a compendium of knowledge that I couldn't begin to fathom. He loved to read and philosophize, and was always eager to fill the gaps in my understanding of the world. Not that I understood everything he said, but Socrates was patient and scholarly... and unlike certain humans I had known, he never demonstrated his knowledge simply for the pleasure of showing me how smart he was. Socrates never spoke just to hear himself speak.

Naturally, I spent every waking moment plotting my escape. I went for long walks with Tam (he was never far from my side) searching the city for things I might use to build a new airplane. I soon learned that hand-tools were nearly impossible to find. The machines that ran the city were so effective at their jobs that the humans living there had long since abandoned manual labor. Instead, they had devoted their lives to learning, to study and philosophy much like Socrates.

I did eventually find some scrap lumber and some steel, and I gathered them together on the broad lawn behind the tavern. I began working on plans to build a new flying machine, something like a plane but smaller; something that would be able to navigate the city and land on the broad paved streets. This wasn't easy for me, as I didn't have Tinker's knowledge of physics and mathematics. What I did have was an intuitive and intimate knowledge of flight, and I was fairly certain I could make *something* that would fly.

Tam warned me that the others would learn of this, and that they would not allow it, but I didn't listen. I had to do something. I couldn't just sit around philosophizing with Socrates for the rest of my life. I at least had to try. I think Tam understood this, though he offered no help whatsoever.

Ironically, Socrates proved to be a storehouse of useful information on the subject. It was he who helped me with design concepts, and it was Socrates' vast knowledge of physics and mathematics that might eventually have helped me to succeed. But in truth, I was wasting my time. Things existed in the city far greater than anything I could ever build. I simply didn't know where to find them. And if I had it wouldn't have mattered, because the Tal'mar were plotting to kill me the first chance they got. It was just a matter of time until they acted.

In retrospect, they must have been spying on us all along. I shouldn't have expected any less, though in truth I had become quite complacent with my life. I filled my head with dreams of my flying machine, dreams of soaring out over the Wastelands and returning to my daughter in the Blackrock Mountains. I allowed these dreams to consume me, as is my nature, and I thought of little else.

Then, one night while I was sleeping, a strange noise in my room wakened me. I sat upright just in time to see a flash of steel. A dark shadow passed by my bed and I heard a grunting noise as two bodies crashed to the floor. As my eyes adjusted to the darkness, I saw Tam rising to his feet, wiping blood from the blade of his short sword. I opened my mouth to speak but he put a finger to his lips to silence me.

I quietly slipped out of bed and drew my dagger from the belt hanging across the back of the chair. Tam motioned for me to follow him and we crossed to the door. Just as I reached for the handle, Tam swung around. His arm swept out, producing a dagger from under his cloak. With a flick of his wrist it shot across the room. There was a crash as it shattered the glass window and the blade impaled the chest of another attacker on the roof outside.

I heard the sound of movement out in the hall. Tam slid the deadbolt into place. He sheathed his sword and quickly strung his bow. He rushed back to the window, pushing the dead Tal'mar's body aside, and climbed out. He beckoned for me to follow out onto the roof. I hesitated for a moment, reluctant to crawl out the window in my nightgown. Then I saw the door handle quietly turning and forgot my modesty. I leapt after him.

We crept across the narrow ledge in front of my window, making our way to the catwalk at the far end of the building. I heard the twang of a bowstring and instinctively dropped to my knees. The arrow thudded into the roof, just inches over my head. Tam stepped in front of me, shielding me with his body, motioning for me to climb over the peak of the roof. Another arrow whizzed out of the darkness, but Tam was ready for this one. I heard a *whooshing* sound and his hand shot out, catching the arrow in midflight.

Tam locked his eyes on the target, raised his bow, and fired. I twisted around to see a Tal'mar drop to his knees on the adjacent roof. He dropped his bow and it skidded down the roof with a clattering sound. The attacker fell forward, clutching his gut as he rolled down the roof. I flinched as I heard him land heavily on the ground.

A primal scream erupted in the room below us and I nearly jumped out of my skin. I had never heard such a noise before. I shot Tam a terrified look and a smile turned up the corners of his mouth. I heard a crash and the sounds of fighting, followed by another scream. Then I realized what had happened. The attackers had found Socrates. A discovery they would quickly learn to regret.

Tam led me across the roof and down the backside. We dropped to the lawn and made our way back into the tavern through the back door. A Tal'mar came running down the stairs just as we entered. The warrior leapt at us waving his sword. In one fluid motion, Tam stepped inside the attack and drew his short sword. I saw a flash of steel as he beheaded the attacker. The body thumped to the ground. Tam stepped over, motioning for me to follow.

Upstairs, we found Socrates gloating over two more corpses. That made six in all. "Is that all of them?" I said under my breath.

"If not, the rest are gone," Tam said. "They won't be back tonight." He turned to face Socrates. "Stay with her. Protect her." Socrates nodded slightly.

"Where are you going?" I said.

"To pay a visit to Lydian. I knew these men. They were his closest followers. This is his doing."

"Do you think that's wise?"

"It is not wise, it is necessary," he said. "Lydian has exposed himself. Tonight I will see to it that no one else gets a similar idea."

He turned and vanished down the hall, and I stood staring at Socrates. "You knew this would happen," I said. "The two of you."

"Of course," the gorilla said matter-of-factly.

"Why didn't you do something to stop it?"

"Because this is how it is done," he said. "This is how it has always been done. Tonight your enemy has a face. He is exposed. Now Tam will make an example of him, and you will be safe."

"You say that like you've done this before," I said.

He bent over and lifted one of the dead Tal'mar, throwing the body over his shoulder. "It has always been so."

Socrates disposed of the bodies while I cleaned the mess. Two hours later, Tam returned. He entered through the front door and went directly to the wash basin to clean the blood from his hands and face. I could tell by looking at him that Lydian hadn't been alone.

I didn't need to ask Tam if his mission had been successful, I could tell that much from his return. There were other questions that bothered me, other concerns. Consequences.

"What will the queen say?" I said quietly as I watched him wash.

"She will say nothing."

"But Lydian was her most trusted advisor. She has known him forever."

"He was," Tam admitted, carefully phrasing the past-tense. "And you *are* her granddaughter."

"Do you think that will save me? I don't think it means that much to her."

"It means more to her than you know. More than she can say. You think too much like a human." He reached for the towel and I saw impatience written on his face. "You have been too long away from your own kind."

"I don't have a kind," I said. "The more I learn about people, the more I don't want anything to do with any of them."

He tossed the towel aside and caught me by the shoulders, staring into my eyes. "You don't get to choose such things. What is it that humans say? *You can choose your friends, but not your relatives?* You may be human Breeze, but you're also Tal'mar. It is time now for you to learn what that means."

I frowned. "What are you saying?"

"Tomorrow we will go to them. While they are still contemplating the meaning of all that happened tonight, we will show them that you are Tal'mar. You will take your place next to the queen. You will *demand it*. And you will make it clear that anyone who challenges you will end up like Lydian."

"But I don't want that!" I said. "I came here to find a way to fight the Vangars and all I've found is a trap. I don't want any of this. I just want to leave!"

"Haven't I made it clear to you yet that this will never happen? I have made a way for you, Breeze. I have given you a chance to live, a chance to bide your time. Perhaps you may see your family again someday, but for now you must forget them. You will do Robie no good getting yourself killed for him."

I turned away, staring at the floor. "Robie is dead," I said. I climbed the stairs to my room, and closed the door behind me. Tam stood in the kitchen contemplating that for some time before I heard him return to his room.

8

The next day, I did everything Tam had told me I would, and I hated every minute of it. I didn't understand at the time why it was necessary, or what it could possibly accomplish. I'd never had any love of politics and I certainly didn't imagine it was a way to take control of my own destiny, but ultimately that was just what happened. By silencing the loudest opposition, Tam had created a vacuum for me to fill.

There were still those who didn't trust me and never would, who felt that I should never inherit the throne and had no right to be among them, but that was no longer a position of strength. Those who felt that way kept their feelings to themselves, or spoke of them at their own peril. It was known now that my enemies died, and few had the fortitude to brave that peril.

At the same time, with Tam's guidance I found a way back into my grandmother's graces. This was something she couldn't have done on her own for fear of the political backlash. With a divided populace, the queen had no choice but to balance her decisions on the edge of a knife. She had to compromise on all things, to find a way to accommodate everyone. This left no room for her to live the life she chose. Her life was given to others.

When Tam and I walked into the council meeting, the room fell to a hush. Tam stood watching as I strode past the council members and the other representatives to take Lydian's empty chair next to the queen. Before I sat, I met the eyes of every person in that room. Every one of them looked away. Even the queen.

I feared at first that this was some sort of rejection, but Tam later explained that she was merely submitting to my political dominance. From that moment on it was clear to everyone in that room that I was now the queen's most trusted advisor, and that she had better take my advice seriously.

That was nonsense, of course. The queen's law was still law and if I had tried to defy her, the populace would have risen up against me. In a way, I had found my own knife's edge to walk. It wasn't a comfortable place for me, but I learned to survive that way. I also came to know my grandmother in a way that never would have been possible otherwise. At times, when we were alone in her chambers, drinking wine and talking of the past, it was almost like we were sisters.

The queen shared her stories with me, her memories of my mother and father, and her knowledge of all things. The only thing she withheld from me was my freedom. This was the one decision she would never revisit. The city in the Wastes belonged to the Tal'mar, and there they must remain, always in secret. This matter she refused to discuss with me. And so I continued to plot.

Unfortunately, I soon came to learn that Tam was right. Escape was not possible. Not with so many watchful eyes, and especially now that so many lives were connected with mine. Those who wanted me dead were frothing at the mouth with hope that I would try to escape so they would have an expedient reason to murder me. Those that supported me... ultimately, I realized that I couldn't let them down. For the first time in my life I had allies, and incredibly, *they depended on me* to do what was best for them.

So the weeks passed and then the months stretched into years. Eventually, I bore another child. I had found enough reason to trust Tam, and I had come to realize that his devotion to me was unshakable. Regardless of what happened, regardless of anything I did, Tam's love for me would never fail. I didn't need to ask him to forgive me for driving him away. All of that was in the past. He was simply happy to have another chance to be with me.

I found other reasons to admire him as well. He had courage, strength, and wisdom. He had all the characteristics of a great leader and a great man. Though I often didn't understand the complexities of his scheming, I found that he never lead me wrong. He knew the Tal'mar in a way that I never could, and I quickly came to understand that I would need his loyalty in order to succeed.

Ultimately though, it was the loneliness that drove me into his arms. When the feelings of loss became more than I could bear and thoughts of my daughter were like distant dreams, Tam won me over. His steadfast loyalty gave me the strength I needed to go on. I found that I did love him, if not in the same way that I had loved Robie. This was a different love, a deep hard-won respect and devotion that was more like friendship than romance, and founded on trust more than anything else.

I took Tam as a mate, and within a year I had given him a son. For all intents and purposes I had become part of the Tal'mar, but my plotting was never more evident than in the name I gave to our child:

Crowasten'Talbresha, *Vengeful Sword of the North Wind*. The other Tal'mar seemed to think nothing of it. Perhaps they thought it was an attempt to win them over, giving my son this old-fashioned, very traditional Tal'mar name. I didn't care what they thought. I only knew that in Crow's eyes I saw the potential for success in all the things I had failed. If I raised him right, and taught him all I knew, Crow could change the world.

9

Like all Tal'mar children, Crow matured rapidly. In months, he had grown from an infant to a small boy, and within a few years he had become an impressive young man. A decade later, he was several inches taller than me and had become the spitting image of his father -save for his unusually tall height and muscular build, which I can only attribute to my human ancestry.

Crow was magnificent. He had all the makings of a great leader. I knew in time he would have the Tal'mar eating out of the palm of his hand, but there were other things to do first. We had long since discovered the treasuries of ancient weapons and machines scattered throughout the city. Among these, we found incredible machines that utilized highly compressed steam for power. Some of these were similar to airplanes. Some were massive, large enough to carry fifty people at once. Others were small, like the cloak-shaped wing that allowed one person to fly with the speed and agility of a bird. There were many, many more, some of them practical, some designed just for entertainment.

As we made these discoveries, I went to extra lengths to make sure my grandmother knew I had no intention of leaving the city. I didn't want her to suspect that I was still scheming against her. In fact, the impression I gave her was true. I had long since accepted the fact that I would never escape on my own. Occasionally, I still dreamed of finding a way, but over time I had seen the truth of the matter: escape was not possible, and even the attempt would put my family in danger.

I had other ideas, though. I had watched and learned from the scheming of the Tal'mar all those years, and I came to recognize the only way to truly accomplish my goals. I felt like a fool for not seeing it sooner. For all those years since my arrival, I had only thought of escape. I had wanted to break free and return to the mountains to find my daughter and Tinker. Perhaps that was the reason it took so long for me to realize that I didn't need to escape at all. I needed to do something entirely different. I had to expose the Tal'mar.

I had to open up their precious city to the entire world, so that they would have no choice but to share it. And I had to do it before the Tal'mar grew too powerful. If I waited too long, no army in the world could force the Tal'mar to share their city. Many children had grown into young men and women already, and their numbers would only increase as time went by. The time to act was now. And thankfully, my son was ready.

Among our discoveries was the collection of flying "wings" that the higher-ranking nobles were allowed to use recreationally. No one seemed to notice the true practical value of these items, that they could transport an individual hundreds or even thousands of miles in a single day. This fact was not lost on me, and I made sure to take advantage of my political position to acquire one of these for my son.

At the time I gave it to him, I presented it as a gift, a toy that might bring him some pleasure. I was careful to make sure he used it properly, of course. He practiced for many weeks at low altitude, over an open field. I took every precaution imaginable. Thankfully, my worries were those of an overprotective mother. Crow took to the skies like a bird. If nothing else, he had certainly inherited my love of flying.

One of the Tal'mar exploratory teams also discovered a large garage filled with four-wheeled vehicles similar to steamwagons or coaches, but with a low profile and large, powerful steam engines. We called them runabouts. They had seating for just two, with only a small space for cargo, but incredibly sophisticated steering and suspension systems. This, coupled with their incredibly powerful engines made them perfect for moving around quickly inside the city.

There were thousands of the vehicles. With only a few hundred Tal'mar families living in Sanctuary, the queen quite logically dispersed the vehicles throughout the city. Whenever a citizen felt like driving, he or she could simply take the nearest runabout to her destination and abandon it there for the next person. Naturally, some popular areas were constantly congested with the vehicles while less popular destinations like the Old Quarter rarely had a single runabout available.

Socrates once confided to me that there was a way to make the vehicles return to a designated area, but he refused to divulge this secret. "The Tal'mar already know everything," he said snidely. "Just ask them. Why should I prove them wrong when they do it so effortlessly on their own?"

One day, I finally told Crow the truth about my past. I took him to a secret place, to the city park where the Creator had been laid to rest. I didn't bring his father. I knew what Tam would say. Tam's one and only concern had ever been to protect us, and I knew he would not approve of the story I was about to tell his son.

I took Crow to the park and filled him in on the pieces of my past that I had kept secret. I told him about how the Tal'mar had trapped me in Sanctuary, and how they refused to use their newfound powers to fight the Vangars to free our kingdom. I told him about Robie and how he died, and about how the Vangars had taken thousands of Tal'mar and humans and forced them into slavery. For the first time ever, I explained to Crow that he had a sister he had never met.

When I was done, Crow was understandably somber. I had protected him from this information for all of his childhood. It wouldn't have done him any good to know these things as a child, it would only have frustrated and angered him as it had done to me. Over the years, I had learned to put my anger aside. I had learned patience. Crow had yet to learn this. He was angry with me.

"You should have told me, mother," he said, pacing back and forth in front of the bench where I was seated.

"I've already explained this, Crow. It wouldn't have done any good."

"But I would have *known*. Don't you see that I should have known? I have a sister!"

"I hope so," I said quietly.

He shot me a horrified look. "What does that mean?"

"Many years have passed. Life in Astatia is not easy. The Vangars are cruel barbarians. Your sister-"

"She's fine," he said firmly. "I know it. I will find her."

"Don't be hasty. *Caution is the key to success.*" That was an old Tal'mar proverb that Crow had heard a thousand times, but like most old proverbs, I don't think he really understood it.

"I have to do *something*," he said, the anxiousness evident in his voice. "I must go get her."

"Sit with me," I said. "Calm yourself. I have a plan."

He dropped onto the bench next to me and stared into my eyes. "Tell me. Whatever it is, I'll do it."

I took a deep breath. "First, you must be cautious. You will be swift and silent and deadly..."

10

Tam and I had moved into the city years earlier so Crow would be closer to the other children. On the night he left, we were living in a large apartment in one of the massive skyscrapers. Tam was sleeping when Crow and I slipped into the stairwell and climbed to the roof of the building.

Crow was eager to be off, but I had to take him in my arms one last time. As I held him, my stomach churned with fear. It suddenly felt wrong to me, sending my son to do this thing. It was too dangerous. Too many things might go wrong.

"Give me the cloak," I said as I hugged him. "I can't let you risk your life like this."

"I'm not a child anymore," he said. He looked down into my face, his eyes sparkling with mischief and adventure.

"I know," I said. "But it's not your war."

"I don't care about the war. I care about my sister. There is nothing you can do or say to stop me mother. I will find her." He stepped away from me wearing a confident smile, and said, "I'll bring her to you!"

With that he was off, spinning through the sky over the city, passing up over the rim of ice and out into the Wastes. Even though he left under the cover of darkness in the middle of the night, the Tal'mar guards spotted him, just as I knew they would. It wasn't long before they were at our door. But before they arrived, I woke Tam and told him what I had done.

Tam was understandably dismayed, but it only took him a moment to recover from the shock. "I knew it," he said, shaking his head. "I knew you would do something like this."

"It's the right thing to do," I said defiantly. "You should be proud of your son. He is very brave."

"It's not him I'm worried about. The nobles will have you killed for this, Breeze. Not even the queen can save you this time."

"I don't care. Let them kill me. In a few weeks, none of it will matter. It's all going to come crumbling down and they'll do what's right whether they like it or not."

He gave me an exasperated look as he pulled on his boots and buckled his sword belt. He snatched his long coat off the hook by the door and then took me by the hand. "We have to go," he said.

The guards were already banging on the door as we went onto the balcony and climbed down to the next level. We rushed into the apartment, which like most of the thousands of dwellings in the city was empty, and we left through the front door. I could hear the guards shouting above us as Tam activated the elevator. Steam vented out of the pipes and the sound of creaking gears filled the shaft. The guards heard, and cried out that we were in the elevator.

"They're taking the stairs," I said in a worried voice as we made our descent.

"They'll never catch us," Tam said.

A few seconds later, the doors opened and we flew across the lobby and out into the street. We climbed into one of the small steam-powered runabouts and went roaring down the street.

I took the wheel. Tam was perfectly capable of driving but being a Tal'mar, he had never fully accepted machines. They had been taboo in his culture for all of his life, and even in Sanctuary, it was difficult to let those old notions go. Tam had also long since learned to accept the fact that I simply must be in control. As the person who helped invent the first airplane and became the world's first pilot, I believe it's my prerogative to drive. Tam knows better than to argue.

Tam flinched as they fired a weapon and the bullet whistled over our heads. "Take the next street," he said. "We'll lose them in the tunnels."

I tapped the brakes and twisted the wheel, drifting around the corner. "They'll follow us," I said. "We won't be able to get out."

"Trust me," he said. "We can't stay in the city."

I sighed, but I stomped on the accelerator and followed his directions. The tunnels were once a sort of subway system. Apparently, the city was once so populated that the engineers built underground train systems to move people around. Of course, once the people were gone the trains were shut down and forgotten. Over the centuries, the place had fallen into decay. Because of the safety risks, the queen had declared the tunnels off limits.

As we reached the area, I swerved to the right and guided the runabout down the broad paved ramp. Darkness washed over us as we passed beneath the streets and entered the massive parking garage next to the tracks. My eyes weren't as sharp as Tam's so I flipped the switch to activate the vehicle's headlight. A hazy yellow ring of light appeared on the ground before us.

"There," Tam said, pointing to the tracks. "Take the tunnel."

We had almost run out of garage and the guards were gaining on us. I looked at him like he was crazy. "We can't drive there!" I said.

"Just do it."

As the edge of the platform loomed ahead of us, I clamped my teeth together and braced myself. We roared through the last parking spaces and past the small building at the edge of the rails. Then the ground disappeared, and for a moment, we were airborne.

I pressed my feet against the floor, pushing back on the steering wheel. Tam put his hands on the dash and leaned back in the seat with a grimace on his face. The runabout landed with a crash. Sparks flew into the air as the suspension absorbed the impact, and the axles slammed against the train rails. The vehicle rebounded and then bounced several times as I struggled to regain control. I activated the brakes long enough to get the steering under control and then hit the accelerator.

We went roaring down the tunnel with the left wheels between the rails and the right wheels bouncing along the ties. Behind us, I heard the unmistakable crash of the guards chasing us in their own runabout. I heard an explosion and saw flash of light over my head.

Tam gave me a worried look. "They're shooting at us," he said. "Go faster."

I winced. I could already feel the suspension rattling loose underneath us. I knew the runabout wouldn't hold together much longer. It wasn't designed to take that kind of abuse. Unfortunately, I didn't have any choice. I pressed the accelerator to the floor. A few seconds later, I saw a tunnel branching off to the right.

"Here," Tam shouted. "Turn here!"

I pulled hard on the wheel, fighting the steering as I tried to force the vehicle over the tracks. The front tires bounced erratically, and Tam had to reach over to help me steady the wheel. I slowed a little and at last, the front end popped over the rail. I stomped on the accelerator again and we shot into the darkness.

"Where are we going?" I said in a worried voice. "We can't take much more of this."

"It's just ahead," Tam said. "A few more seconds."

I cast a worried glance over my shoulder and saw the guards racing down the tunnel behind us. I saw another set of lights appear in the darkness behind them, and then another.

"Now!" Tam cried out. "Stop!" I slammed on the brakes, and he leapt out of the vehicle before we had even stopped. "This way," he said, flying up a narrow set of stairs onto a concrete platform. I leapt after him.

We climbed a short stairway and entered a long, narrow foot tunnel. I heard a crash behind us and realized that the guards hadn't realized we had stopped. They had rear-ended our vehicle. We paused to look back at the platform and saw bright orange flames licking up around the doorway.

"That will slow them down," Tam said with a grin. "Keep moving."

The passage wound around and branched out several times before Tam finally guided the way up a long staircase. We ascended into a small, windowless building. "Where are we?" I said.

Tam pushed the door open and brilliant light flooded into the room. I winced, averting my eyes as they adjusted to the brightness. When I could finally see without it hurting, I looked out and saw a vast endless plain of ice and snow stretching to the horizon. I gulped, remembering how I'd nearly died out there. I felt a tremor of fear and tried to force it down.

"We're facing southwest," Tam said. "If we start walking in that direction, we'll eventually reach the mountains. If we live that long."

"On foot?" I said.

"I have no wish to make that journey unless we have to. For now, we'll hide here. If the guards find us, then we'll do what we have to. Our odds of surviving are better out there than they are in the city."

I stared out into at ice, my heart hammering in my chest. "It's all up to the children now," I said.

Blood & Steam, Part Two:

Chapter 13

At dawn the next morning we were running down the eastern slopes of the Blackrock Mountains, twenty of us in all, and the Vangar dragon ships were visible in the sky behind us. We had traveled all through the night, moving as quickly as possible, stopping only for a bite of food or to tend to our wounds. We had a good lead on the airships. They hadn't zeroed in on us yet, but we were at a serious disadvantage traveling on foot.

Tragically, we had been forced to leave several men behind. One of them had simply been overwhelmed by exhaustion and collapsed. The others were fighting minor injuries that sapped their strength and slowed the pace of the entire group. When it became clear that they could no longer keep up with the rest of us, we did all we could to insure their survival. We left them with food, weapons, and the tools to build lean-tos and fires. We also left them with the promise that we would come back for them as soon as possible. Then we pressed on.

As we reached the foot of the mountains and headed out across the plains, the ice-cold wind hit us like a splash of water and I heard gasps all around me. We sank to our knees in the snow and I knew then that we only had a few hours at best. None of us were prepared for the cold. We weren't dressed for it and we certainly weren't used to it. It was late summer and our bodies had become acclimatized to the warm southern weather. Had we been prepared, we still wouldn't have had the strength to push through the snow and that driving wind for long. If the airships didn't catch us first, that wind would be the death of us.

A short while later, one of our group called out that the airships had spotted us. I turned and saw that they had indeed changed course and were making directly for us. We'd had the benefit of darkness and the cover of trees through the night, but with the rising sun and our transition out of the mountains we had become highly visible marks against the spotless white plain.

"Move faster!" I shouted. "Keep running! Don't make yourselves easy targets."

I was asking the impossible. This group had already been pushed to their limits. It was a miracle that they could walk, much less run. It wasn't long before we started falling apart.

"I can't go anymore," Mal said at one point. "I can't feel my feet." He dropped to his knees in the snow and started weeping.

"Keep moving!" I shouted. "Everyone, keep moving!"

The others obeyed, but Mal didn't move. I grabbed him by the shoulders, trying to force him to his feet, but it was a wasted effort. He looked up into my face and through the tears said, "Go on without me. I'll catch up after I rest."

I saw the pain and futility written across his face and knew that he wasn't going to get up. Not after he'd rested; not ever. He was going to lay down in the snow and die. I slapped him across the face so hard it left a welt on his cheek.

"Move!" I shouted. "Get to your feet, slave!"

I grabbed him by the collar and pulled. To my surprise, he actually stood up. "Good, now move. Move!"

"Yes," Mal mumbled under his breath. "A little more." He took an awkward step, and then another, leaning into the movement so that he it looked less like he was walking than falling forward and catching himself at the last moment.

I scanned the rest of the group and didn't see any signs of immediate trouble, except for Kale. It wasn't actually Kale, it was Nena. She had run out of strength, and in all his stupid masculinity, Kale had decided to carry her. She was draped over his arms, curled tightly against his chest. Her eyes were closed and I thought she might be sleeping. I wanted to tell Kale to drop the stupid girl and let her freeze. Better her than him. She had been offered the chance to stay behind more than once. She could have been sitting in a lean-to huddled next to a warm fire waiting for help, but she had insisted on coming with us. I thought better of it and bit my tongue. I rushed to catch up with the group.

As we pushed on, I focused on the others in the group, trying to keep an eye out for trouble. When I saw someone falter I was immediately there, encouraging, even helping if I had to. Likewise, Crow was putting all his energy into helping the others. I could tell that he was healing them. When they stumbled or began showing signs of faltering, Crow touched them and I instantly saw a change come over them. It warmed my heart to see him using his abilities so generously, but I also knew that he couldn't keep it up forever. Crow didn't have the strength to heal us all. He couldn't support the entire group in that manner for long.

Then, sometime midmorning, I threw a glance over my shoulder and saw a dozen Vangar airships bearing down on us. I nearly started crying myself. Instead, I clenched my fists and forced my frozen legs to keep moving. Less than an hour later, the Vangars started firing at us.

The first few shots were test rounds. I could see the ships struggling against the wind as they tried to line up their cannons and I noted a certain irony in the fact that the same wind that was killing us was also saving us. When the first cannon fired, we heard the boom in the distance and a second later, an explosion of snow blossomed up half a mile to our right. That spurred us on, but our spirits couldn't have been any lower. The endless white horizon loomed ahead, taunting us with our inevitable fate. If the Vangars didn't kill us, we were all going to freeze to death. Already, many in the group were suffering frostbite and showing symptoms of hypothermia and I could see Crow's strength waning fast.

Then someone up front yelled, "I see someone! Help is coming!"

I had been lurking at the back of the group, doing my best to keep everyone moving. I ran to the front and saw two dark shapes on the horizon. Crow leapt into the air and *whooshed* up ahead. Some of the men cheered.

"Keep moving," I said warily.

Another cannon shot went off, this one nearly as far off as the first. I kept marching, stubbornly putting one foot in front of the other, oblivious to the crunching sound of the snow under my feet and the howling of the wind in my ears. I was cold, shivering. I felt numbness creeping through my limbs.

I watched Crow rocket across the snow and land next to the people up ahead. As he touched down, I saw a another group appear in the distance. They were a mile away or more, but they were moving fast. They had already caught up to Crow and the others before we were even halfway there.

The wind carried the broken sound of raised voices, and I could tell that there was some sort of trouble. As we got closer, I could make out a dozen Tal'mar fighters spreading out to encircle Crow and his companions. Instead of retreating, Crow drew his daggers and settled into a defensive posture, putting himself between the Tal'mar and their captives.

That was when I put it all together. When I saw Crow risking his life to defend them, I knew who the people in the snow must be: his parents. *Our mother.* Suddenly I forgot everything else. I left the group and broke into a full-out run.

The Tal'mar saw me coming. Two of them turned, training their bows on me. The female -my mother- dropped to her knees in the snow and her partner bent down to help her. Emotions welled up within me that I hadn't experienced since the night Tinker died. Crow had warned me that the Tal'mar would be furious with our mother. He'd told me that we needed to get back to the city as soon as possible. Perhaps we were too late.

As I neared the group, I drew my revolver. I came up to them exhaling heavy gusts of steam, my heart pounding like a drum. I fixed my sights on the Tal'mar who seemed to be in charge. "Back off!" I shouted. "Get back or I swear I'll kill every one of you."

The Tal'mar warriors stared at me, fingers twitching on their bowstrings. They didn't make a move. For a few moments, it was a standoff. We all stood there, nerves as tight as harp strings, weapons ready to fire at the drop of a pin. I dared a glance at Breeze and Tam, and I was horrified to see the ice-blue color of their skin. Tam's thin facial hair was a beard of ice. My mother's eyes were closed, her eyelids white with frost. My finger tightened on the trigger as I realized I may have arrived too late.

I heard voices behind me. Someone shouted, "Get them! Get the Tal'mar!"

The slaves broke into a run, charging towards us as if they could actually fight.

That is courage, I thought with a grim smile. A group of ex-slaves, frostbitten and starved, mere hours from certain death, but still willing to fight to the bitter end. The Tal'mar didn't know how to react to this. Could they open fire and kill a bunch of half-starved, unarmed men? Even if they did, they might still be overwhelmed by sheer numbers.

I couldn't help but smile as I watched a shiver of diffidence pass through them. They weren't watching me anymore, they were looking at each other. They were looking at their leader who seemed to have his tongue frozen in his mouth, and at the wall of angry slaves about to come crashing down on them. The best was yet to come.

At that very moment, one of the airships let loose with her cannons. Ten shots went off in quick succession, the loud booms echoing like thunder across the sky. Cannonballs struck the ground all around us, explosions of snow shooting up into the air. The Tal'mar fell into a shambles, stumbling backwards, a few of them actually falling to the ground. They'd been too focused on their captives to notice the cluster of dragon ships hovering over the horizon.

"Retreat!" someone shouted. It wasn't the leader. They broke ranks and began fleeing to the north.

Crow bent over to check on our mother. "She's been shot!" Tam said. "Take her to safety, Crow. Take her to Socrates!"

Crow lifted Breeze in his arms and hurtled into the sky, spiraling slowly because of his damaged cloak. Once he had settled into a controlled flight path, he fired the jets and rocketed over the heads of the retreating Tal'mar.

I helped Tam to his feet and saw him staring at the bloody spot on the snow. His skin was like ice to the touch and his teeth were chattering. "Will she survive?" I said quietly.

He took a deep, shuddering breath. "I removed the arrow. I could do no more."

"Crow will heal her," I said confidently. "Can you walk?"

He took a step and immediately stumbled. I reached out, catching him before he dropped. I pulled Tam close, throwing his arm over my shoulder. I glanced at the others and saw that they were all watching us.

"Let's move," I shouted. "Follow the Tal'mar!"

We banded together, cold and hunger forgotten in the rush of fear-fueled adrenaline. We pushed against the driving wind, our long-forgotten hope suddenly renewed by the promise of civilization and shelter. Behind us, the Vangars fired another volley. One of the men went down and it was clear that he wasn't ever going to get back up. I shouted at the others to keep moving.

"There," Tam said in a hoarse voice a short while later. He tried to raise his arm to point, but he didn't have the strength. I followed his gaze and saw the outline of a whitewashed building, barely visible against the backdrop of snow. I headed straight for it.

When we reached the building, we saw the Tal'mar footprints vanishing behind the door. I tried to open it, but they had locked it behind them. One shot from my revolver did the trick. The lock shattered, and a warm wind rushed up around us as I kicked the door open. A cheer went up among the slaves. I knew better than to wait for the Vangars to get their guns sighted in on us. I awkwardly helped Tam down the stairs, until we at last came to the maze of tunnels in the earth below.

"What now?" Kale said. He was still carrying Nena, though she didn't seem any worse for wear.

"Let's rest here," one of the other slaves said. "It's warm."

The others murmured in agreement, but Tam said, "No! Not safe... that way."

"You heard him," I said. "Let's go." As we started to move, I shot Kale a look. "I think you can put her down now," I said.

Kale bent his head over, gazing into Nena's ridiculously pretty face. "I'm okay," he said with a smile. She sighed and pulled closer to him. I tried not to vomit.

Thankfully, Tam had enough presence of mind to keep us on the correct path back towards the city. Without his guidance we would have been lost down there forever. A short while later, we came upon the crash in the subway.

"What the devil happened here?" Kale said. "This mess looks like the steamwagon I pushed off a cliff when I was younger."

"Younger?" I said, cocking an eyebrow at him. "That was last spring."

"Aye. I'm much older now," he said, smiling brightly. "Speaking of which-"

"Keep moving," I said, cutting him off. Even with Nena in his arms, he was still trying to flirt with me. He must have been doing it so long that it was a habit.

We gathered some scraps of wood from the crash and used them as torches to light our way down the tunnels, gradually making our way through the subterranean labyrinth. I was astounded by the cleverness of the place. The subway's creators had burrowed massive holes right through the earth, reinforced them with concrete, and then lined them with miles of tracks similar to the Vangars' freight trains. We clearly understood what the tunnels were for, but we couldn't imagine how they had been made. Tam wasn't sure, either.

"Socrates knows," he said, half-delirious. "Socrates knows all."

When at last we came to the end of the tunnel and reached the platform, we heard the whooshing sounds of massive steamjet engines echoing down the ramp. We stopped, staring at each other, more than a little frightened by the sound. A moment later, we heard the thunderous rumble of distant explosions.

A smile came to Tam's lips. "You've done it," he said. "The Tal'mar are fighting the Vangars."

We climbed up the ramp out of the dark subway, and the warm rays of sunshine washed down over us. We stepped out into the street, staring up at the tall, gleaming buildings, each of us overwhelmed with emotions. We all cheered, and tears began streaming down our cheeks. Kale absently set Nena on the ground and turned in a slow circle with his jaw hanging open. He didn't even notice Nena's indignant stare. I had to suppress a grin.

"Grandpa's beard," he muttered. "I've never seen such a thing!"

"Crow was right," I said quietly. "He never could have explained this to me."

I heard a beeping sound and lowered my eyes in time to see a street sweeper come around the corner. I had my revolver in my hand in a flash. I trained my sights on the thing, ready to face its attack.

The machine didn't even seem to notice us. It rounded the corner, dropped a broad scrub brush to the ground, and began spraying water. The steam engine at the back of the machine chugged quietly as it idled down the street past us, and then disappeared around the next corner. I lowered my weapon and turned to see Tam grinning at me.

I was about to question him about the strange machine but at that moment, Crow appeared out of the sky. He landed next to us wearing a somber look, and I was instantly worried.

"Our mother?" I said cautiously.

"She will be fine," he said. "I will lead you to her. We shouldn't be on the streets. If we come across any Tal'mar, they won't understand what's happened. It's not safe."

"I understand," I said. "Help me with your father."

I took Tam's arm again, and Crow picked up the other. "Let's go," I called to the others. Everyone move out!"

They obeyed. As we started walking, it suddenly occurred to me that somehow I seemed to have become their leader. I narrowed my eyebrows thoughtfully, wondering just how that had happened.

Crow took us to the Old Quarter on the outskirts of the city. By the time we reached *The Black Rose*, the sounds of battle had faded entirely. Crow was certain this meant that the Vangar airships had already been defeated. It would have seemed improbable a few hours earlier, but having witnessed Sanctuary's machinations and awesome technologies firsthand, none of us doubted Crow's opinion. After all, we couldn't even guess what sort of weapons the Tal'mar might possess now. Based on what we had seen of the city so far, its defenses were probably quite impressive.

As we entered the inn, Crow explained that our mother had lived there once, many years before. "When she first came here, father took her to this tavern. They lived here with Socrates for nearly a year."

"Socrates," I mumbled. "Who is this person the two of you keep talking about?"

Crow smiled. "I can't explain, sister. You will understand when you meet him."

We entered *The Black Rose* and found Breeze lying on a sofa in the main room downstairs. A fire was burning in the fireplace and the smell of food wafted out of the kitchen. Sitting in the chair next to her, reading from an old leather-bound manuscript, was a creature that I could only assume was Socrates. My eyes widened as I saw him and I sensed several of my companions go stiff. Socrates calmly lowered his book to gaze at us.

"Socrates," Crow said. "This is my sister River, and her companions."

"River," Socrates said with a slight smile. "It's a pleasure to finally make your acquaintance." He rose from the chair and held out his hand. As he moved, several people in our group flinched. I boldly stepped forward and shook hands with him. I smiled as I felt his leathery flesh against my skin and gazed into those deep golden eyes.

"Well met," I said politely, trying not to stare at the machinery poking through the smooth midnight blue fur on the side of his head and his arm. I was reminded of the overseer, and yet at the same time I wasn't. I could tell from his eyes and his handshake that Socrates was nothing like Rutherford. I wasn't sure how to treat him, though. His appearance led me to believe he was some sort of animal, but he was clearly mechanical as well. I thought he might be a combination of the two, like the sentinels.

Socrates was dressed in short breeches without boots, and wore a fine white shirt with a dark gray vest over the top. He had rolled up the sleeves of his shirt and I saw what appeared to be bits of dough matted in his fur. His countenance was that of an animal, but his clothing, mannerisms, and speech were quite human. I couldn't get over the enigma.

"I've never met someone like you," I said, unable to contain my curiosity. "What is your race called?"

Socrates laughed gently. "I suppose you would call me an automaton. I am a machine."

As the others saw Socrates speaking and came to realize that he was no threat, they visibly relaxed. He went on to explain that there were many other machines like him in the city, a fact that Crow immediately disputed.

"There is none other like Socrates," he said.

Socrates bowed his head slightly. "You flatter me. I must admit, that I am the only autonomous, sentient machine. I am the Creator's greatest invention. But I digress, and there are more important matters at hand. As you can see, I have given Breeze a sedative and she is resting. Will the rest of you share a meal with me? I've prepared roast fowl with freshly baked herb bread, and vegetables sautéed in a light butter sauce."

My eyebrows shot up. Crow just smiled. Needless to say, we didn't need any convincing. Kale and I help-ed Socrates lay out the food while Crow and his father tended to the rest of the group. Many had fingers and toes that had gone completely black with frostbite. Without healing, they would have lost those digits and possibly entire limbs. For the last few hours out in the snow, Crow simply couldn't keep up. Now that he could rest and replenish his energy, these healings were almost trivial.

The meal Socrates had prepared for us was a feast, though we were all so hungry that we ate faster than our taste buds could process the flavors. Socrates took a few bites, but no more. When he saw me watching him, he explained, "As a machine, I obviously do not need food. I do however, have the capacity to taste. I like to sample foods and observe how the flavors change. I process this information and store it for future reference. Cooking is something of a hobby of mine."

We all marveled at that, of course. Socrates claimed to be a simple machine, and yet he was clearly so much more. His ability to work, to create, even to learn seemed to imply that Socrates was more than the sum of his parts. As the evening progressed, I began to suspect Socrates' nature had as much to do with starfall as anything else. He was a brilliant creation of course, but he was definitely more than a machine.

Halfway through the meal, Breeze woke and joined us. I heard a noise and saw her standing in the door-frame, staring at me. I rose from my chair, watching her, wondering what I should do or say. I can't even describe what that was like. I hadn't seen my mother since I was a toddler, and all my life I had believed her dead. Now here she was, almost a stranger to me, and yet somehow familiar. I knew her face, her eyes. Especially her hair.

I wanted to rush over to her but I was suddenly unsure. What if she didn't accept me? What if I had somehow disappointed her? I felt a lump in my throat as she walked across the room and stood before me, staring up into my face. The entire room went silent and I couldn't even breathe. Then she shook her head and in a breaking voice said, "I'm so sorry."

She threw her arms around me, pulling me close, and I closed my eyes as her scent washed over me. My mind filled with broken memories of staring up into those eyes, of that hair falling down around me. Before I knew it, tears were streaming down my face. I tried to find words to tell her that it was okay, that none of that mattered, but no sound would come.

At last, she pulled away to gaze up into my face. "I never should have left," she said. "I'm, so very sorry."

"No," I said shaking my head. I started to say more but my voice broke and I didn't have the strength to force the words. I was trying hard not to cry, not to let the others see me, but it was already too late for that. I pulled her back into my arms and held on for a few more seconds, a sense of warmth and familiarity that I had never known filling me. I raised my eyes to glance around the room and saw all the faces staring at us, smiling, some of them even crying.

"Well, I suppose we'd better sit down and let the rest of you eat," she said when we finally parted. We all laughed at that, and with the sound of our laughter the weight of the moment seemed to lift.

Breeze settled down in the chair next to me and began asking questions. She wanted to know everything about me; about my childhood, my youth, and everything else that she had missed out on in her absence. I answered her questions and when I was too slow to respond, Kale was quick to help. I had forgotten that Kale had known my mother when he was young. I saw right away that they had a deep bond, the sort of connection that two people could only have after they've been through hell together. It was touching in a strange sort of way, seeing the smiles on their faces as they revisited their old stories, and it slowly dawned on me that in a way, Kale was as much family to my mother as he was to me.

It was with great sorrow that I had to tell my mother about Tinker's death, and the effect on her was considerable. My mother wept, and I couldn't help but join her. She rose from her seat to put her arms around me and when I looked up, I saw tears in everyone's eyes. Even big, strong Kale.

After that, we made several toasts in Tinker's honor. Breeze and some of the others shared their wonderful memories and stories about him. My favorite was the story of how Breeze -as a very young girl- had stolen one of Tinker's cannon charges thinking it was a rock. She threw it at his barn and nearly knocked down an entire wall.

I believe I bested her story with my own tale of getting into Tinker's vials of chemicals and powders in my youth. I mixed them together into a random potion that burned down our shanty and nearly set fire to all of Dockside. Tinker spent the next year trying to recreate my potion because he wanted to know what combination of chemicals could start a fire without a spark. We all shared a good laugh and another round of drinks over that.

In all, it was a wonderful, joyous evening. Possibly the best of my life. For a few brief hours, we forgot all that we had suffered and lost, and we celebrated the fact that we still had each other. And then, just before midnight, the Tal'mar came for us.

Chapter 14

Kale was reciting the tale of how he'd become a steamshovel operator when they arrived. Halfway through the story, I saw Crow tense up. I followed his gaze and saw movement outside the front windows. Kale sensed our mood and immediately fell silent.

My hand instantly went to my revolver, but Crow shook his head. "Leave it here," he said. He rose up, eyeing the others. "Leave your weapons on the table and follow me. Do not try to fight. We are outnumbered a hundred to one."

It was a sober and disappointing end to our celebration. I glanced around the room and saw the others looking at me, wondering if they could trust Crow. I placed my revolver on the table and rose to my feet. "Do as he says," I instructed. Grudgingly, they discarded the knives, swords, and other miscellaneous weapons they had collected from the mountain camp. Then, one by one, we filed through the door after Crow.

Tal'mar warriors lined the street, waiting for us. The met us with swords drawn and arrows knocked to their bowstrings. The one who was in charge stepped out in front of us and said, "You will follow me."

"One moment," said a voice behind us. I turned to see my mother appear in the doorway. She came down the steps and passed through the crowd, only glancing at me as she passed by. "Put your weapons away, Lordain," she said.

He smiled wryly. "You no longer have the authority to command me, half-breed."

Breeze thrust her hand out, grabbing him by the throat. The other Tal'mar tensed up around us, but she didn't even seem to notice. She pulled him close to her face, staring right into his eyes, and said, "Tell them to put down their weapons or I will kill you."

A few breathless moments passed. As I watched them, I realized that some sort of struggle was going on between them. It was something powerful, something invisible. The energy radiated out from them like heat, and it made the hairs stand up on the back of my neck. I saw grim determination on Lordain's face as he locked eyes with her, and I sensed that he was battling her in some way. This went on for about ten seconds, then Lordain's face changed and I saw something else in his eyes: fear.

He dropped his hands to his side and lowered his eyes. "Drop your weapons," he said.

"But Lordain-" one of the warriors protested.

"Do it!" he shouted. "Drop your weapons."

Breeze let him go and he turned away, furious and ashamed. He walked up to the fighter who had challenged him and took the man's sword from his grip. "Don't question me again!" he shouted, flinging the sword to the ground. It clattered across the cobblestones and then lay still at their feet. Slowly, the others around them began dropping their weapons. I stared at my mother in awe, still unsure as to what exactly she had done. Without a backward glance, she began walking down the street. We all fell in line behind her.

The Tal'mar warriors closed in to follow behind us as Breeze led us through the city. We followed her for three miles, finally entering one of the massive buildings downtown. The walk had taken us less than an hour, but it seemed like days. Every corner revealed some new amazing secret, some ingenious machine or architectural wonder. Tense as our situation was, I found myself less worried about where we were going than what I might pass up. There were too many wondrous things to take in. I wanted to stop and see them all.

When at last we reached the building where the queen waited for us, hundreds of Tal'mar were there, lining the street and packing the inside like rats on a sinking ship. My mother led us down a long, wide hallway and into a large elegant ballroom. The queen sat in a throne at the far end of the room. Silently, we approached her. No one moved to stop us.

"I told Lordain to take you prisoner," the Tal'mar queen said, eyeing Breeze up and down.

"I didn't let him," Breeze said defiantly. "This is my daughter, River," she said. "She is a brave warrior." She turned, waving me forward. I walked up to her side and she took me by the hand.

The queen cast a judgmental look at me and then drew her gaze back to my mother. "And how is this relevant?"

"She is your great granddaughter, you fool," Breeze said. "She is your kin, your very blood."

"She is a human," the queen said distastefully.

I winced. I hadn't ever finished reading my mother's journals, or I might have known the ordeals she faced as a child. Listening to our grandmother speak, I suddenly began to understand. "You're not my grandmother," I said, loud enough that everyone could hear me. "You're a bitter old witch."

The Tal'mar around us gasped. A slight smile curved my mother's lips. "She's too much like you," the queen said dismissively. "Regardless. On to the matter at hand. Breeze, you have conspired against the throne. You have led our enemies to our fortress. For this, you must die."

"No!" shouted a voice at the back of the room. I heard a grunt and a shriek and saw the crowd part as Socrates came ambling into the court. He rushed across the floor to stand next to my mother. The queen rolled her eyes.

"I have not invited you, beast," she said.

"I did not invite you into my city, but still I have tolerated your presence!" he said angrily.

Again, gasps and murmuring behind us. The queen frowned and a deeply menacing look crossed her face. "How dare you speak to me with such insolence. You forget your place, machine!"

"You forget your place, woman," he said. He turned, waving a giant furry hand at the crowd behind us. "You all forget your place."

Suddenly he leapt forward and took hold of the queen. A primal shriek escaped his lips as he yanked her off the throne. The guards rushed forward, but didn't dare move against him. He still held her in his powerful grip, and with one quick movement, he might snap her neck.

Socrates reached out with his right hand, lifting the massive throne in the air. He threw it down, shattering it into a million pieces on the hard marble floor. "You came unbidden to *my city*," he shouted. "You welcomed yourselves into *my home*. You treated *my kind* as your slaves. I quietly tolerated all of this. I thought my creators had returned, but I now see that I have been deceived. You are not my creators. You are a thousand generations passed, and none for the better. You are a weak and arrogant people!"

As he spoke, I heard shouts and strange noises behind us. I turned to see an entire herd of gorillas ambling into the hall. I could tell by looking at them that these beasts were mechanical. They weren't like Socrates, though. Not really. (I would later learn that Socrates had designed many of these creatures himself, to help monitor and protect the wildlife around the city. This was one of the jobs the Creator had given him.) More machines streamed in behind the gorillas, scattering out to fill the court. I recognized some of them as automatons I had seen tending shops and cleaning the streets.

It was perfectly clear to everyone there that the machines had come at Socrates' bidding, and they would do whatever it took to defend him. I had the sinking feeling that things were about to get violent. As usual, Socrates was one step ahead of us all.

Socrates shoved the queen, and she fell awkwardly to the floor in front of us. I shot my mother a worried look but her face was serene, perhaps even pleased.

"I welcomed you into my city and you took it as your own!" Socrates yelled, casting his gaze back and forth over the audience. "You ignored me while you established a new government and appointed your queen to rule over us. Today, it ends. You no longer rule this city. This is no more your queen."

"You can't do this," the queen said, pushing to her feet. "Guards, kill him. Kill them all!"

The gorillas closed in threateningly, and reached out to take the guards' weapons. "I don't think you heard him, grandmother," Breeze said. "You're not the queen anymore." She turned to face the rest of the crowd. "There will be no more queens and kings. Nobility is not a birthright. From this day forward, the only nobility will be that of the actions and characters of our people. Freedom is not a privilege to be granted or withheld at the whim of our leaders, it is *our* birthright."

She turned to face Socrates and he nodded respectfully. "From this day forward," she said, "we are all free."

"Lordain," Breeze said, turning to face him. "Gather the Tal'mar together and choose three leaders from amongst you. You must reach your decision by anonymous vote. When you have chosen your leaders, send them to me. Grandmother, I suggest you go with them. While you're gone, bear this in mind: the machines of this city are Socrates' family, Even the buildings themselves obey his command. Their loyalty belongs to Socrates alone, and they will be watching you."

Having little other choice, the Tal'mar filed out of the room to go make their decision. It was obvious that they were not happy. I turned to face my mother and saw her smiling.

"You planned this entire thing, didn't you?"

"I've had a lot of time on my hands," she said, laughing.

I stared at her and then at Socrates, who had been watching us quietly. "What now?" I said. "Will this really work?"

"Oh, I'm sure some of the Tal'mar will start conspiring immediately," she said. "I also expect them to vote for the same nobles who have just been relieved of their powers. Still, there is a chance they might surprise me."

"Do you think they will try to fight?" I said.

"That would be unwise," Socrates said. "This city is more than just machines. At times, I think Sanctuary has a consciousness all its own."

I stared at him. "I wouldn't have believed it, if I hadn't met you," I said.

Socrates smiled that weird apish grimace. "Then I am privileged to have opened your mind."

The next day, the Tal'mar leaders came to us. As Breeze had expected, my grandmother, her advisor Lordain, and one other high-ranking noble had been elected into positions of power. For our part, we had to do the same. We chose Breeze and Tam, and Crow. Some of the others had tried to nominate me, but I wanted nothing to do with it. Socrates also turned down their nominations. For Socrates however, the reason was different.

"I must act as judge," he said. "Someone must have the ability to break tie votes among the counsel, and to overturn the council's laws if they are unfair."

"It's all so complicated," I said.

"It may seem so, but it is necessary," he said. "Soon, when the humans have discovered this city, we will hold another vote. The council we elected today is only temporary."

We gathered back in the throne room, in full view of nearly two thousand witnesses. This also was Socrates' doing. He insisted that all laws and decisions be passed in full view of the public. He called the meeting to order by pounding a loud gavel on the table we had placed in the middle of the room.

"The council is chosen," he said. "Today we enact a new republic. Over the coming weeks we will proceed to set forth the rules governing this council, but our first priority is the matter at hand: What will we do with the Vangars?"

"Half their fleet is destroyed," Lordain said. "As her last act, our queen sent battleships to overwhelm their forces and take control of the air city."

"And of the survivors?" Socrates said. "What will you do with them?"

The council members all looked back and forth at each other as if the thought had never occurred to them. "We should kill them all!" someone in the crowd shouted.

"That would be most efficient," Lordain said. "Imprisoning the Vangars would be a drain on our resources."

"May I suggest another possibility?" Socrates said. "It is my understanding that the Vangars have wrought great destruction on the cities and lands of Astatia."

"It is true," said Crow. "I have seen it with my own eyes."

"Then perhaps they should repair the damage they have created."

The council members looked back and forth at each other, all surprised by the suggestion. "What exactly do you have in mind?" said Lordain.

"I suggest we give them a choice. They can either work as slaves for a period of ten years, repairing the damage they have done and rebuilding your cities, or they can submit to capital punishment."

The Tal'mar exchanged a few whispers and quickly reached a conclusion. "We agree," said my great grand-mother.

Socrates turned to face my mother and the other members on her side of the table. "What say the rest of you?"

"We agree," Breeze said.

Socrates hammered the gavel down on the table. "Then it is done. The law is passed. Now, on to other matters... when will we schedule our first general election?"

By the end of that meeting, it was clear that Socrates was very schooled in the art and science of politics. Somehow, the Creator had ingrained in Socrates' memory banks the knowledge of thousands of years of history. It was perfectly clear to me that our new empire would do just fine. Of course, there were many changes to come.

When the Tal'mar fighters first appeared over Avenston in their massive steam powered battleships, the citizens didn't know what to think. Rumors quickly spread about what had happened to the armada sent after us into the Wastelands, and within a few days everyone knew that the Tal'mar had attacked and taken control of Juntavar. But there were more surprises to come.

Over the following weeks, the council laid out the foundation of a new kingdom that would swallow up all of Astatia, including the Isle of Tal'mar, the Border-lands, the Wastelands, and the city of Sanctuary. In the process, they defined a basic constitution of rights and privileges, leaving most of these to the voting public. They formed an army of volunteers that rounded up the Vangars and put them to work in chain gangs that spanned the continent, from Silverspire to the Blackrock peaks and as far south as Bronwyr.

In the midst of this process, we held our first official election. My mother wasn't interested in retaining her place on the council, but she did accept a position as a judge. Strangely, it was our grandmother who convinced her to do it.

On the day of the election, the former queen withdrew her name from the list. "I never wanted to be queen," she said, speaking before a large audience. "I was groomed from the day of my birth. I was taught a certain way of behaving, of speaking, even of thinking. Never in all my many years have I entertained the hope that I would truly be free. Yet today I stand before you, a slave that was bound not in iron but in gold and silver. Today, like you, I choose to be free."

She went on to endorse my mother as High Judge of the state of Anora. Breeze could do little but graciously accept the position. To be honest, she embraced it with surprising enthusiasm. She explained her feelings to me one night while we were eating with our friends on a patio at the top of a tower overlooking Sanctuary. She had been working hard with the council for several weeks, hammering out the logistics of running the new kingdom and all of its inherent challenges. There were many details to consider, from the consolidation and organization of government to the distribution of technology and power. At last she was about to hand those challenges off to her successors, and assume the role of a powerful judge.

"I have always been a dreamer," she explained to me. "I learned as a child to escape my suffering by dreaming of a better world. When I had achieved some of those dreams, I crawled into an airplane and vanished into new dreams. All the while, I was trying to find my place, yet I was never actively *looking* for it. I understand this now. Socrates has taught me a great deal about government, and about the work a judge must do. I think I finally understand my place in this world."

"I think you'll be a fantastic judge," I said. I didn't bother pointing out the irony that she would now hold power over all the people who had made her life so miserable. I don't know if she even considered the situation in those terms, but I know I would have. In fact, if I could have been a judge for just one day, I'd have shown the Vangars a thing or two, and the Tal'mar as well.

Despite Breeze's new title, the city of Anora was never rebuilt. The region from Anora all the way south to Riverfork became known as a state, one of many in our new kingdom. States and counties were divided by region and populace, so as to more easily manage our votes, and so that people wouldn't have to vote for a sheriff who lived hundreds of miles away. It was a good system; one that Socrates assured us had been used successfully many times in the past.

My brother had a role to play in this new empire as well. He had only ever known Sanctuary, and his experiences in the rest of the kingdom hadn't impressed him. Sanctuary was his home. To that end, he became the first official mayor of the city. It was a largely diplomatic position, as Sanctuary would never be dangerous and brutal in the way that Avenston was, but the position acknowledged Crow's importance and he ran unopposed in the election. Breeze was thrilled, and of course, we were all very proud of him.

At one point, Kale located a locksmith shop on the north end of the city. He took me there as a surprise, and happily told me I could finally have my slave collar removed. As we stood in front of the robotic machine that was going to open the lock, I pulled away.

"What's the matter?" he said.

I looked at him and then reached up, feeling the collar at my throat. "I want to keep it," I said.

He frowned. "River, I don't understand. Is there something-"

"I just want to keep it," I said.

I didn't have the words to explain it to him. Just touching the thing reminded me of Rutherford and Wulvine and all of the things they had done to me. But it also reminded me of what I had done to them. It reminded me that no one, no matter how strong or powerful they were, could get away with what they had done. I'd watched Rutherford die and I had gazed into Wulvine's lifeless eyes. Those memories brought a smile to my face. I didn't ever want to forget that lesson.

In the days and weeks that followed, the Tal'mar begrudgingly accepted their new government. In fact, those who had managed to survive under the Vangars' reign openly and happily accepted it. They knew better than to trust the old ways and they were more than happy to abandon the yoke of privilege and class warfare. While there may have been a few seeds of discontent among those who were once called "nobles," there wasn't any sympathy or respect for that attitude.

They soon learned to work and prosper like the rest of us.

We also set up a regular schedule for airship travel back and forth between Sanctuary and the other cities. Naturally, everyone wanted to see the fabled city, but we had to manage it in such a way that the other cities weren't abandoned. To that end, the council adopted a proposition that allowed a certain number of visitors to Sanctuary per week for the first year. That way, everyone would have a chance to see the city, but they wouldn't be tempted to just abandon their old lives and homes on a whim. After all, if our new kingdom was to be successful, it would need to grow quickly rather than consolidate back into Sanctuary. The council had more ideas in that regard as well, but I didn't pay much attention. The details of running an empire were simply a bore to me.

Analyn Trader left her tunnels for the first time in years to climb aboard a dirigible and fly to Sanctuary. It took some convincing, but Breeze made a special trip just for her. They met like you would expect, in a joyous reunion full of tears and celebration. After a few days, Analyn moved into an apartment in Sanctuary just across the street from one of the city's expansive libraries, where she dove into her lifelong passion for history. Soon, she became Sanctuary's official historian and the Chief Custodian of all the city's libraries. Just for fun, she also taught history lessons to the young visitors who came to the library several times a week with their schoolmates.

A few days after the election, Kale came to me. I was packing to travel back to Avenston. As endearing as Sanctuary was, I wanted to go home. I missed the familiar streets, the dark alleyways, and the Dockside breezes of my home. I heard a noise and turned to see him standing in the doorway of my apartment.

"Leaving?" he said.

"Yes. I suppose you'll be staying here with what's-her-name."

"Who, Nena?" he said, wrinkling his nose. "Nah, she left days ago. Missed her parents too much, or so she said. Personally I think there was some country bumpkin that was on her mind."

I grinned at that. "So what will you do then?"

He shrugged and leaned up against the doorframe. "I was about to ask you the same thing."

I could hear from the tone in his voice that he was asking about more than where I was going. He wanted to go with me. I sighed, trying to find a tactful way to say I wasn't interested in a relationship. "Kale, I've told you before you're like a brother to me."

"Correction," he said. "You *have* a brother now. Which makes me more like an, uh... an acquaintance."

I looked him up and down. It was easy to see why Nena had taken such an interest in him. Kale was a strong, good-looking man. A little too cocky perhaps, but that could be trained out of him. I wasn't looking for that kind of work, though. Not yet. I was young. Adventures waited. I was about to say something like that when a young messenger boy pushed past him and ran into the room.

"River, Breeze needs you!"

There was something so urgent in the boy's voice that I dropped everything and went running after him. Kale took up the chase behind me. We took the stairs up to the next floor and then crossed the street by way of a long, glass-encased catwalk. As we ran through, I caught a glimpse of the airships coming and going over the city and the thousands of people moving through the streets. I could hardly believe the city had changed so much in just a few weeks. It seemed everyone in the kingdom wanted to see Sanctuary.

The boy took a hard right at the next building and led us around a long balcony. From there, we took an elevator that ran down the outside of the building to the main floor. As we descended, I couldn't help but look longingly over the city. The spires were gleaming in the afternoon sun, the wall of ice beyond shimmering bright blue.

"I'm going to miss this place," I said.

"You don't have to leave," Kale said.

"Yes, I do."

"Avenston, then?" he said. He was prying, trying to find out where I was going so that he could follow me. A slight smiled turned up the corners of my mouth.

"I suppose, for now. It won't be the same without Tinker, though. I don't know if I can really call Avenston home anymore."

At last, we reached the main floor. The boy led us past the marble stairs and into the grand foyer. This was the capitol building, the new seat of government for our new kingdom. Hundreds of people were coming and going, admiring the exotic architecture, watching the workers put up signs indicating where their newly elected representatives could be found.

The messenger boy led us through the maze and into a small conference room with a modest brass table and matching chairs. Breeze was there along with the entire council and a dozen other important officials. Socrates was there also, and he seemed to be the focus of their attention. They paid little notice to us as we entered the room.

"Are you sure this is absolutely necessary?" one of the men said.

"What will we do without you?" someone else said.

Socrates stood at the head of the table. He held up his hands to silence them. "Ladies and gentlemen, you have all you need. You have your council and your judges, and you have the support of your people. There is no going back now. Continue what you have begun. Finish the rebuilding, so that we may bring peace and freedom that serves as an example to the entire world."

"But what about you?" someone shouted. "We need you!"

"That is not true. You will do fine without me. You know what you must do. The empire is like a boulder rolling down a slope. It is your job to guide its path. Never rest."

"When will you return?" someone said.

"When I can."

I leaned over to whisper in my mother's ear. "What's this about? Why is Socrates leaving?"

Breeze sighed. "We took an inventory of the starfall liquid that powers the city. The scientists have warned us that our supply of the element will run dry within a decade. Maybe sooner, depending on how much we distribute."

"I don't understand. Starfall isn't the only fuel available. We can still use coal and lumber and Black-rock steel."

She turned to face me. "All of those resources are finite. What will we do when we run out of coal? Or when we've cut down all of the trees and mined all of the ore? If we're going to be different than the Vangars, we must begin now."

I considered that. I had to admit, I had wondered myself how we could possibly avoid that future. "I understand," I said, "but what does that have to do with Socrates?"

"Socrates is a highly sophisticated machine. When we run out of fuel, we can't just throw another log on the fire."

My eyes widened. "You're saying he's going to die?"

"Sadly, yes. Unless we can find a replacement for starfall. That is why, with his wisdom and knowledge of the world, it makes the most sense for Socrates to take up that journey. No one has more to lose than he does."

I stared at him for a moment, suddenly realizing how much Socrates had come to mean to me. I had only known him a few weeks but he truly was a marvel. He was a machine that spoke and reasoned like a man, and yet looked like a beast. He was the most amazing creature I had ever known.

Before I realized what was happening, Socrates had said his parting words and left the room. I stared at him through the glass as he wandered down the hall and into the foyer, followed by a flock of admirers. My mother touched my shoulder.

"Is something wrong?"

"I don't know," I said. I turned to face her. "Mother-"

"I understand," she said with a gentle smile. "I'll be waiting for you when you return."

I threw my arms around her and kissed her on the cheek. Then I dashed out of the room and went chasing after Socrates. He was just about to exit the front of the building as I came running up. "Wait!" I called after him. "I'm coming with you."

Socrates looked up as he heard my voice and shot me a beaming smile. I rushed up to him. "I'm coming," I said breathlessly. "I want to help."

"Are you certain? It may be dangerous."

"This place is too boring anyway," I said. "When are we leaving?"

"As soon as we're ready."

"And where are we going?"

"Wherever the world takes us."

"I'll get my things."

I raced back to my apartment to gather my meager possessions. I found my bags lying on the bed, just as I had left them. I carefully removed the cutlass that had been a gift from my mother and buckled it around my waist, and I gathered up my pistol to hang it from my belt. I had few other belongings: a set of new clothes, a few miscellaneous treasures that I had collected during my exploration of the city - that was about it.

I threw the pack over my shoulder and raced back to the capitol building. Socrates was waiting for me in the street out front. "This way," he said, gesturing towards the elevator. We stepped inside and Socrates activated the switch, guiding the elevator to the basement. I frowned. I had expected us to take a vehicle of some sort, possibly even an airship.

"Where are we going?"

"All journeys begin somewhere," he said. "This is where ours begins."

The elevator stopped and the doors parted, opening up to reveal a wide concrete subway station below the capitol building. My jaw dropped as I saw a massive steam locomotive idling on the tracks in front of us. It was similar to the Vangars' steam locomotives, but only in a superficial way. This locomotive was much bigger, so tall in fact that it nearly reached the roof of the tunnel, and so broad that it swallowed up two entire sets of tracks. It was made of gleaming black steel with brass and copper pipes and fittings. Brass lanterns were attached to the sides of the cab and brass filigree decorations raced along the boiler and up and down the pillars in front of the cab.

Towering smokestacks rose up along either side of the boiler, not just one or two, but half a dozen on each side. Their tips glowed menacingly as sparks drifted out, floating lazily up toward the ceiling. A number of railcars stretched out behind the locomotive, down the tunnel and out of sight behind us, each as large and impressive as the steam engine itself.

I couldn't speak as I stared at the thing. It was so massive, so eerily powerful and dominating that it seemed like some prehistoric wild beast snorting flames and rumbling the earth with its sheer power. I wanted to run up to it and touch it, to explore the wonders that most certainly waited inside those railcars, but I was afraid to move or even speak for fear of shattering the illusion.

"Introducing the *Iron Horse Express*," Socrates said with a smile. "This will be our home."

"It's beautiful," I said in a breathless whisper.

I heard a shout behind us and turned to see Kale running out of the elevator. He had a bag thrown over his shoulder and a broadsword strapped to his back. "What are you doing?" I shouted at him, narrowing my eyebrows.

"Looking after my interests," he said slyly as he joined us. "Besides, I'm not going to let you have all the fun. We're making history here, you know."

"He's right about that," Socrates said. "You're going to see things your kind hasn't seen in thousands of years, if ever."

"You've seen it, though," I said. "Do you think the world has changed so much?"

"Never underestimate how things may change," Socrates said wisely. "The world is a whirlwind waiting for you to turn your back. Just when you think you have it mastered, you are in the greatest danger imaginable."

He sighed in a humanlike manner and then clapped his hands together. "Well, then. Shall we?"

Kale and I couldn't help but grin as we followed Socrates across the station and climbed the stairs up to the massive platform. I glanced ahead and saw the bright lights of the tunnel twinkling in the distance, and a chill ran down my spine.

"What happens when we run out of track?" I said.

Socrates smiled as he twisted the control valve, releasing the built up steam pressure into the engine. There was a loud hiss followed by the slow, deep drumming of the lifting cylinders. Slowly, the wheels began to turn.

The End

COMING SOON!

Watch out for the upcoming adventures of
Socrates the Steampunk ape
in
"<u>Aboard the Great Iron Horse</u>,"
coming December 2013!